T0168916

Hollywood Troubleshooter

Hollywood Troubleshooter:
W. T. Ballard's Bill Lennox Stories

Edited and introduced by
James L. Traylor

Bowling Green University Popular Press
Bowling Green, Ohio 43403

Acknowledgements

Special thanks to Hilary Cummings, Curator of Manuscripts, Special Collections and Kenneth W. Duckett, Curator, Special Collections, both of the University of Oregon Library, Eugene, for their invaluable assistance with material from the Tod Ballard collection; also thank you to Bill Blackbeard of the San Francisco Academy of Comic Art for allowing the use of the issues of *Black Mask* containing the stories reprinted in this volume; but most of all my special thanks to Phoebe Ballard for her generous co-operation and approval of this project. Finally, to my wife Janice, my heart-felt appreciation for her assistance and endurance through the entire project.

The following stories are reprinted by special arrangement with Blazing Publications, Inc., proprietor and conservator of the respective copyrights and successor-in-interest to Popular Publications, Inc., The Pro-Distributors Publishing Company, Inc. and Fictioneers, Inc., in cooperation with the Estate of W. T. Ballard:

"A Little Different," *Black Mask,* September 1933. Copyright © 1933 Blazing Publications, Inc. All Rights Reserved. Copyright © 1933 by The Pro-Distributors Publishing Company, Inc. Copyright Assigned to and Renewed © 1961 by Popular Publications, Inc.

"A Million-Dollar Tramp," *Black Mask,* October 1933. Copyright © 1933 Blazing Publications, Inc. All Rights Reserved. Copyright © 1933 by The Pro-Distributors Publishing Company, Inc. Copyright Assigned to and Renewed © 1961 by Popular Publications, Inc.

"Gamblers Don't Win," *Black Mask,* April 1935. Copyright © 1935 Blazing Publications, Inc. All Rights Reserved. Copyright © 1935 by The Pro-Distributors Publishing Company, Inc. Copyright Assigned to and Renewed © 1963 by Popular Publications, Inc.

"Scars of Murder," *Black Mask,* November 1939. Copyright © 1939 Blazing Publications, Inc. All Rights Reserved. Copyright © 1939 by The Pro-Distributors Publishing Company, Inc. Copyright Assigned to and Renewed © 1967 by Popular Publications, Inc.

"Lights, Action—Killer!" *Black Mask,* May 1942. Copyright © 1942 Blazing Publications, Inc. All Rights Reserved. Copyright © 1942 by Fictioneers, Inc., a Division of Popular Publications, Inc. Copyright Renewed © 1970 by Popular Publications, Inc.

For information address: Blazing Publications, Inc., C/O Neil J. Rosini, Esq., Franklin Weinrib Rudell & Vassallo, P.C., 950 Third Avenue, 7th Floor, New York, New York, 10022.

Copyright © 1985 by Bowling Green University Popular Press

Library of Congress Catalogue Card No.: 84-72510

ISBN: 0-87972-316-5 Clothbound
     0-87972-317-3 Paperback

To Phoebe, Cora and Alison

CONTENTS

W.T. (Todhunter) Ballard

Tod Ballard: An Appreciation

TOD BALLARD WAS A TRUE PROFESSIONAL, writing convincingly in many styles and from different viewpoints. He was extremely prolific, writing hundreds of short stories and articles for the pulp and slick magazines, numerous screenplays and teleplays, and almost one hundred western and mystery novels. He was able to portray the police, the PI and the criminal with equal believability. Although he never won any MWA (Mystery Writers of America) awards, he was good enough to win the WWA (Western Writers of America) Spur Award in 1965 for the best novel of the year, *Gold in California!* His crime novels are always rewarding; not the least of his achievement is his ability to engage the reader with his characters, making the reader care what happens to these people—crook, cop or PI. Ballard wrote some near classic detective novels, ones which warrant rediscovery for their unacknowledged role in the development of the hard-boiled detective tradition.

Ballard was born in Cleveland, Ohio, and graduated from Wilmington (Ohio) College with a degree in chemistry in 1926. He was a practicing writer from 1925 on. Leaving a job with an Ohio newspaper chain at the start of the Depression, Ballad became a stringer for the Cleveland *Press*. While there he met, quite by accident, an acquaintance of Al Capone's younger brother who was trying to establish a small "family" business. Later, Ballard was able to use this first-hand experience in writing crime stories.

In California Ballard's first break came when he was spotted by Major Harry Warner, an old friend from Cleveland. Ballard told Warner he was doing freelance writing and presented him with a copy of the current issue of the dime pulp *Detective Dragnet* in which one of his stories appeared. Warner was impressed enough to give him a writing job at First National Studios at $75 a week where he worked for eight months until Jack Warner heard him make a derogatory remark and summarily fired him.

By 1932 Ballard had also left a job with Columbia Pictures and was living with an uncle and aunt in Los Angeles still trying to support himself in the pulp market. One night he heard an advertisement on the radio for the first movie version of *The Maltese Falcon*. The movie credits led him to the pulp magazine *Black Mask* to which he promptly wrote and mailed the first Bill Lennox short

1

story. Captain Joseph Shaw mailed him a check less than a week later and hooked Ballard as a pulp writer.

This first short story and many to follow featured Bill Lennox, a troubleshooter for the fictitious General Consolidated Studios. Lennox was patterned after Ballard's friend Jim Lawson who repeatedly saved the rambunctious son of Universal's Carl Laemmele when he was in trouble with the police. For many years thereafter Ballard sold Shaw about ten stories per year.

Ballard was a methodical craftsman. After his initial success with *Black Mask* he set a goal of writing ten pages per day even if these were later discarded. During his pulp career he wrote about one million words per year.

After publishing short stories for about ten years, Ballard entered the book market with Bill Lennox: *Say Yes to Murder* (1942), *Murder Can't Stop* (1946), *Dealing Out Death* (1948) and much later the paperback original for Belmont, *Lights, Camera, Murder* (1960), published under the nom de plume John Shepherd. The Lennox books were quite successful, two of them still in print in the 1960s. In all, the four Lennox books sold more than one million copies.

Ballard's *Say Yes to Murder* (1942), the first Bill Lennox novel, set the standard for the Hollywood murder mystery. Ballard's gift for this type of story is his careful depiction of scene and his emphasis on character in a genre which usually does not rely on such realism. Ballard invented a cast of characters that later became almost cliches of the movie industry: Sol Spurck, the crusty head of General Consolidated Studios; Nancy Hobbs, Lennox' long-suffering girl friend who, of course, can never marry him; cops named Spellman and Stobert who are not quite as condescending toward Lennox as the typical cops of the hard-boiled detective novel; and various actors, actresses and movie industry hirelings who have personality in addition to being part of the machinations of murder.

In *Say Yes to Murder*, Lennox investigates the murder of Leon Heyworth, a drunken actor that Lennox finds stabbed and lying under the bed of actress Jean Jeffries, granddaughter of Lennox' old friend Mary Morris. Ballard presents the murder as a problem of separating illusion from reality, a method quite effective in presenting Hollywood's artificiality.

Lennox is extremely faithful to Spurck and the studio. With the help of Jake Hertz, a studio minion, and an empty piano box, Lennox moves the body from Jean's apartment, attempting to keep Mary Morris' name out of the papers. Lennox doesn't think about the consequences of such an illegal act until he's actually done it.

Along with a superior sense of timing and scene, Ballard's novels show great intricacy in plotting. In this novel, the vital clue to the solution of the mystery is identity. All the characters are in show business, with consequent multiple personas. Lennox' primary task is wading through the maze of personalities.

The second Lennox Novel, *Murder Can't Stop* (1946), presents another view of Hollywood infighting but with a different location—Skull Lake, a mountain retreat used by the studio. Here Dick Cullen—Chairman of the board of Pinnacle Pictures, General Consolidated's chief competitor—is killed and Lennox, babysitting a dipso actor, is accused of the murder. Before Lennox and "close personal friend" Nancy Hobbs wade through the maze, five people are dead, all mysteriously connected with an old mining claim in Tonopah, Nevada. Here, personality development and well-constructed action sequences keep the plot believable.

In *Dealing Out Death* (1948), Lennox is accused of the murder of Robert Moore, a writer married to sexpot Renee Wilson. Ballard's tongue is firmly in cheek when he has Lennox declare he'd known "too many authors to have any respect left for the profession." Although James Sandoe in his essay "The Private Eye" notes that the novel is "a little corpse-heavy at the end," he admires Lennox because "he doesn't have to flex his biceps to prove that he's strong."

Through *Lights, Camera, Murder* (1960) a pattern emerged: there are no great conspiracies, just people caught up in situations in which human fraility causes their downfall. In his final caper, Lennox is hunting the murderer of homosexual actor Joe Moss, killed on location in Mexico where General Consolidated is filming a picture called "The Strangers."

Ballard uses the Hollywood movie colony as a microcosm of the plastic world in which art and artifice keep truth at a distance. *Lights, Camera, Murder* is atypical of Lennox novels of the 1940s for its frank portrayal of sexual relations (Lennox admits a long affair with Nancy Hobbs and has a short affair with one of the actresses, Candy Kyle, while on location) and its more somber tone. The murders in this novel are not the amusing deaths of the earlier Lennox adventures. Lennox is older, wiser and sadder. The relationships depicted are more open and realistic, yet the novel is not as much fun as the three previous Lennox exploits. As Ballard himself said in Steve Mertz's 1977 *Armchair Detective* interview: "Bill Lennox ... had outlived his usefulness. We'll let him rest in his own time frame."

Between the late 1940s and the middle 1960s, Ballard worked primarily writing western novels and scripts for movies and television. Ballard and close friend Robert L. Bellem, famous as the creator of Dan Turner, Hollywood Detective, collaborated on many projects. Ballard and Bellem had adjoining offices in downtown Pasadena, working on novelettes (as the 10,000 word stories were called), movie and TV scripts. They sold stories to such TV series as *Shannon* (1961), *Superman, Will Bill Hickok, Cowboy G Men* (all early 1950s), *Death Valley Days* (1964-65; mostly scripts for future President Ronald Reagan), *Shotgun Slade* (1959), *Dick Tracy* (1951) and *Manhunt*. Tod was the plot man; Bellem rewrote Tod's first draft.

The enthusiasm absent from the last entry in the Bill Lennox series reappears quite renewed in Ballard's crime novels of the late 1950s and 1960s. The Tony Costaine and Bert McCall thrillers (written under the pen name Neil MacNeil) recapture the spark of the earlier Lennox cases and utilize more realistic sexual relationships and a broader social range of characters than those of Lennox's Hollywood set. The Costaine/McCall adventures are also fun to read. As with all Ballard novels, plotting is intricate, engaging and fair. The characters, especially McCall, are eccentric in an amusing way and the situations are not merely thriller fluff. For example, in the first MacNeil novel, *Death Takes an Option* (1958), Constaine and McCall investigate a suicide which can in no way be construed a murder—yet still must be. Achieving such a trick is an auctorial treat to be admired.

The Costaine/McCall stories verge on fantasy in that they were written for an audience perceived as being more concerned with action, sex and fast-paced story than with character and straight-forward plotting. There's also a good deal of humor in these exploits, most of it derived from McCall's prodigious drinking habits (he buys and drinks it by the case), his height (he's 6'4" in the early books but "grows" to 6'5 3/4" in *The Spy Catchers,* 1966), his Scottish background (he has flaming red hair and a tendency to play the bagpipes), and his serial love affairs (in *Two Guns for Hire,* he's forced to pose nude for an Amazonian lady artist in order to successfully seduce her).

The Max Hunter series (all paperback originals for Permabooks) is a departure from the Ballard norm; the protagonist is a Las Vegas police lieutenant. The books are written in the first person and present crime from the viewpoint of the police. In addition, the characters who appear in the Hunter series are closer to the actual human condition. These novels resemble other Ballard crime stories for they, too, are straightforward in presentation but complicated in plotting.

Pretty Miss Murder (1961), the first in the series, presents a variation of the Laura theme. Hunter—certainly an appropriate name for a sheriff—meets briefly a young woman named Flora Thomas who is in Vegas for the cure, a quickie divorce. She's applying for a job and must be fingerprinted by the police. Hunter, impressed by her beauty and presence, makes a note to look her up. Later that same day, she's found murdered and Hunter is shaken. He takes on the case personally, even journeying to her home town in an attempt to follow the trail which led to her death. Everything which he discovers points out that Flora was a girl that "everyone said was headed for murder." Yet Max cannot believe it. He even forms an uneasy alliance with mobster Johnny Blessing who is also tracking down her killer because Flora's husband owed him $250,000.

The next two Max Hunter exploits reveal the same humane quality. In *The Seven Sisters* (1962), Max tracks a mad bomber who kills an odd little man known as the Duke, an aging astrologer who left a clue to his murder with the seven members of the world's oldest profession that he called the "seven sisters."

In *Three for the Money* (1963), Max's friendship with captain of homicide Joe Kane is severely tested after he discovers that Kane has the $200,000 missing from the estate of recently murdered Las Vegas con man Frenchy Melman. Three different wives turn up to claim Frenchy's money. Max is saddened and perplexed to discover that Frenchy also had a fourth wife: Joe Kane's wife Kitty.

There is a strong sense of compassion and concern for man in the Max Hunter novels. Unlike Bill Lennox, Tony Costaine and Bert McCall, Hunter is all too human. His cases are more based in reality. It's an admirable series, tersely written, one that involves the reader personally.

Ballard's last private eye novel was *Murder Las Vegas Style* (1967). The story returns to familiar *Black Mask* territory with its hard-boiled detective, mysterious and untrustworthy women, and fast, violent action. Mark Foran—a $50 a day PI from LA—is hired by Colonel Preston Fremont to journey to Vegas to break up the marriage between his niece Carol and Chuck Benton, a fortune hunter with Mafia connections. By the time Foran and Colonel Fremont arrive, both Carol and Benton are dead, leaving unanswered the question of who died first and would therefore inherit Carol's $2 million trust fund.

Stylistically, the novel is a reflection of the pulp format. Mark Foran—the foreign mark in Vegas—is not a typical Ballard character. He's an amalgam of Ballard's entire writing career and his association with all the legends of the *Black Mask* era—Dashiell Hammett and Raymond Chandler especially. The action is psychologically and physically violent; there are six deaths, three of them innocent victims, the other three coincidental partners in murder.

The plot is a variation of an old pulp theme: easy money and the resulting corruption. All the classic Ballard touches are here, and it may be considered the epitome of his detective writing career. There's the mysterious and deadly atmosphere of Las Vegas, with its emphasis on big money and unreality. There are the easily available women, both the young and the middle-aged who are still randy under the influence of wealth. That lust for money even overrides the sexual gymnastics which become merely side issues, an easy diversion from the real obsession: get the money. It's an altogether compelling and rewarding hard-boiled novel, a must book for the Ballard aficionado.

In all Ballard wrote about twenty crime/detective novels spanning the years 1942-1973. Early in his book publishing career, however, he recognized that the public's taste for detective novels was changing. By the mid 1940s, Ballard had moved into the new field of western fiction and by the 1950s was writing more westerns than mysteries, becoming quite active in WWA. From 1951-1977 he published over seventy western novels under various pen names.

Left to Right: William R. Cox, Thomas Thompson and W.T. Ballard at a WWA Convention in the late 1950s.

The famous picture of the West Coast *Black Mask* writers, January 11, 1936.
Back: Raymond Moffat, Raymond Chandler, Herbert Stinson, Dwight Babcock, Eric Taylor, Dashiell Hammett. Front: Arthur Barnes, John K. Butler, W.T. Ballard, Horace McCoy, Norbert Davis.

Writing for the Pulps

Todhunter Ballard

IN THE EARLY 1970s, Todhunter Ballard wrote the following reminiscence, originally planned as part of a projected series for Argosy. *Although it was never published, Ballard's sketch of life writing the pulps is a treasure of information about an era which will very shortly be inaccessible to memory. Preferring to preserve Ballard's unique style, I have made only the slightest editorial changes.*

*   *   *

It has been said that for every successful writer there must be one editor who believed in him, an assessment I heartily endorse. It was certainly true in my case, for until I began to work for Joe Shaw at *Black Mask* I was drifting without any real direction.

Captain Shaw was quite a person. Besides his great talent as an editor he had been a successful businessman, then joined Herbert Hoover in the effort to feed starving Europe at the end of the first world war. When he returned to New York after that stint, having always wanted to write, he took a story in to Phil Cody, then editor of *Black Mask.*

Phil did not buy the story, but he hired Shaw as editor, and under "Cap's" shepherding the magazine flowered. He developed such writers as Dash Hammett, Ray Chandler, Erle Gardner and a host of others, and reoriented the direction of the American detective story.

Without the freedom for growth Shaw gave his "boys" we might never have had Sam Spade, The Thin Man, Marlowe, Perry Mason and their fraternity.

Before I had heard of *Black Mask* I was working in Hollywood, writing an occasional free-lance detective story for Street and Smith, Fiction House and other magazines. Then one evening my uncle turned on the radio and I heard a "trailer" advertising a movie

8

called *The Maltese Falcon* starring Richardo Cortez.

From the snatches of dialogue I suddenly had to see that picture. I saw in the dark house and watched characters who thought and spoke in the way I had been wanting to write but had been unable to sell to the markets I knew of. Cortez was not as powerful as Bogart was in the later remake, but he was convincing, and there was a credit line on the film saying the story had originally appeared in *Black Mask*.

I left the theater, stopped at the corner drug store, bought a copy of the magazine and read it cover to cover on the streetcar ride home. By the time I finished I knew that was my market. I was particularly impressed by a Jerry Tracy story, a yarn about a New York reporter, and I began casting about for a character for myself. I considered a Los Angeles reporter, but that was too close to Tracy, then I remembered a friend who worked for a major studio. He was head of the foreign distribution department, but the studio chief used him for every chore from piloting visiting distributors and theater owners around the lot to getting Junior out of Lincoln Heights jail. My friend jokingly called himself the studio trouble shooter, which was just what I needed.

His name was Lawson and I liked the sound but could not use that, of course, so I ran down the L's in the phone book and settled on Lennox. William Tecumseh Lennox, Trouble Shooter for General Consolidated Studios, was born at midnight. By eight o'clock the next morning I had ten thousand words about him.

I mailed the story and ten days later had a letter from Joe Shaw. He liked the manuscript; true it had a couple of minor holes that he wanted plugged, but in the meantime he would not hold up the check. To a writer in the bottom of the depression that alone was enough to endear him to me.

The check was for two hundred and fifty dollars—two and a half cents a word. I had been working for one cent or less and usually on publication. I was rich. So rich that I lost a hundred and a quarter at the Caliente race track. But the headiest part of the sale was that I was working for Joe Shaw, writing copy in which I could believe.

I wrote eight more Lennox stories in the next six weeks and Shaw bought them all, then told me Phil Cody, who had moved up to president, said the Ballard inventory was big enough and not to buy more from me for some months. But over the years Shaw remained at *Black Mask* I sold him more copy than any other writer, using three noms and different characters, and after he left and Fanny Ellsworth became editor I continued to outsell the others.

One incident with Fanny amused me. She had been highly successful with *Ranch Romances*, but she knew nothing about detective stories. In one she bought from me I hid a villain in some bushes near Hollywood Boulevard and La Brea to kill someone with a sawed-off shotgun. Fanny objected, wanting me to use a forty-five instead because a shotgun would be too noticeable.

One of Shaw's greatest strengths as an editor was his ability to impart a spirit of high morale to his writers. He made us all feel that we were the elite, the chosen few, and as a result drew from us our best work and a devotion that I have not seen equalled in the business. He made us a sort of family, invited the boys who lived in the New York area to parties at his Scarsdale home and encouraged those of us on the west coast to have periodic dinners together. I still prize a picture taken at one of those dinners at the old Knickabob on Western Avenue so a copy could be sent to Cap: Dash Hammett, Ray Chandler, Horace McCoy, Eric Taylor, Bert Davis, Herb Stinson, Johnny Butler, Dwight Babcock and myself.

Not that the crowd ever treated Joe with reverence. They were always putting him on in one way or another. At one dinner Shaw attended on the west coast, Peter Ruric, who wrote *Fast One* under the nom Paul Cain, and McCoy ganged up, outdoing each other with outrageous brags of their adventures in various whore houses. Poor Joe, he could write a book called *Blood On The Curb*, but he couldn't tolerate four letter words, particularly in polite society. Then the gag to shock Joe backfired on the pair when another writer topped them with his own true story. He piped up saying he had been raised in a whore house, one operated by his mother and an aunt up on the Oregon coast.

Hammett had another way of needling Joe. He had wangled a five hundred dollar personal advance from Shaw, then wouldn't pay it back although at the time he was carrying away the MGM treasury in dump trucks. I don't know whether he finally paid up.

I never really knew Dash, none of us did with the possible exception of Horace McCoy who shared an apartment in San Francisco with him for a time. McCoy was an ex-police reporter from El Paso, tough as they came but one of the nicest people I ever knew. He told one on Hammett that Dash never denied. It seems they had hit a dry period when neither could sell anything, then Dash got a check from Shaw for a couple of hundred bucks. They had no bank account so Dash took the check down to cash at the Chinese restaurant where they ate. In the restaurant was a claw machine, one of those gadgets where you try to fish up prizes out of a bed of hard candies. Hammett was gone so long McCoy got worried and went to find him, walked into the restaurant as Hammett put the last nickel of the whole two hundred into that claw machine. The Chinese was so sorry for him that he opened the machine and gave Dash a tin cigarette case.

McCoy would live in wait for an audience, then say, "Dash, show us your two hundred dollar cigarette case . . . . "

As a lot of writers are, Dash was a compulsive gambler. I have no idea how much he lost during the opening season at Santa Anita, but Hollywood was sure the track would have failed in its first year without Hammett.

I used to go with him to the Colony Club, the Airport Gardens, and four or five joints along what became the Sunset Strip, but I never learned much about him. I knew he had come from Baltimore and had worked for the Pinkerton agency, but that was all. He did not talk about himself.

McCoy on the other hand was an extrovert. You knew what he had done, who his girl friends had been, how much dough he'd made. He never pretended. After he went to work for Columbia Pictures he used his first pay checks to buy a Cadillac of which he was inordinately proud. He wouldn't park it on the street for fear someone might run into it, so he parked it at the Muller Brothers tire store where they also washed cars. I ran into him on the street one day and asked what he was doing.

"Washing cars at Muller Brothers," he said.

I laughed at him. "Down to washing your own Cad?"

"Downer. I got laid off last week and I'm broke. I'm washing cars for fifty cents an hour."

Whether he was making fifty cents an hour or a thousand a week McCoy was always the same. He wrote one very good book, *They Shoot Horses, Don't They?* of which a picture was made with Jane Fonda, but McCoy did not live to see it.

Joe Shaw was never arbitrary, and he did not always trust his own judgment. Once he sent me a manuscript and asked me to read it and tell him whether he was nuts to believe he had discovered a near genius. I found the dialogue somewhat contrived, for the writer invented his own slang, but the characters jumped out of the pages and in most cases were bigger than life. That was the first submission to Shaw by Raymond Chandler.

Two or three years passed before I met Ray personally and found him and his wife very shy, quiet and retiring. He had been raised in England although he was American, and some of the

English reticence had clung to him. When he wrote that first story and sent it to Shaw he knew so little about the business that he justified every line on a page the way columns are justified by a linotype.

There are many anecdotes on the west coast boys. One of the crowd was Carroll John Daly, a small man so cold blooded that he kept the oil heater going in his Santa Monica office in August and worked in an overcoat. His Race Williams must be rated as one of the most bloodthirsty characters in the pulps, written with Daly's tongue in his cheek. Shaw phoned him one day to protest a new, utterly unexplained character that had abruptly appeared more than half way through Daly's latest opus. Shaw was in a hurry to schedule it and wanted answers.

Daly's voice took on a long suffering note. "Cap, the character hadn't yet broke out of prison when I wrote the first half of the story. How could he appear until he was free?"

Joe walked into the trap. "When did he break out?"

"Read your afternoon paper," Daly told him. "He broke out this morning."

Daly hung up, leaving Shaw no choice but to run the story as was. I never heard any complaint so I guess his readers took the late arrival in stride.

Eric Taylor was a Canadian who loved to cook. The first time he invited us for dinner he spent two days making a sauce. So my wife tried doubly hard on our return dinner, making elaborate hot hors d'ouvres, having them ready in the oven to toast as soon as the guests arrived. Eric got hung up at the studio and they were two hours late, hours we spent getting well oiled. Next morning we found the hors d'ouvres still in the oven, soggy and limp. So much for trying to impress your peers.

One day I got a telegram from Shaw: "Missing last four pages mss. Please air mail at once."

It put me in a quandry. I had just mailed one story that could not have yet reached New York and the one preceding it should already have been set up in type, so to be on the safe side I mailed both endings. Two days later came another telegram from Joe: "Mistake. Wire meant for Dwight Babcock, Tujunga. Please deliver it to him."

That was pure Shaw. Instead of wiring Dwight direct I was to be the messenger boy. We didn't know Dwight but my wife and I sallied forth to find him. We could find no street address but at that period the section around Tujunga and Montrose had few streets. We questioned the local store, the postman, people along the way and finally located a trailer set on the edge of an arroyo.

Babcock was not at home but his wife, a cute little blonde, was much impressed that we had brought the wire all the way from Pasadena. Two days later the Babcocks showed up at our place, Dwight to introduce himself and thank me. They brought along Norbert Davis and both writers became my very close friends.

Babcock was still very young, a salesman for a wine concentrate company, moonlighting in a dance band and writing in what time was left.

Davis had graduated from Stanford Law School but had sold so many stories through his school years that he never bothered to take the bar examination. He was big, six feet four, a gentle, delightfully whimsical man who unfortunately died too early to achieve the promise of his early work. Even so, his work for *The Saturday Evening Post* was classic.

Most writers tend to cling to other writers. It's a lonely profession and people in other lines of work have no conception of the problems that confront the writer. In the early thirties we formed a little dinner club we called the Fictioneers with twenty original members. Any writer who came to Hollywood was invited to join and hundreds revolved through the meetings. We kept no records, charged no dues, and innocently laid down one rule ... no business was to be discussed. It was Eric Taylor's rationale that, "You don't catch a bunch of plumbers telling each other about the joint they wiped, so why should writers waste the evening talking shop?"

We did talk shop, of course, but there was none of the jealousy or back-biting I found in New York. For one thing, when you can walk into a magazine office at will to sell a story and gather market news you tend to be suspicious of the next guy who can do the same thing and plug your market. But on the coast three thousand miles away information was hard to come by and every scrap and rumor any of us collected was shared with everyone else.

Our cooperation went further. Whenever any of us got a check for a little more than bare subsistence we would climb into the car and make the rounds to find which of the brotherhood was not eating. Cleve Adams originated that practice. He was the Fictioneer's first secretary and had something of a father complex, was always ready to help anyone.

As a case in point, Rogers Terrill, editor of Popular Publications, made a business trip west, was staying at the Ambassador and talking to a parade of writers. Like the access to editors in New York this sudden access on the coast generated jealousy. Some of Rog's prime contributors lived in the area, Harry Olmstead, Cliff Farrell and others, plus a number of women writers.

Rog told me privately that one group wanted to take him to dinner in the old Spanish section, which did not interest him. His time was short and what he wanted most was to slip away with half a dozen of us for a visit to one of the gambling boats then anchored off the coast.

Cleve had a new Cord with more room than my car and I asked him to come although he had never yet sold to Rog, most of his copy going to Munsey's. That evening we went up to Rog's room to pick him up and found a donnybrook in full swing, with several factions warring over the prize. I thought they'd tear the poor guy apart.

During the thirties the gambling boats offered cheap excitement. A three-mile launch ride for a quarter across Long Beach or Santa Monica harbor, an excellent dinner free on a good sized ship, drinks for a quarter at the bar and music to dance to if you chose. Of course, you were expected to lose at the crap, roulette, and twenty-one layouts and you did, but our system was to allot five dollars to be lost, figuring that the dinners and boat rides were well worth it.

Rog, though, lost a couple of hundred. I felt pretty sick about that but Terrill shrugged it off, his eyes shining. As we rode back across the moonlight harbor he stood up in the rear of the launch looking like Washington crossing the Delaware, swelled his chest and grinned at me, saying fervently,

"Tod, thanks. Tonight I have looked into the bright eye of danger."

Such histrionics were part of what made Rog a great editor. He lived his part and really believed it. There was about as much danger on a gambling boat as at a church ice cream social. They were gangster run, certainly, but much too profitable to risk frightening customers away.

One writer however did damn near get into trouble on Tony Carnero's *Rex*. Glen Wichman was a mousy, half bald druggist who had turned to writing westerns and was one of Street and Smith's highest paid performers. He had been raised in Needles on the desert and knew what he was writing about.

On one particular night we went out to the *Rex* alone, unsuspecting that Earl Warren, then attorney general and looking forward to a political future, had ordered the boat raided. When the police launches began circling it Tony's crew held them off with streams of water from the fire hoses, but one of them spotted Glen and decided he was an undercover agent for district attorney Burton Fitt's office.

Glen was grabbed by a pair of crew men and hustled to a cabin where gangster type lieutenants interrogated him. He said he was a writer and they laughed at him. "Hell," said one, "That's what I used to tell the cops in Chicago."

Glen brought out his Authors' League card and they laughed harder, tore it up and told him he'd have to do better than that. Getting desperate, Glen fished through his wallet and came up with his pharmacist's license. They took it, looked it over at length and were impressed. It was obviously old, probably thirty years, and one of the hoods admitted that no detective and certainly no writer would try to pass himself off as a druggest if he weren't.

Another close friend was Bob Bellem. I have no idea what his output was, but it was enormous. He wrote most of *Spicy Detective, Saucy Detective* and had his own book, *Dan Turner, Hollywood Detective*, writing the full contents every month. In addition he and I turned out *Super Detective* for Trojan Publishing Company. This was a meal ticket worth four hundred dollars a month to each of us. It took me three days on a dictaphone to do the rough, then Bob did the polish.

So it was with considerable surprise that one year I received from the company a tax report showing that they had paid me over forty thousand dollars.

Bob had a similar report, not for the same sum but for a hell of a lot more than he had collected. We squealed to Frank Armor like a pair of stuck pigs. Come to find out, two of the assistant editors had dreamed up a neat little racket of their own.

They had gone back into the magazine's files, pulled stories, changed the names with a lead pencil, rerun them, vouchered them through to Bob and me and some other contributors, had the checks drawn, taken them down to their favorite bar, forged the endorsements and cashed them.

Bellem was a former newspaperman from Philadelphia, Tulsa, San Jose and Pasadena. He and I wrote the *Dick Tracy* television show for Herb Molton. Then Bob went as story editor on *A Man Without A Gun*. He contributed to the *FBI* series and with me did a number of *Death Valley Days* for Ronnie Reagan.

Speaking of television, Tommy Blackburn moved from the pulps to the screen and he and I wrote the original six *Wild Bill Hickok* scripts, then Tommy jumped to the *Davy Crockett* show for Walt Disney.

Another one on me. My wife and I were at Tommy's the night he brought home the first rough cut record of the *Ballad of Davy Crockett* and played it for us. There was no arrangement yet and she and I looked at each other, not knowing what to say. When we got down off the hill he lived on, high above Burbank, I exploded.

"Blackburn must have lost his mind. If Walt uses that song the program will be the laughing stock of the town."

The ballad, of course, skyrocketed to the top of the Hit Parade and stayed there for months, proving that while I may know a little about writing stories, I sure don't know anything about music.

There is another story involving Rog Terrill. On his trip to the coast he went down to see Walt Coburn near San Diego. Walt was one of the most prolific men in the western field and son of old Pat Coburn, an early Montana sheriff. He used to tell it that the old man would set a water glass of whiskey on the kitchen table at night and the first of his boys to get down and build the fires in the morning got the whiskey. With that background it's no wonder that Walt enjoyed the bottle, but his wife saw to it that he had difficulty accommodating the habit.

He and Rog took off for Walt's summer cottage in Arizona and arrived there on a chilly afternoon. Coburn had cleaned out his office before leaving the camp in the fall and stuffed the discarded papers into the iron stove. Now he added wood and put a match to it.

The room had hardly begun to warm when the stove exploded, blew its door past Rog's ear, and there was a scramble to keep the place from going up in flames. Coburn's red-faced explanation was that he had a standing order with a Mexican neighbor to keep him supplied with Tequila. The man had hidden a quart in the stove and Coburn had stuffed the papers in on top of it and forgotten it. Rog wrote to me later that a greenhorn wasn't safe in the West even today.

And then there's a man who stands at the forefront of the pulps, Erle Gardner, whom I knew rather well. I do not know how many Perry Mason titles there are, and those people who never read one of his books certainly know the television program. Gardner was a man of immense energy and enthusiasm. Tom Curry tells of the early *Black Mask* days when the eastern writers would gather in Grand Central Station and catch the train to Scarsdale to Joe

Shaw's parties. Tom claims you could hear Erle from one end of the train to the other, talking at the top of his voice.

He was still talking when I met him. He had been a writer and clerk in the Ventura district attorney's office and picked up an unconventional legal education. Shaw wrote me that Gardner was living in an apartment above Vine Street, sent me his phone number and told me to call. I did, Gardner said to come up at six and we would go out for dinner.

When I got there I was greeted by one of his three secretaries who said Erle was dictating, had a couple of chapters to finish and then would join me. She disappeared. I could hear his big voice somewhere offstage. I began to burn. He had made the six o'clock date, I had rushed to be there on time, and now he expected me to cool my heels while he did two chapters. I wondered how long he would be at it.

The voice came through a curtained arch. I walked to it and peered through the curtain and had my first look at Erle Gardner. He sat on a couch, bent over his knees, a dictaphone horn cupped in both hands, talking so fast that I could not follow the words. Ten minutes later he came out. I don't know how long those chapters were but I'm sure they were spoken faster than any two others on record by any other writer.

Gardner has to have been the greatest salesman in the business. I am sure of only one sale he did not make, when he tried to talk me into doing a book on the heyday of the magazine market. We were having dinner at the old Alexanderia Hotel with the editor of *Liberty*, Bill Lingle, and his assistant, Dick Carroll. Carroll had been the Wonder Boy, the youngest story editor Hollywood had ever known when he was at Fox, and later he became editor of Gold Medal Books. At the moment he and Lingle were arranging to publish serially Gardner's first book, and they had asked him to bring me along with the idea that I might do a serial for them using my character, Bill Lennox.

I asked what they would pay and they said four hundred-fifty for the magazine rights and I would be free to place the hardcover book rights. Crime Club was paying two hundred-fifty for books at the time. Together I would make seven hundred dollars for a fifty thousand word manuscript. Shaw was paying me four-fifty for twelve thousand words. I told them I couldn't afford to work for them at those prices.

Gardner took over the sales pitch, leaned forward, hooked a finger in the breast pocket of my coat and nearly pulled me across the table.

"Books," he said. "That's the way you have to go. You want to be a lousy pulp writer all your life? In ten years I'll have thirty books under my belt. What will you have?"

I couldn't see that far ahead. I didn't do the book. It was ten years before the death of the pulps forced me into the book field, and he was right. But I wouldn't have liked to miss the excitement of the pulps and their people.

Introduction

MANY OF THE HARDBOILED WRITERS of the *Black Mask/Dime Detective* school have had short story collections reprinted. In the 1940s and 1950s fans of the private dicks could obtain copies of Paul Cain's *Seven Slayers*, Frederick Nebel's *Six Deadly Dames*, George Harmon Coxe's *Flash Casey*, several collections by Raymond Chandler and the Dashiell Hammett short stories collected by Ellery Queen.

There were even several famous anthologies which offered stories by otherwise unavailable authors: Joseph T. Shaw's *Hard-Boiled Omnibus* (both the longer 1946 hardback and the somewhat shorter 1952 paperback edition), Ron Goulart's valuable collection *The Hardboiled Dicks* (1965), Herbert Ruhm's *The Hard-Boiled Detective: Stories from 'Black Mask' Magazine 1920-1951* (1977) and Bill Pronzini's recent *Detective and Mystery Stories from the Great Pulps* (1983).

Yet with all these collections available, there was not a single short story by W.T. Ballard in print. It's quite true that Tod Ballard's most famous character, Bill Lennox, is not strictly speaking a PI. Still, he has all the elements except for carrying the license and he was one of the most popular characters in *Black Mask*, appearing twenty-seven times between 1933 and 1942.

This volume is just a sampling of Bill Lennox, a selection for both the connoisseur of crime and the lover of good, fast-moving crime/adventure stories. As the title of Lennox's first adventure—"A Little Different"—indicates, by 1933 even Cap Shaw was aware that the hardboiled formula needed enhancement. By this time, Hammett was no longer writing for *Black Mask*; Raymond Chandler had not entered the field; Carroll John Daly was showing signs of declining popularity (at least with the editors); and Erle Stanley Gardner was concentrating on his new Perry Mason novels. Shaw himself would edit *Black Mask* for only three more years before becoming an agent.

Of course three Bill Lennox novels were available to the public in the 1940s and sold quite well. Even so, the short story appearances of Ballard's Hollywood Troubleshooter have a different sort of charm from that of the novels. *Black Mask* writers often spoke of their freedom to develop character in their tough guys. There is a sense of immediacy with Lennox; the reader likes Lennox. He's hardboiled enough to satisfy all but the fringe element, yet has a respect for women which is atypical of the normal pulp orientation. One of Tod Ballard's achievements as a pulp writer is his ability to portray realistically a sense of love between characters. There are chiseling harpies and heartless bozos in these stories but these types are not protagonists. Lennox is as warm a pulp character as can be found. He romances girl friend Nancy Hobbs through nine years in the pulps and eighteen more in novels, obeying all the dicta against a hardboiled character's marriage, yet still revealing the real commitment which is a characteristic element of a Ballard PI. His stories quite often conclude with the "happy" ending of a marriage proposal, following closely on the identification of the murderer who has been trying to keep the protagonist from such a marriage declaration.

The stories in this collection present Bill Lennox at key points in his career. We first see him in his debut appearance in *Black Mask*: "A Little Different" (September, 1933) and "A Million-Dollar Tramp" (October, 1933). In these stories, we find all the now familiar characters of the Ballard created Hollywood milieu: Sol Spurck (the egotistical but mostly benign movie studio mogul), the seemingly unchanging actors and actresses who wage their fierce little battles over roles and image (the names change but the character types rarely do), Nancy Hobbs ("pert and chic, plainly pleased with Lennox," his long term and long suffering girl friend/lover who spends most of her time trying to get Bill to quit the studio and write the great American novel), Jake (one of a long line of studio minions who help Lennox get studio hams and vapid female stars out of trouble, usually murder) and Sam Marx (the archetypical Jewish attorney). Later (in "Gamblers Don't Win," April, 1935 and "Scars of Murder," November, 1939), we meet Captain Floyd Spellman (the not so dumb cop who regularly appears as Lennox's friend and nemesis).

The final Lennox short story, "Lights, Action—Killer!" (May, 1942), shows Ballard planning his character's first book appearance. This story, while having all the characteristic pulp touches (one of the characters is murdered by being sliced in two in a sawmill), marks a change in emphasis. There is even more characterization than usual with Ballard. We learn that Lennox was a student at Northwestern and had been a newspaperman in Chicago, the same facts which Ballard reworked into his first book appearance in *Say Yes To Murder* (1942). Ballard correctly believed that people read stories about believable people. All his stories, no matter how pulp in orientation, have this common element of humanity.

Lennox succeeds for this reason. He is comfortable territory, a likable character in fast moving, literate, yet tough stories. The stories display a confident sense of period, reflect their era very well, yet retain a timeless sense which makes them accessible. The original *Black Mask* readers enjoyed and highly regarded them. You will too.

A Little Different

By
W. T. BALLARD

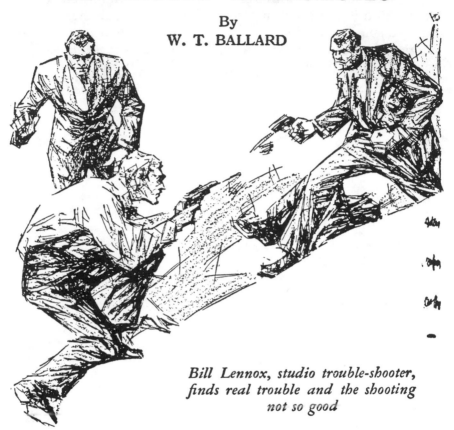

Bill Lennox, studio trouble-shooter, finds real trouble and the shooting not so good

ILL LENNOX nodded to the gateman and climbed on to the shine stand, just inside the General gate. The shineboy grinned, his white teeth flashing in his dark face. "When is you all gwine tuh star me, Mister Lennox?"

Bill said, absently: "Pretty soon, Sam. Lean on that brush, will you; I'm in a hurry."

"I'se leaning." The boy ducked his head and went to work briskly. A big gleaming car came through the gate.

Bill could see the woman on the rear seat, a dazzling blonde with dark eyebrows. He watched the car sourly until it halted before the star's bungalow dressing-room. The blonde descended, assisted by her maid, and disappeared. Lennox said something under his breath, found a quarter which he tossed to the boy, and climbed from his seat.

Sol Spurck, head of General-Consolidated Films, put his short fingers together and stared at Lennox as the latter came into his office. "Where was you yesterday?"

Lennox looked at him without visible

emotion. "Out, Sol. Out doing your dirty work."

The short figure behind the big desk shifted uncertainly. "I told you that you should watch out for that dumb cluck Wayborn. He's in a jam."

Lennox shoved his hands deep into his trousers pockets and sat down upon the corner of the desk. "What, again?"

Spurck seemed to explode. "Again— again! Always that guy—"

"Save it." Lennox's voice was very tired. "What's he done now?"

"Am I a mind reader—am I?" Spurck had come to his feet and was bouncing about the office. "What is it that I pay you for—what is it? Must I do everything—everything? I tell you that Wayborn's gone. Fifty thousand they want—fifty thousand for that——"

Lennox said: "Remember your arteries, Sol. Who wants fifty grand and for what?"

Spurck was wrenching open the drawer of his desk. He pulled forth a dirty scrap of paper and shoved it at Lennox. "Find him—find him quick. Are we half through shooting *Dangerous Love?* I ask you. Can we shoot without Wayborn? But fifty thousand for that *schlemiel.* I wouldn't pay fifty thousand for Gable yet, and they ask it for a ham like Wayborn."

Lennox said: "You wouldn't pay fifty grand for your grandmother," and stared at the piece of paper. On it were printed crude letters with a soft pencil. They said:

"We've got Wayborn. You've got fifty grand. Let's trade. Go to the cops and we drop him into the ocean. More later."

Lennox looked at his boss. "Where'd this come from?"

Spurck threw up his hands, appealing to the ceiling. "He asks me riddles yet. Mein Gott! He asks me riddles."

Lennox said, roughly: "Cut it. Where'd this come from? Who's seen it?"

His voice seemed to quiet the little man. Spurck returned to his chair and lit an enormous cigar with care. "No one has seen it," he said in a surly tone. "I found it on the floor of my car this morning."

"How long has Wayborn been gone?"

Spurck shrugged. "Yesterday, he was here. Today, he is not. Find him? Yes—but fifty thousand—no. Ten maybe. Not one cent over ten."

Lennox said: "I suppose you know what this will mean? The picture is half in the can. If we don't find Wayborn, we shoot it over and Price is three days behind schedule now."

Spurck's eyes were narrow. "Why did you let me use Wayborn? That ham— what is it I pay you for?"

Lennox said: "Because I'm a fool"; he said it bitterly. "Because I stick around this mad house and keep things going. Some day, Sol, I'll quit this lousy outfit cold. I'll sit back and watch it go to the devil."

Spurck grinned. He'd heard the threat before, many times. "Find him, Bill." He reached across and patted Lennox's shoulder with a fat hand. "Find him, and I take you to Caliente. That's a promise yet."

2

BILL LENNOX, trouble - shooter for General-Consolidated Studio, walked through the outer office. Trouble-shooter wasn't his title. In fact, one of the things which Lennox lacked was an official title. Those in Hollywood who didn't like him, called him Spurck's watch-dog. Ex-reporter, ex-publicity man, he had drifted into his present place through his inability to say yes and his decided ability in saying no.

His searching blue eyes swept about the large waiting-room. A world-famous writer bowed, half fearfully. A director whose last three pictures had hit the box-office paused for a moment to speak to him. Bill grunted and went on. As he walked down the line towards the row of dressing-rooms he was thinking quickly. Wayborn was gone. They needed him for *Dangerous Love*. No one seemed to know anything about him.

Lennox paused before the door of the third bungalow and knocked. A trim maid opened the door. Her eyes were uncertain when she saw who it was. Bill said: "Tell Miss Meyer that I want to see her."

The maid's eyes got more uncertain. "I don't think—"

His voice rasped. "You aren't paid to think. Tell Meyer that I want to see her at once."

Elva Meyer's eyes were cold, hostile beneath her dark brows as he walked through the door. She was seated before her dressing-table, but there was as yet no greasepaint on her face. "Well?" Her voice was colder than her eyes.

He was staring at her blonde hair. "I'm not so hot," he said, helping himself to a chair. "When did you see Wayborn last?"

The eyes flecked, glowed for an instant. "I told you some time ago that I was perfectly capable of looking after my affairs without your help."

"Yeah?" He'd found a loose cigarette in his pocket and was rolling it back and forth between his strong fingers so that the tobacco spilled out at both ends. "Well, sweetheart, it so happens that I'm not sticking my schnozzle into your playhouse at the moment. You and Wayborn were at the *Grove* last night, then you turned up at the *Brown Derby* about one—"

She pushed back her chair, noisily. "I'm not going to stand this any longer —your jealous spying is driving me insane. I'm going to Mr. Spurck."

He said, "Nerts! You'll get damn' little sympathy from Sol today, honey. He left it at home, wrapped in moth-balls— but you're getting ideas under that peroxide-treated mat of yours. I'm not checking on you because I'm still interested. I'm washed up, baby, washed up. You're not the first chiseling tramp that forgot my first name after I boosted them into lights, and I don't suppose that you'll be the last. I always was a sucker

for a pretty face with nice hips for a background; but this is strictly business. *Dangerous Love* should be in the can by the last of the week. It won't be unless Price can shoot."

She said: "I've been here all morning, waiting." She said it in the tone of one who does not like to wait.

Lennox grinned. For the first time in days he was enjoying himself. "You're good, baby," his voice mocked her. "You're plenty good. You should be. I found you, trained you, but you aren't good enough to play love scenes by yourself. Wayborn isn't around. He's been snatched."

She made her eyes wide. "Snatched?" she said, slowly. "You mean—"

His voice rasped with impatience. "Quit acting. You read the papers. You know what snatched means. They want fifty grand and they won't get it."

She sank back into her chair as if her legs suddenly refused to support her. "This is terrible. When did it happen?"

His eyes were sardonic. "That's what I'm asking you, sweetheart. You were with him last night. He hasn't been seen this morning."

Her eyes blazed and she made two small white hands into little fists. "You're lousy, Bill Lennox. You can't tie me into this." Her voice threatened to break. "Ralph took me home at one-thirty. I haven't seen him since."

His eyes searched her face. "I guess you're in the clear, kid." He sounded almost regretful. "Wayborn's boy says that he came in around two, but that he went out again, without his car."

She gained assurance at his words. "But what will Spurck do? He'll have to pay the fifty grand."

"Will he? You don't know Sol, sweetheart."

"But he can't junk the picture. Why, he's spent more than that on publicity."

Lennox shrugged. "We'll reshoot it if Wayborn doesn't turn up." He was on his feet; the girl came out of her chair.

"But he can't leave Ralph to—to—die. It isn't human."

Lennox's voice grated. "Want to pay the fifty grand yourself?"

She stared at him. "I pay the fifty thousand? Don't be absurd."

"There's your answer," he told her. "That's the way Sol feels, and Wayborn isn't Sol's boy-friend."

She said, angrily: "You're getting nasty again; but Sol will have to pay. I'll go to the papers, to the police."

"Do that," he suggested, "and you and me will be going to one swell funeral; that is—if they find the body."

3

 ANCY HOBBS was eating in Al Levy's when Lennox came through the door. She nodded to the empty chair, and he sank into it. "Hello, Brat."

She smiled at him. "You look worried, Bill."

He ordered before he answered. "And you look swell. Why don't you go into pictures instead of writing about them?"

She said, "Because I know too much. You have to be dumb to get by, like Elva Meyer."

He scowled. "Seems I saw an interview in a fan magazine where you said that she was just a home girl—"

Nancy laughed, not nicely. "She is. Anybody's home girl. Look at the ones she's wrecked."

He said: "Lay off! I'm trying to think. I can't when you chatter."

She was silent with no sign of resentment. He broke a piece of bread savagely. "Wayborn's been snatched."

Her eyes were narrow. "What is it? A publicity gag?"

"I wish to.—— it was. The dumb cluck is gone; someone wants fifty grand."

Her eyes were still suspicious. "I don't trust you, Bill; not since you pulled that burning-yacht stunt."

He didn't grin. "I'm out of that racket, sweetheart. I've got to find Wayborn. The picture's half in the can and the big slob looks like a million. Sol is howling his head off."

She said: "Why don't you chuck it, Bill—pull loose? You used to be a decent pal; now you're nothing but a two-timing mugg. Get loose. Shove off to New York. Write that book. You've been writing it in your mind for ten years."

His mouth twisted with a shade of bitterness. "What would I use for money, sweet?"

She stared at him. "You're getting three fifty—"

He spread his hands. "It goes—I'm living on week-after-next now. Sol lets me draw ahead."

"Sweet of him. He knows that he can hold you as long as you're broke. Listen, Bill. I've got a few dollars that aren't working their heads off. I'll stake you. Get the Chief tomorrow and get the hell out of this town."

For a moment he was silent, then he patted the back of her hand. "It won't work, babe. I gotta find Wayborn. I gotta get that damn' picture into the can; after that, we'll talk about it."

She sighed, knowing that she had lost. "This Wayborn thing? It's on the level?"

He said: "So help me."

She sat there, playing with her fork, thinking. Finally she looked up at him. "Better see Red Girkin."

He stared at her. "Who's Girkin? What is this?"

She said, in a tired voice: "I'm helping, pal. Helping as I always do. Go on. See Girkin. He's got an apartment on Van Ness off Melrose." She gave him the number.

He said, roughly: "What do you know, babe?"

She shook her head. "Just a hunch. Go see him. Stall." She gathered her bag and gloves and rose. "You can pay my check, that is, if you have enough."

He said, absently: "My credit's good, but Nance, what's the—"

"For a smart guy, you ask plenty of questions. You wouldn't believe me if I told you."

She was gone, leaving him staring after her. Lennox said something under his breath, then went on with his dinner. Afterward he took a taxi.

The cab dropped him at the corner of Melrose and he walked to the apartment house. A row of brass-bound mail-boxes stared at him from the tiled-lobby wall. One of them, number five, had the name, W. C. Girkin. There was another name, but Lennox did not notice it. He pushed the bell viciously. The door at the bottom of the carpeted stairs buzzed as the catch was released from above. Lennox pulled it open and started up the steps. At their head a man in a light, close-fitting suit waited.

The man said: "What the hell?"

Lennox stared at him and said: "Hello, Charley."

Charley took a thin hand out of his right coat pocket and wrapped the fingers around those of Lennox. "I'll be a so and so. How are you, pally? How'd you know that I was in this burg?"

Lennox started to say that he hadn't known, then stopped. "I know things," he grinned. "What's the matter? Cops in the big town get rough?"

The other shrugged. "Pal of mine had a doll out here. I drifted out with him. Jeeze. What a country!"

Lennox said: "Some of us like it. You ought to have blown in a year sooner. Could have used you in a gangster picture."

Charley said, "Me?" and made his eyes very wide. "You've got me wrong, pally. I'm just a business man with ideas. But come on. Red will think they've put the finger on me." He turned and led the way towards the door of number five. The door was closed and he knocked, three knocks close together, another after a slight pause. The door came open and

Charley said: "Okey, just a pal. Meet Red Girkin. This is Bill Lennox."

The red-headed man said hello without evident pleasure. He was big, with heavy shoulders and a rather short neck. He sat down on a chair before the small built-in desk and went on with his game of solitaire. Once he swore to himself and turned over a pile of cards to reach an ace. Charley said: "What are you doing in Suckerville?"

Lennox laughed. "That's one for the book. You'd make a swell gag man."

The other nodded slowly. "There's money in these hills, Pal. Like to cut you in."

The red-headed man at the desk said: "Shut up." He made it sound vicious.

Lennox looked at him with narrow eyes, then back at Charley. "Your friend doesn't like me."

The thin man grinned. "Don't mind him; it's just the bad booze. Lemme have your number. I might put you on to something swell."

4

ILL LENNOX said to Spurck. "I haven't found the slob yet, but I know who's got him."

Spurck was excited. He came out of his chair and bounced around the corner of the big desk. "You know—you know, and you don't go to the police yet?"

"Listen, Sol. Why don't you try thinking once in a while before you open that mouth of yours? I know who's got Wayborn, but I don't know why and I don't know where he is."

"Who's got him?"

"That's one thing that it isn't wise for you to know. These boys are tough, Sol. It don't mean a thing to them that you're the biggest shot in the industry. They'd as soon rub you out as look at you. In fact, they'd a little rather. You never won any beauty contests, you know."

Spurck sat down at his desk again. "What do we do, then?"

"We pay fifty grand."

"You're crazy!"

"Sure, I got that way, working for you. We pay the fifty grand, finish the picture, and then I try to get it back. If I don't, we spread the story all over the front page and charge the fifty grand to publicity. What the hell else can we do?"

Spurck swore. He raved. He almost cried, but Lennox paid no attention. "Take it and like it," he said. "You've spent more than that on New York flops and kept nothing but the title. Have you heard from the gang?"

The little man pulled out his desk drawer and found an envelope which he handed to Lennox. "They want I should bring the money down to Redondo, in a suitcase. I should bring it myself, and I should not bring the cops; no one but me and my chauffeur."

Lennox said: "Okey. Go to the bank and get the dough in small bills as they say. Don't be a sap and mark them. Then take a ride to Redondo tonight."

Spurck rolled his eyes. "It ain't that I'm afraid, you understand; but I don't like it, I'm telling you."

Lennox grinned. "I'm your chauffeur, Sol. I wouldn't miss this party for a lot."

At seven o'clock Lennox swung the Lincoln town car out of the driveway of Spurck's Beverly Hills home. Dressed in brown livery, borrowed from the chauffeur, he was hardly recognizable as he cut across towards Inglewood and picked up Redondo Boulevard.

In the back seat Spurck, with a black bag clutched between his fat knees, was nervously watching the passing traffic. Lennox stepped the car up to sixty and watched the back road in the rear-view mirror. At Rosecrans Avenue a Chevrolet coupé swung in behind them and followed them through Manhattan and

Hermosa. Lennox slowed down to twenty and the coupé slowed down also. As they reached Redondo city limits, the Chevrolet speeded up and ran them to the curb. Two men were in the coupé, hats drawn low over their eyes. Lennox saw that the one beside the driver carried a riot gun across his knees.

For a minute, the road was empty, no traffic coming either way. The man with the riot gun said: "Keep your hands on that wheel, mugg."

Lennox obeyed, a thin smile twisting his lips for a moment. He knew that voice, knew it well. The man with the gun said to Spurck: "Toss the bag over, quick!"

With trembling fingers, Spurck obeyed. The driver of the coupé opened the bag, inspected the contents. "If these are marked, guy, it's curtains for you. Okey, Charley."

The man with the gun nodded. "Keep driving through Redondo and up through Palos Verde till you come to where the road ends and another road goes off to the left and into Pedro. Drive out in the field at the end of the road. You'll find your ham along the top of the cliff, tied up. We were set to push him over if you didn't show up." The coupé's motor speeded up and they jerked away, swinging left at the next street.

Spruck moaned: "Fifty thousand!" He sounded out of breath.

Lennox put the Lincoln in gear. They went through Redondo, climbed the hill beyond and skirted the ocean until they came to the road's end. Five minutes later, with the aid of a flashlight from the tool-box, Lennox found Wayborn. The actor was tied securely, lying flat on his back so close to the cliff's edge that had he made any effort to free his bonds, he might have rolled off. Aside from chafed wrists and stiff ankles, he appeared none the worse for his experience, nor was he even thankful. "You might have gotten here sooner," he told them, in a peevish voice. "I assure you that it was far from comfortable lying here, bound hand and foot."

Spurck exploded. For five minutes he called the actor everything that he could think of. Wayborn listened silently, then climbed into the car. Lennox grinned to himself as he turned the Lincoln towards town.

5

TAN BRAUN, Spurck's nephew, walked back and forth across his uncle's office. He was slight, with black curly hair and long eyelashes. He looked like an actor and wasn't. He was production manager for the studio.

"It's strange," he said, "that Lennox advised you to pay that money. I wish that you'd have asked me about it." He pouted as a small boy pouts when his feelings have been hurt.

Spurck threw his hands wide. "Ask you? What good does asking you get me? Does it bring back Wayborn? Does it catch Price up with his schedule? It was you that wanted Wayborn ——that ham. It was you that held up the schedule three days, changing the story. Maybe you would have got him back and saved us fifty thousand—you—"

Braun said, harshly: "At least I'd have marked the money. You say Lennox wouldn't let you do that?"

Spurck's face became crafty. "Which shows what you know. Me, I got a list of them bills from the bank. Every number. A copy I have made which Lennox takes. If we had marked the bills, they might have killed Wayborn when the picture is only half shot, to say nothing of retakes. Such ideas you've got."

Braun's voice was stubborn. "You could have hired private detectives."

"A swell idea, when the barn door is closed and the horse is—"

"Anyhow," his nephew's voice rasped, "I've hired some. They're waiting outside now."

Abe Rollins and Dan Grogan came in. Grogan was big with a flat Irish face. Rollins was small, dark, with shifty eyes and too white teeth. He said: "Please tuh met yuh, Mr. Spurck. Braun's been telling us about your trouble. Don't worry, we'll turn these muggs up." He examined the two notes from the kidnapers. "I'd like to talk to Lennox," he said. Spurck hesitated, then pressed one of the buttons at the side of his desk.

Bill came through the door and nodded slightly to Braun. His blue eyes narrowed as they went over the two detectives; then he looked at Spurck. "What's eating you now, Sol?"

Spurck explained. As Lennox listened, his eyes got narrower. Then he looked at Rollins. "Okey. What do you want me to tell you?"

The man cleared his throat with importance. "Did you recognize either of the men in the Chevy?"

Lennox hesitated, then said: "No. Their faces were shadowed by their hats. I couldn't have recognized my grandmother."

"Yet you told Mr. Spurck that you knew who had Wayborn?"

Lennox said: "Yeah, I also told him that I'd try to get the fifty grand back, if he let me work it my way. I didn't figure that he'd run in a couple of lame brains to mess things up."

Rollins' face got red, Grogan shifted his feet. "Don't be too smart, fella," Rollins warned. "You're not in the clear on this thing, not by a damn' sight."

Lennox said: "Now isn't that just too swell? You'll be telling me next that I framed the whole play and got the fifty grand myself."

"That's not such a bad idea," Rollins snapped. "Maybe you did. As I remember it, you advised Mr. Spurck to pay the money."

"That's right, Bill, you did." Spurck sounded excited.

Lennox looked at him. "So you got me tagged as a kidnaper too. Okey, Sol, get your own fifty grand back. I'm quitting, washed up." He swung towards the door. Rollins' voice stopped him.

"Not so fast, punk." The detective's hand was in his coat pocket, shoving the gun forward against the cloth.

Lennox shrugged. "You seem to be running the set." He turned back into the room.

Spurck said: "Just a few questions, Bill. Don't get sore."

Rollins said: "Isn't it true that you are always broke?"

"Ask Sol," Lennox advised. "He's my banker."

"And isn't it true that you told Mr. Spurck that you knew who had Wayborn?"

"What of it?"

"You may be asked to explain that statement at the D. A. office." Rollins' voice was threatening.

"Nerts!" Lennox found himself a cigarette and lit it.

"And isn't it also true that you offered to drive the car to Redondo? I should say that you insisted that you be allowed to drive; yet you made no effort to follow the kidnapers after the money had been passed?"

Lennox shrugged. "Go right ahead, bright boy. Wrap me up in cellophane and deliver me at San Quentin; but while you're talking, the muggs are spending Sol's dough." Spurck groaned, and Lennox laughed.

6

NANCY HOBBS said: "So you finally quit." She said it in the tone of one who hears about a miracle and does not believe.

Lennox nodded. "Can you feature that? After all I've put up with from that fat slob he accuses me of kidnaping. There's one of his funny-looking dicks outside this joint now. I'm getting important."

She said: "Now's your chance to get out of this town. No," as he started to speak. "I know you're broke, but I've still got a stake."

He was silent and she read refusal in his silence. "Too proud to borrow from a woman?" There was a jeer in her voice. "You've done worse."

He said: "It isn't that, Nance. You're a pal. I could borrow from you, but I can't scram with this hanging over my head. I'll get Sol's fifty grand back, then I'll take a powder; but I can't go until I do. I said that I'd find that dough and I will."

"Don't be a fool," her voice was hoarse. "These boys play rough. If they get the idea that you're gumming their game, they'll plant you in a ditch."

He looked at her with narrow eyes. "What boys, Nance? You seem to know a lot about this play."

"I know plenty about this town that I don't print in fan magazines," she told him. "I get around."

"Words," his voice was harsh. "Why not pass out some names."

She said: "Girkin. I gave you that once."

"Where's he tie in? A cheap New York hood."

"He used to hang around the New York club where Elva Meyer undressed," she said, softly. "That wasn't her name then, but she's the same girl that you promoted into lights."

"Is this straight?"

"Did I ever give you a wrong steer, Bill?"

Lennox was silent for a moment, then he shrugged. "That's nothing to keep me awake nights. Girkin may be a big shot in New York, but he doesn't rate out here."

"Doesn't he? I saw him on the boulevard yesterday with French and they didn't act like strangers."

Lennox swore softly. "French of the *El Romano Club*, huh? Nice people."

The girl smiled with her mouth, but

her eyes were serious. "Friend of yours, isn't he?"

Lennox shrugged absently. "So long." He rose. "I'll be seeing you in New York."

She rose also. "You're not losing me, Bill Lennox. I'm in this if you are." She followed him into the street. He grasped her thin wrist in strong fingers.

"Don't play the sap, sweetheart. It would be just that much tougher, having you along."

A cab cruised by. He let go her wrist and jumped to the running-board. The next moment he was inside. "Go ahead fast," he told the startled driver. The cab lurched forward. Lennox peered through the back window. He saw Grogan cross the pavement and wave wildly to an approaching taxi. Lennox found a five in his pocket and passed it to the driver. "There's a guy following us. Lose him."

The driver grinned and turned sharply into Vine, right on Sunset, left at Highland, crashing a signal. Finally, at the corner of Arlington and Pico, he pulled to the curb. "Where to?"

Lennox said: "Take me to Melrose and Van Ness." The driver shrugged and turned towards Western.

Lennox got out at the corner and walked to the apartment house. He rang the bell of suite five, got no answer, tried nine and was answered by a buzz from the door. He jerked it open and started up the stairs. A woman's voice called: "What is it, please?"

Lennox said: "I pushed the wrong bell. Sorry." Her door slammed, and he paused before number five. He knocked without response, then tried the knob. The door was unlocked. He opened it cautiously and stepped into the small hall. For a moment he stood listening. There was no sound in the apartment. He closed the door softly and went along the hall to the living-room door. There he stopped and said something under his breath. The door

was partly open. Through the crack he saw the figure of a man sprawled in the middle of the rug. His quick eyes went about the room, then he pushed the door wide and crossed to the body. The face, twisted with fear and pain, was that of Charley, and he was very dead

7

ILL LENNOX found nothing in the apartment that interested him. There were no papers in the desk, nothing, in fact, except a soiled deck of cards. He went into the bedroom and looked through the closets. Two suits hung there, flashy garments of extreme cut, nothing more. He walked back to the living-room and stopped just inside the door. There was a man looking at the body, a man with a gun in his hand, who said: "Now isn't this swell?" The man was Grogan.

Lennox didn't say anything and the private dick laughed.

"Imagine finding you here." His voice held a note of gloating self-satisfaction. His gun came up so that it bore on the second button of Lennox's vest. "Get the paws in the air, nice boy."

Lennox obeyed, and Grogan picked up the phone. "Gimme Hollywood station, and make it snappy." His eyes never left Lennox's face, the gun did not move. "That you, Bert? Grogan of Rollins and Grogan. Yeah, listen. Is Lew there? Swell. Let me talk to him, will yuh? Hello, Lew, Grogan. Listen. There's a stiff in an apartment on Van Ness." He gave the number. "It's close to Melrose, apartment five. Yeah, I got the mugg. He's standing against the wall with his hands in the air. Make it snappy." He hung up and grinned at Lennox. "Nice weather we're having."

Lennox didn't say anything. He

stood there with his hands in the air. They stood there seven minutes, then a siren moaned below, heavy feet made noise on the stairs, and three men in plainclothes came in. The leader nodded to Grogan and looked at Lennox, then at the huddled body on the floor.

He said: "What's going on here? Who's the stiff?"

Grogan shrugged. "I don't know who he is. I was trailing this bird. He came up here and I sneaked up after him. When I got here, he was searching the joint."

The city detective's eyes went to Lennox. "Well, what's the story?" His voice sounded bored, uninterested.

Lennox shrugged. "When I got here, Charley was on the floor with a knife in his guts. That's all I know."

Grogan pursed his lips and made a funny sound of disbelief. The homicide man said: "Charley who?"

"Bartelli."

"Where's he from?"

"New York."

Two other men came through the apartment door. One said: "What's going on here, Lew?"

The other looked at Lennox and said: "Hello, Bill." Lennox recognized Alder, of the *Post*.

The city detective said: "So you know this guy?"

Alder's eyes widened. "Sure, everybody knows him. He's Bill Lennox of General-Consolidated. What's it all about, Lew?"

The city man looked hard at Grogan. "Thought you said that you were trailing this dude?"

Grogan shifted his weight from one foot to the other. "I was, Sol Spurck's orders."

Both reporters looked interested. Lennox snapped: "Be careful, you fool."

The city detective looked at him. "When I want to hear you talk, I'll ask you. All right, Grogan. Go ahead with the story and don't skip anything."

Grogan said: "Well, yuh see, it's this way. Ralph Wayborn was snatched—"

"Snatched?"

"Yeah." He went on and told the whole story. The reporters looked at each other. "So I was trailing Lennox to find where he had the dough planted, and I walked in on this."

The city detective said: "So we've got a kidnaping charge on you along with a murder rap."

Lennox said, in a tired voice: "That man's been dead hours. If you birds would think before you open your mouths, you'd know that. Grogan here is my alibi. He can swear that I wasn't in this place five minutes before he walked in." Lennox smiled sweetly at the now silent private detective.

8

NANCY HOBBS said: "So you wouldn't listen to me and you get yourself into a worse jam." They were seated before the Hollywood Station in her car. "Will you go to New York now?"

"Such ideas you have, Brat. I'm going to get that fifty grand."

"You'll probably get a knife about where Charley got his."

"At least that would be a new experience. Who was it that said there is nothing new under the sun?"

She swore whole-heartedly and stepped on the starter. "Where do we go from here?"

"You don't go anywhere," he told her.

"I suppose I'm to hang around, ready to bail you out?" her voice was sarcastic.

He grinned without mirth. "That's a thought," and unlatched the door at his side. "I'll be seeing you." He turned up the collar of his coat against the cold wind from the ocean and walked rapidly along. A block farther down he hailed a cab and climbed in.

"Know where the *El Romano Club* is?" The man didn't and Lennox gave him the address. Fog was beginning to roll in from the southwest. The street lamps looked fuzzy and the auto lamps glowed with funny rings. Lennox lit a cigarette, snuggled his chin deeper into his coat collar, and stared at nothing.

The *El Romano Club* is located on the top of a storage building. The attendant looked at Lennox, nodded, and motioned him to the elevator. They shot skyward, stepped out into a hallway with blank concrete walls. There were doors off this hall. Lennox knew that some of them opened into storage rooms. The door at the end seemed to open automatically as he stepped before it. He said: "Hello, chiseler," to the man that stood aside for him to enter.

The man grinned in what he thought was a pleasant manner. "Evening, Mr. Lennox. How are you?"

Bill said: "Pretty lousy, Bert. Big crowd tonight?"

The man shrugged expressive shoulders. "Fair. What can you expect with the studios on half-pay?"

Lennox nodded and tossed his hat and coat to the hat-check girl, " 'lo, gorgeous."

She gave him a dimpled smile. "Hello, Bill. You look like the devil."

"Sure, that's because I've been working for him so long."

He went down the short, carpeted hall and into the main room. The room was large, high-ceilinged and comfortably filled. Three roulette wheels set in line, occupied the center. In the far corner were a group of men and one woman about the crap table. Chuck-a-luck and the half-moon blackjack tables were ranged against the wall. Lennox crossed the room, conscious that people were turning to look at him. A blonde who a week ago would have rushed across the room to attract his attention, presented a pair of too prominent shoulder blades for his inspection.

Lennox's lips thinned. "Just a friendly town," he thought. "When the knife falls, everyone helps you down into the gutter." He paused before the grilled window of the cashier's cage and, picking up a pad of blank checks, filled one in for five hundred.

The man behind the grill took it in his soft white fingers and pretended to study it. Lennox watched him with narrowed eyes. "Don't you read English?"

The cashier said: "You're sure that this is good, Mr. Lennox?"

Lennox said: "Hell, no; it isn't good, and you know it, but you've cashed a hundred like it. I've never failed to pick them up, have I?"

The man shrugged. "Sorry. My orders are not to cash any more checks."

"You mean any more of mine?"

Again the shrug, as he pushed the check towards Lennox. Someone behind him snickered. A voice said: "Did you hear that Sol was getting himself a new office boy?" Several people laughed.

Lennox apparently had not heard. He said: "Is French here?"

The cashier shrugged for the third time. Lennox picked up the check, folded it carefully and slipped it into his pocket as he crossed one corner of the room, went around the end of the metal bar and through a curtained doorway. Before him was a wide hallway with a door at the end. A young man with too black hair was seated on a chair in the bare hall, reading a confession magazine. He dropped the magazine and came to his feet with cat-like grace. "You can't come in here, you."

Lennox said softly: "I'm coming in, lousy. Out of the way."

For the space of a half-minute neither moved. The black-haired one's hand was in his pocket. He said, slowly, distinctly: "You don't rate around here any more, Lennox. Take a tip and get out."

Bill's smile was very thin. "That's where you have your cues mixed, handsome. I still rate, plenty. I'm seeing French, and he's going to like seeing me."

The other's voice was confidential. "Why don't you get wise? When you're through in this town, you're through. Go out easy, pal. I wouldn't like to throw you out."

Lennox hesitated, shrugged, and half turned. The other relaxed slightly. Suddenly Lennox's right shoulder sagged, his left came up, and his right fist crossed to the gunman's jaw. The black-haired one went down with a look of surprise and pain. Lennox caught him, eased him to the floor, knelt on his chest, pulled the gun from the side pocket and got another from the shoulder-harness. There hadn't been much noise.

"Now I'll give you a tip," he said, in a low, grim tone. "This town isn't healthy for you. Remember that killing at San Clemente? The D.A.'s office might hear something about that if you aren't out of the village before morning."

He straightened his coat, pocketed the two guns, and went on down the hall to the door. Looking back, he saw the gunman get slowly to his feet. Lennox stuck a hand into his pocket. The man looked at him once, then disappeared into the gambling room.

There were voices in the room beyond the door. One that Lennox knew said: "But, French. How was I to know they had a list of the numbers?"

"You fool! That's what you should have found out. A hell of a help you are. Why didn't you tell me sooner?"

"Because I couldn't get away sooner. My uncle kept me at the studio until late. He's half-crazy."

"Yeah." French's voice had a biting quality. "Now get out of here and don't let anyone see you go. I'll call you when I want you."

A door closed somewhere within the room, and Lennox retreated down the passage towards the gambling room. His eyes were narrow, but there was a thin, half-mocking smile about his lips. The voice he had heard belonged to Stan Braun, Sol Spurck's nephew.

He came back along the passage, taking pains to walk heavily.

"Hello, handsome," he said to the empty hall. He didn't shout, but his voice was loud enough to carry to the room beyond. "The boss in? Yeah, well, don't move, rat. This thing in my hand isn't an ornament."

He covered the remaining distance to the door in quick strides. It wasn't locked and he pushed it inward, only far enough to slip through. A man was just stepping around the flat-topped desk, a man with a young, cold face, and gray hair. He stopped when he saw Bill, his face showing no emotion, his eyes very narrow.

"Hello, Lennox! Didn't Toni tell you that you weren't wanted?"

Lennox's smile was almost child-like. "He did mention something like that, but I didn't believe him."

The gambler took a step backwards and sat down in the desk chair. "Maybe you'll believe me?" The direct, prominent eyes measured Lennox carefully.

Bill walked slowly towards the desk. He took his hand from his coat pocket, calling attention to the fact by doing so very slowly. "The cashier turned down my check. I got the idea that it was your orders."

The man at the desk shifted his weight slightly. "We've had plenty of trouble with your paper, Bill. That bank account of yours is like a sieve, a rubber one."

Lennox said: "You never howled about my paper before. It's always been covered."

The other shrugged expressively. "Spurck always took care of that. I hear that he isn't taking care of it any longer."

"Meaning?"

"Just that. You're off the gold standard as far as Spurck is concerned. Sorry, Bill. If ten will help you?" He drew a large roll from his pocket and hunted through the big bills slowly, insultingly.

Lennox grinned. "Thanks, French, but I'll eat tomorrow." He turned towards the door, then said, across his shoulder: "Don't mind if I hang around a while? I always did like raids."

The man at the desk laughed. "So you'll have me raided. Your mind's getting twisted. You've got yourself mixed with someone important. There isn't a cop in town that would dare touch this joint."

"Like that?" Lennox's voice sounded interested.

"Like that," French told him, blandly.

9

ENNOX went back into the main room. Toni, the slick-haired gunman, was not in sight. Lennox stopped before the bar and spun a half dollar on the polished surface. The white-coated bartender shoved across a scotch and soda, with a twisted bit of lemon peel in the bottom. Lennox tasted his drink, then, hooking his elbows on the edge of the bar, he considered his next move. The blonde, who had given him her back when he first came in, swept past with a black-haired youth in tow. She turned her head.

"Why, it's Mr. Lennox. My dear, I didn't recognize you."

He said, sourly: "It's your age, sweetheart. Age dulls the eyes."

Her face reddened beneath the rouge and she moved hastily away. Someone tugged at Bill's arm. He turned to see Frank Howe. He'd gotten Howe a job in the publicity department six months before. Howe was a little drunk, but it affected neither his speech nor actions.

"Listen, Bill," his voice was a hoarse whisper. "I heard that lousy cashier hand you the runaround. This is my lucky night. Beat the wheel, I did." His hand disappeared into his pants pocket and came out with a crumpled stack of bills. "Money no use to me. Never had any, don't know how to handle it—hey, bartender, a drink. I'm burning up."

Lennox said: "Thanks, kid," he was genuinely touched. Out of a hundred people in the room that he had helped at one time or another, Howe was the only one who seemed to remember. "No can do. Get you in trouble with Spurck."

Howe said: "To hell with Spurck. To hell with the whole lousy industry. Swell job. You take some tramp from behind a lunch counter and build her up until she's writing autographs instead of orders."

He shoved the bills into Lennox's hand and went away from the bar, his drink forgotten. Lennox watched him go. The bartender brought the glasses. Lennox drew a crumpled bill from the wad in his hand and started to hand it over. Then he stopped, stared for an instant at the number on the bill and put it into his pocket. He found some loose silver, paid for the drinks and drank both of them.

That done, he crossed the room and disappeared into the men's lounge. There was a shine stand in the wash-room. He crawled on to the stand and watched the kinky head bob as the boy applied the brush. After a moment, he drew a sheet of paper from his inside pocket and compared the numbers on the bills with those on his list. Five of them tallied. He put the five bills into his breast coat pocket, and shoved his white silk handkerchief on top of them, then thumbed through the rest of the roll.

As he counted them he whistled softly. There were four hundred dollars left. Certainly Howe had been lucky. Lennox knew him well enough to know that the ex-reporter seldom had four dollars at any one time. He paid the shine-boy and climbed from the stand. As he emerged into the main room a newspaper man with two girls walked past.

Lennox said: "Know Frank Howe?"

The man nodded.

"Didn't notice which table he was playing at a little while ago?"

The man nodded again. "Yeah, the center one. He was on thirteen and it came up. He let the money ride and she repeated."

Lennox said: "Thanks," and looked about.

A man came out of the passage which led to French's room. Play stopped at the first table while the man exchanged cases of money with the croupier. This was repeated at the other tables. Lennox frowned. He started forward, then stopped. For perhaps a minute, he stood, undecided, then moved towards the center table. He had the idea French was withdrawing the bills which bore numbers that were on Lennox's list.

As he stepped to the table, the rat-eyed croupier glanced at him sharply. Lennox apparently did not notice. He watched for several minutes, then bet twenty dollars on black. Red came up and he bet forty, only to be rewarded by double-O. He switched and played the middle group of numbers, won and let it ride. He won again, and shoved the whole pile on to black. Black appeared. He gathered up his winnings and moved towards the crap table.

The lone woman had the dice when he reached the table. He put twenty on the line and watched the green cubes dance across the cloth to turn up a five and six. He picked up his winnings and transferred them to no-pass. She threw snake-eyes.

French came through the curtained door at the end of the bar. He stood for a moment just inside the door, a striking figure, his shirt front gleaming, his gray hair carefully brushed, then he walked across to the crap layout, just as Lennox picked up the dice.

"You're through, Bill."

Lennox turned slowly, deliberately to face him. The room was suddenly quiet. Everyone was watching, breathlessly. Lennox said: "Meaning?"

"Just that," French's voice held a flat quality which was almost metallic. "We don't want your play here. We don't even want you."

The dice rattled in Lennox's hand. He shoved the whole pile of currency on to the line and sent the green cubes dancing across the table with a twist of his wrist. They turned up, six and one. Lennox's eyes met the crouper's. "Pay off, mister."

The man hesitated, his eyes went to French. The owner nodded imperceptibly and the man counted out bills beside those which Lennox had laid on the board. Bill gathered them up slowly, stripped two tens from the pile and tossed them to the croupier, then folded the rest and slipped them into his pocket.

"Okey, French. I thought that you were yellow." His voice carried across the silent room. "Now I know."

He walked calmly towards the door. No one said anything, no one moved. He got his hat from the check girl, slipped into his overcoat and tossed her a folded bill, then he rode down in the elevator. The elevator man said: "Take it easy, Mr. Lennox." There was a gun in his hand.

Lennox grinned, "You, too, Mac?"

The man shrugged. "Orders." He stopped the car at the second floor and opened the door. Two men stepped in, one of them was Toni. He smiled when he saw Lennox. "If it isn't my little boy friend." He ran quick hands over the other's coat and removed the guns. "Come on, mugg. This is where you get off."

Lennox obeyed. They went along a poorly lighted passage and down a flight of stairs. Lennox said: "I never knew how French got rid of people he doesn't like."

Toni grinned. "There's lots of things you don't know. One of them is how to keep your mouth buttoned. In there." He pushed open a steel door and shoved Lennox into a curtained touring car. "Hey, Frank!" he called to the driver. Lennox turned his head a little and the gunman brought the barrel of his automatic crashing down on Lennox's skull. "That's for clipping me on the jaw," he muttered, as he shoved his way into the car.

10

CONSCIOUSNESS came back slowly. Lennox groaned, moved slightly, then lay still for several minutes, his eyes open, staring about the dark room. To the right, a window gave an oblong of lighter sky. Morning could not be far away. He raised a hand to the side of his aching head, felt the knob

there, the hair, matted with dry blood.
Sounds from another room reached him
indistinctly. A cry, a thump as if a
heavy object had been thrown against
the wall, then the door opened. Instinctively, Lennox closed his eyes. Light
showed against his lids.

French's voice said, from a distance.
"Take the —— in there and let him
think it over."

Heavy feet made noise in the room.
There was a groan, a hoarse laugh, and
the door slammed. The groans continued. Lennox opened his eyes. The
room was again in darkness. Cautiously
he swung his feet from the couch and
sat for a moment, his head in his hands.
Then he rose, swayed, and looked about.
There was a huddled shape in the chair
beside the window. Lennox blinked at
it and said, cautiously:

"Who're you?"

The groans ceased. The room was
quiet except for the labored breathing
from the chair. Lennox moved closer.
His head was clearing.

"Come on!" his voice was louder than
he intended. "Who *are* you?"

His hand fumbled in his pocket and
found a box of matches. He struck one
with fingers that shook. The match
flared, and Lennox stared at the battered features of Red Girkin. He said:
"My ——!" and let the match drop to
the floor. "They don't play nice, do
they?"

Girkin swore heavily, tonelessly. "Let
me alone."

Lennox's voice got sharp. "Your play-
mates will be back in a few minutes to
give you another dose. What do you
want?"

The gangster said: "Go to hell!" He
said it indistinctly, as if his lip got in the
way.

Lennox managed a laugh. "Boy, you
love punishment. Come on! Who dec-
orated Charley with the chiv?"

"Charley?" There was a new note in
Girkin's voice. "What about Charley?"

"Only that he's dead."

"Say, who are you?"

"A pal of Charley's. Don't you remember? Bill Lennox. I was up at
your place the other day."

The man in the chair said slowly:
"Yeah, I remember, and Charley's dead.
You sure?"

"I found him on the rug with the chiv
in his side."

"That damned French."

"So it was French?"

"I'm not talking."

Lennox got mad. "Listen, sucker!
Why don't you get next to yourself? Do
you think that they've been pounding
your pan because they love you? It's a
wonder that you aren't in a ditch by
now."

The man in the chair found a laugh
somewhere and managed to turn it on.
It was a poor effort. "They'll keep me
until they find out what I did with the
ten grand, the dirty —— They can
beat me, but I don't talk."

Lennox tried a shot in the dark. "Still
figuring that Meyer will help you?"

The gangster started to swear again.
"That tramp! She got me into this,
then she tied a can to me."

It seemed that the flood gates had
opened. He talked and talked; finally he
got to repeating himself. Lennox turned
away and walked towards the window,
his lips very thin, his eyes bright.

Suddenly the door opened, a light
switch clicked, and Lennox swung about
to see Toni. The gunman said, with
surprise: "Look who's come to. Hey,
chief! The boy scout's awake."

French's voice growled: "Bring him
in."

Lennox took a quick step towards the
window. Toni seized his shoulder, forcing him towards the door. With a shrug,
Lennox relaxed. "Okey! You win."

Toni said: "We win every time, mugg.
Start walking."

French sat in a leather chair. His
coat was off and the gray hair mussed.
There were pouches under his eyes and
he looked very tired.

"Well, Bill—"

Lennox said: "Not so hot. Your

boy friend here swings a mean gun."

French said: "Little boys who play outside their own yards get hurt sometimes. Why the hell can't you keep your nose clean?"

Lennox shrugged. "Mind if I sit down?" he moved towards a chair.

The gambler's voice cracked. "Stand still."

Lennox let his eyes widen slowly. "What is this?"

French said: "It's your show-down," he came out of his chair, and they faced each other. Toni shifted his feet, grinning loosely. "What did you tell Frank Howe?"

Lennox hid his start of surprise. "What did I tell Howe? When?"

The gambler growled: "Don't stall, Lennox. You and Howe talked it over last night at the bar. You gave him something and he went away fast. The boys didn't tell me about it until later. They haven't found him yet, but they will. Come on! What did you tell him?"

Lennox grinned. He was beginning to understand why he was still alive. French thought that he had told Howe something at the club, something about the money, perhaps. Lennox said: "I gave him some dough to take home for me, some dough to put in a safe place."

"You—" the gambler took a step forward, his hands clenching at his sides. "Where is he?"

"That's a little mystery you can solve for yourself." Lennox grinned carelessly, much more carelessly than he felt. There was a desk in the corner of the room. He stepped sidewise towards it. French said:

"Stand still, you."

Lennox nodded. "Okey, French, I wouldn't try anything with you." He took another step. "I'm in a jam, I know it. I've been around long enough to know when my number is coming up. What's it worth to you for me to get Howe on the phone and call him off? Does it buy me a ticket to New York?"

French said: "Yes," quickly. He said it too quickly. Lennox knew that New York meant a wash in San Fernando Valley, but—

"Okey! Gimme the phone."

French's eyes searched his. "Don't try any funny stuff," he warned.

"Would I try any funny stuff when Toni has his gun on me."

He crossed to the desk and, picking up the phone, called the first number that came into his head. As he waited, his hand toyed with a heavy glass inkwell hidden by his body from the other men. Toni still stood beside the door. He had his gun, but he let it hang carelessly at his side.

"That you, Howe?" Lennox demanded, as a sleepy voice asked what the hell he wanted. The voice protested that it wasn't Howe, that he had never heard of Howe, and that if he did now, it would be too soon. Lennox paid no attention.

"Listen, boy!" he said, making his voice sound serious. "That money I gave you, you know, those——"

He picked up the inkwell and half turned so that he could see both French and Toni. "What'll I have him do with them?" he asked the gambler.

Toni's eyes switched from Lennox to his chief's face for an instant and in that instant, Lennox dropped the phone and threw the glass inkwell. He threw it underhanded, threw it with all the force that he had.

It caught the gunman just above the temple and he went over on to the rug without a sound. Lennox sprang at French. The gambler was tugging at his coat pocket. He had his gun half free as Lennox's fingers closed about his wrist. French tried to jerk free, couldn't and struck Lennox in the face with his free hand. Lennox grabbed his throat and tried to force the gambler's head back. French was too strong.

Slowly, ever so slowly, his hand came from the pocket, bringing his gun with it. Desperately, Lennox clung to the man. French hit him again, squarely on the nose. Tears started from Lennox's eyes, his fingers sank deeper into French's throat. The gambler swung about, carrying Lennox with him, and then across French's shoulder, Bill saw something which almost caused him to relax his grip.

The door into the other room had opened. Girkin, on hands and knees, was crawling towards the gun which lay on the carpet at Toni's side. Even as Lennox saw him, Girkin's hand reached the gun, closed over it, and he reeled to his feet, his eyes burning with hate, staring at French.

The gun came up slowly. Lennox cried out. He was never sure afterwards exactly what he said.

"French!" Girkin's voice cut across the room.

Lennox's fingers slipped from the gambler's throat. Girkin's gun flamed and French stiffened. Lennox threw himself sidewise, out of the line of fire. French paid no attention to him. It was as if the gambler had forgotten his existence. He turned slowly and, as he turned, Girkin fired again. French staggered, went to his knees.

His gun came up, and Lennox saw a hole suddenly appear between Girkin's eyes. The gunman pitched forward without a sound.

French stared at him, coughed twice, went over on his hands, and then set-

tled to the floor. For a minute there was silence in the room, then Lennox bent above Toni, and noted that he was still breathing, but unconscious.

Lennox rose, found a handkerchief, and dabbed at his bleeding nose; then he looked around the room. Behind the desk, a wall safe, its door half open, attracted him. He crossed to the safe and drew out bundles of currency. In all, there were thirty-five thousand dollars. He found a newspaper, wrapped up the money and moved towards the door. Everything was quiet. Evidently there was no one in the house. He wondered vaguely why the shots had not attracted attention.

Outside, it was broad daylight. The house, he saw, was set far up on one of the hillsides north of Beverly. He walked down the long, curving roadway without seeing anyone. He walked for a long time, his head aching dully, the sun growing warmer on his back. Finally he reached a drug-store and called a cab.

11

HE shine-boy looked up as Lennox came through the General gate.

"Morning, Mr. Lennox."

"Hello, Sam." He went on across the lot towards the executive offices. Steps sounded on the concrete behind him. Nancy Hobbs' voice called.

"Oh, Bill!"

He turned and managed a grin. "How 'r' you, Nance?"

She said: "I've been hunting for you since I heard you were out of here, looking every— Your face! What's the matter? What happened?"

"I've been playing house with the boys," he grinned. "Come in while I see Sol, if you want some fun. Then you can drive me to the station."

She followed him towards Spurck's

office. "So you're really going to pull out?"

"You said it. Just as soon as I see Sol."

"I'll wait out here," she said stopping in the reception room. "And Bill, don't let him talk you into anything."

He stopped also, and patted her shoulder. "Don't worry, sweet, I'm washed up." He went through into Spurck's office. Spurck's secretary was beside the big desk taking dictation. Spurck came to his feet.

"Bill?"

"Mr. Lennox to you," Bill told him. "Get Elva Meyer and that precious nephew of yours in here. I want to see them."

Spurck said, "But—your nose!"

"Never mind my nose. Get them."

Spurck swung on the secretary. "What is it you're standing there for? Get them—can't you? Must I do everything about this plant yet?"

"Yes, Mr. Spurck." The secretary bobbed, and disappeared.

Spurck said: "Where have you been? All night, I don't sleep, wondering."

Lennox clipped: "Save it until Braun gets here." He helped himself to a cigarette from the box on Spurck's desk and stood, rolling it between his fingers so that the tobacco spilled out a little at each end. The door opened and Elva Meyer came in. "You wanted—" she stopped when she saw Lennox.

Bill said: "Sit down."

"I—er—"

His voice snapped: "Sit down!"

She sank into a chair. Spurck looked at her, then at Lennox, started to speak, then changed his mind. Again the door came open and Braun entered the room. His face changed when he saw Lennox, losing its color; his lips grew almost pallid. "Hello, Bill?" he managed.

Lennox nodded. He crossed to the desk and tore the newspaper wrapping from the package. Money spilled out upon the desk. Spurck made a glad sound, deep in his throat. Braun and the girl exchanged quick, startled glances.

Lennox said: "There's thirty-five grand there, Sol. You'll have to take the rest out of Braun's salary."

Spurck, who had been fingering the money, looked up quickly. Braun made a strangled noise. "You can't ——"

Lennox said: "Shut up! Listen, Sol! This relative of yours has been bucking the wheel. He dropped plenty to French. French had his paper for fifty grand and was threatening to come to you. Someone got the bright idea of snatching Wayborn and soaking you fifty grand to get him back. They figured that you'd call Braun in and let him handle it, but you didn't. You showed the letter to me." He stopped and lit the cigarette.

"Meyer here has been playing around with Braun when people weren't watching. He told her about his jam and the Wayborn idea and she put him in touch with Girkin. Girkin and Charley did the dirty work—"

"It's a lie!" Braun was on his feet.

Lennox said, coldly: "See this nose?" He touched it with his finger. "The man that gave me that is dead. Shut up!"

Braun sank back in his chair with a sick look.

Lennox went on:

"Girkin thought that Meyer was still his moll. He didn't know that he was washed up there. When he found out, he held up ten grand. I don't know where it is. Neither did French. They grabbed Girkin and tried to make him talk. They searched his apartment and stuck a chiv into Charley's ribs when he walked in on them. That's about all."

Braun said: "You can't prove it, you can't prove it."

Lennox looked at him. "For the first time in your life, you're right. French and Girkin are dead, but I don't have to prove it. Sol knows."

Spurck was looking at his nephew. "Loafer!" he shouted. "Loafer! Get out!" He waved his arms wildly. Braun tried to say something. Spurck moved around the desk towards him. Braun went out fast.

Lennox said: "That will be about all, Sol. I'm washed up here. It's New York and some rest for me."

Spurck said: "But listen once, will you? I——"

NANCY HOBBS had been waiting a long time. She looked at her watch again, just as the door opened and Lennox came out. She told him: "You'll have to hurry. There isn't much time."

He didn't meet her eyes, "I'm not going today, Nance."

"Bill!" she was facing him, her hands on his shoulders, forcing him to look at her. "You've let Spurck—"

He shrugged wearily. "Sol's got a new idea for a picture. All about an actress who has her leading man kidnaped to raise money for her boy friend so that he won't have to go to the big-house. Sol says that it's the best idea in years. That it is 'superb, stupendous, colossal.' That's just the usual bunk talk, of course, but I think that I'll hang around and see how it turns out. A few weeks won't matter, and this picture may be a little different."

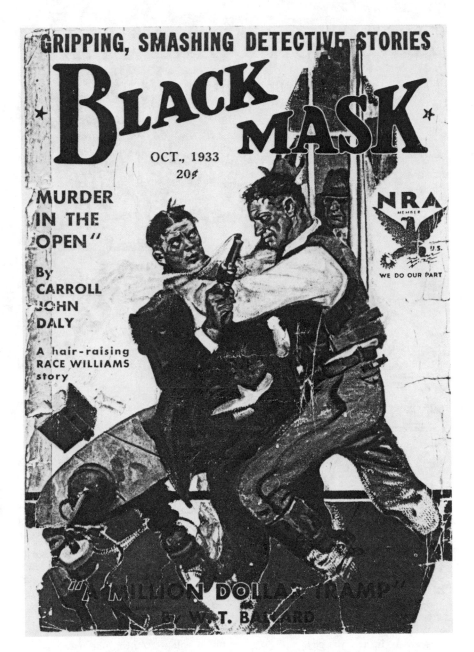

GRIPPING, SMASHING DETECTIVE STORIES

BLACK MASK

OCT., 1933
20¢

MURDER
IN THE
"OPEN"

By
CARROLL
JOHN
DALY

A hair-raising
RACE WILLIAMS
story

NRA
MEMBER
U.S.
WE DO OUR PART

"A MILLION DOLLAR TRAMP"
BY W. T. BALLARD

Ballard's first cover appearance with *Black Mask*

A Million-Dollar Tramp

By W. T. BALLARD

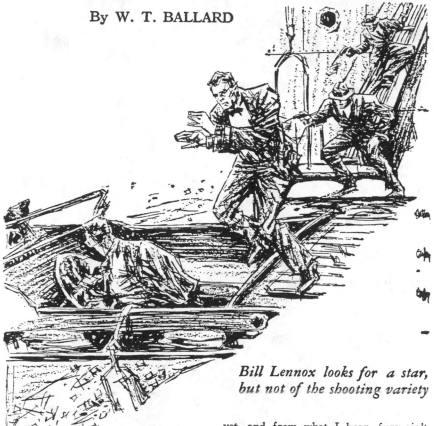

*Bill Lennox looks for a star,
but not of the shooting variety*

ILL LENNOX, trouble-shooter for the General Consolidated studio, sat in the dark projection room and watched the rushes of their latest picture. When the lights came up he dropped his cigarette to the floor, stepped on it, and yawned.

Sol Spurck, boss of the West Coast studio, looked around his large cigar at Lennox. "I tell yuh, Bill, we got something. If that ain't an extra special feature, I'll go back to the fur business

yet, and from what I hear, furs ain't what they once was, you understand."

Lennox yawned again. "Why shouldn't it be a good picture? If that back-stage story has been made once, it's been made a hundred times. Mac-Nutt did the script. Arthur the dialogue, and Hendrix the music. Buzzy staged the routine, and you spent enough to buy the Chicago Fair."

Spurck ignored this. "Jean Hammond will wow them," he predicted. "I tell you, Bill, that girl is hot."

"She's been hot too long," Lennox said, as he rose, "but there's a bet in the picture at that; the little girl with the big eyes that steps out of the chorus

42

and sings a number in the last reel. Who is she?"

Spurck shrugged. "Am I the casting director?" he wanted to know. "Always you are chasing girls with no reputation yet, no box office draw."

Lennox did not argue. As he left the projection room, he passed Carlson, the director. Carlson was big with bushy hair and heavy eyebrows. He said, "How'd it look, Bill?"

"Lousy; but it's box office. The exhibitors will probably send you an orchid. By the way, who's the lassie with the big eyes and the educated puppies that sang the number in the last reel?"

Carlson hesitated, then shrugged. "Just an extra. Billy Walters was slated for that, but her tonsils got tangled up with a knife and this kid begged me so that I gave her a chance. Not so hot, huh?"

Lennox did not bother to answer. He went along the passage to his own office and shoved open the door, violently. A girl seated at his desk looked up with wide eyes. "My gawd—Bill! Save the hinges."

He said: "Hello, Nance! What brings a fan writer out this way?"

She shrugged. "I came out for a bit of news, and then stopped to say howdy. I was hoping for decent company, but your mood doesn't seem to be right. Has someone been spoiling your temper again?"

He lifted her bodily from the chair, sat her on the corner of the desk, and took the place vacated. "They make me mad," he complained. "Here is a kid with looks, a voice, and educated feet. Add a little sex, and it spells wow, and neither Sol nor that dumb kluck Carlson can see her."

Nancy Hobbs looked at him with narrowed eyes. "I know the signs," she said, half to herself. "You're about to pick out some unknown tramp and educate her for pictures. I thought that you'd sworn off that pipe dream. Haven't you been burned enough?"

"But this kid has class. I tell you, Nance, the trouble with pictures is—"

She said, wearily. "I've been writing for fan magazines for three years, and you try to tell me the trouble with pictures—"

He scowled at her. "You always were a smart brat. You should have been a gag man."

"You give me enough laughs without that," she said, sliding from the desk.

"But seriously now, Nance," he said, and his voice was enthusiastic, "this looks like real money, and I'll cut you in. I've some preliminary work to do first; get her lined up, put a stop on her thinking for herself and leave that to me. Then when I'm ready you can write a swell gag on her. How about it?"

Nancy Hobbs laughed, not nastily, but nicely, with a suggestion of sympathetic pity.

"Poor old Bill," she said. "When this bum throws you down, come around and cry on mama's shoulder."

He swore at her as he watched her go, waited until she closed the door then picked up the phone.

2

THE girl with the big eyes was named Irene Schultz. Bill shrugged at the name, but that was easy. Hollywood was no respecter of names. He hung up the phone and went out through the main gate on to Sunset. For a moment he hesitated, then turned and walked west. At the corner he flagged a cab and gave the driver the address. The Schultz girl, according to the casting bureau, lived on North Windsor.

Lennox paid off the taxi and looked around. The address he had was the second door in a bungalow court. He rang the bell and waited. He waited a long time, then pushed the bell again. Steps clicked across wood and the door opened two inches, held in place by the night chain.

Through the aperture Lennox saw her, and his eyes quickened. Without makeup, she was prettier than she had been in the film. There was a troubled something in the depths of her eyes that made his smile widen. That appealing look was worth a million to General, if Lennox knew his box office, and there was no one in the colony that knew it better.

He said: "I'm Bill Lennox, from General Consolidated. I want to talk to you a moment, Miss Schultz."

Recognition came into her eyes and Bill saw the pulse in the white throat quicken. "Oh—Mr. Lennox! I didn't recognize you."

Bill said: "That's all right, Kid. Open the door. I never was good at talking through cracks."

She hesitated, then slowly the door closed, he heard the chain unlatched and it opened again. The girl was in a wrinkled wash dress. Her brown hair was mussed, and she wore no stockings. "I wasn't expecting visitors," she told him, and he thought she said it kind of shyly.

Bill said: "Never mind that. I've seen them in worse and next to nothing. Grab that chair over there and listen; but first, how much common sense have you?"

She said, uncertainly: "I don't get you."

He shrugged. "How long you been out here?"

"Nine months. I was in vaudeville for two seasons."

"So that's where you learned to pick them up and lay them down. Listen, bum! You've got something, see? You didn't look so bad in that *Footlights* piece, but you're no world-beater. If you'll listen to papa, you can go over. If you go getting ideas of your own, you'll be just another pretty girl, dealing them off the arm in a dairy lunch. What about it?"

She said: "Please, could you come back sometime, or could I see you in your office?"

Quick suspicion leaped into his eyes. "Who's been talking to you, Kid? Has some other studio—"

She said hurriedly: "It isn't that; it's something — something else. Honest, Mr. Lennox, I won't talk to anyone else about pictures till I see you, but you gotta go now. You gotta."

She was going to cry. Tears were not far behind those big eyes.

Bill said, suddenly: "What's the matter, punk? Hungry?" He found a crumpled bill in his vest, but she shook her head violently.

"I worked four days last week. I've got plenty, but please go."

He rose with a shrug. "You're the doctor, Kid. Come to see me when you're ready to talk."

He turned towards the door. Halfway across the room, he stopped and swore softly. The curtain which divided the room they were in from another room had blown aside slightly, exposing a man's foot. Lennox stared at it with narrowed eyes, then he took two quick steps forward.

The girl got in his way, trying to hold him back. There was fear in her eyes, more than fear, terror. "Please, oh please!"

Lennox pushed past, reached the curtains and parted them. The man lay on his back, his arms outstretched, his face distorted. Lennox knew that he was dead before he saw the knife wound in the side, just beneath the heart. The body was rigid and it was evident that the man had been dead some time.

Lennox straightened and swung on the girl. She wasn't looking at him, but at the body. Her shoulders drooped, and her head hung forward helplessly. "I didn't kill him, so help me—I didn't!" she babbled.

Lennox said, his voice brittle: "Who is he?"

She shook her head. "I don't know. I don't—"

He seized her wrist, drawing her

towards him. "Stop lying. Who is he?"

She said: "Bert Rose, but I didn't kill him. I don't know who did, I found him, there."

Lennox dropped her wrist and stepped back. Suddenly he was tired, very tired. A burning sensation of anger crept through him, anger against the girl, against fate. He said:

"Let's have the story; not that it matters. The thing for you to do is call the cops if you haven't already. With a face like yours, and those legs, you're a cinch with any jury."

Desperation stopped her sobs. She moved forward and caught his arm. "But I didn't kill Bert. You've got to help me—why should I kill him?"

Lennox shrugged. "Lots of reasons, sweetheart; but then, women don't need reasons for killing. Sometimes they just do it."

"But I didn't, I tell you. He was here, dead when I came in. I wasn't home last night, I spent the night at a girl's apartment."

She was crying again, not loudly, but hopelessly. In spite of himself Lennox studied her. Either she was a swell actress or this was on the level. Either way, it didn't matter. Again anger burned through him. A million-dollar bet, shot to hell because this Rose had gotten himself killed in her apartment. Lennox stared down at the man's body. The dead face seemed to grin up at him sardonically, adding to his anger.

He found a cigarette, loose in his coat pocket, and lit it. For two minutes he smoked furiously. The girl had turned away. He watched her back with thoughtful eyes, noted the way the hair curled away from her neck, the carriage, the—"Why not?" He was talking to himself not her, yet she turned.

The man on the floor meant nothing to him. The fact that he was dead meant less. All Lennox saw was the girl, her appeal, not to his emotions but to the box office. He may have weighed the consequences of his act, but it did not

stop him. It was a gamble—everything was a gamble, for that matter, if you wanted to do anything big; but he thought he could make it a safe gamble. He crossed the room and grabbed up the phone, dialing a number.

"Let me talk to Jake."

The girl was watching him now; hope struggling with fear in her eyes. Lennox's voice was harsh. "Jake, this is Bill. Listen, grab a truck, better make it a van, and an empty piano box. Get over here as soon as you can," he gave the street and apartment number. "Yeah, that's right. No, come alone and for gawd's sake, don't give your right name when you rent the truck."

He hung up and swung to the girl. All the lethargy had gone from his movements.

She said, wide eyed: "So you're going to help; but is it safe, having someone else know?"

He grinned without mirth. "Jake's okey. He'd do a stretch, if I said the word. But get this now: I'm not doing it to help you, I'm doing it because when I start something, I finish it. I started out to make you a star and by Judas Priest I'll make you one if I have to conceal evidence in a dozen killings. Get your things together. As soon as Jake comes, we're leaving and you're not coming back—here. First we'll go down to the studio and get your name on a contract, then we'll find a place for you to stay, but you've got to understand this: From now on, you don't have a thought of your own, you don't open your mouth until I give the okey. Is that a promise?"

3

OME hours later, Bill Lennox turned in at *Sardi's*, found a table, and ordered, then opened the evening paper and looked at it casually. A quarter-column item in the lower right-hand corner caught his eye. "Gambler's body found in San Fernando Valley."

He read it through with pursed lips. A dead man, identified as Bert Rose, dealer on one of the Long Beach gambling barges, had been picked up that afternoon on a side road a mile and a half from Sennett City. Rose, who, the paper stated, had served two years in San Quentin for attempted robbery, had been stabbed. The police surgeon stated that the man had been killed sometime during the night, and it was thought that he was the victim of a gang killing.

Lennox folded his paper and tasted his soup. From the paper, he judged that Jake had done his work well. Jake wouldn't talk, that much Lennox knew. It seemed that Bert Rose was a closed incident.

A group of younger film players came in noisily and passed Lennox's table. He nodded to them half-consciously, comparing them with the girl whom he had put under contract that afternoon. They didn't compare, and he smiled to himself. Irene Schultz was a thing of the past. Lennox grinned as he thought of her new name, Marian Delaine. The name sounded phoney, but then, most Hollywood names sounded phoney and most of them were.

He'd gotten her an apartment in a quiet house, just off Franklyn, and she had orders not to communicate with any of her former friends. Lennox wasn't taking chances. He rose, and moved towards the door. On the Boulevard he stood for a moment, his hat shoved well back, a cigarette dangling from the corner of his mouth. Lights were on, but he stood in a shaded spot.

"Lavender Lane, hell!" he muttered, "Just Main Street with mascara and rouge."

He moved to the curb. A taxi swerved in close to him, its rear door open. From behind, a hand between Bill's shoulders pushed him forward and he went to his knees on the cab floor. The door slammed and they moved away from the curb, fast.

Bill said, "What the hell?" and struggled to the seat. A man at his side pressed a round, hard circle against his ribs.

"Take it easy, Lennox."

Lennox took it easy. The cab went right at Highland, swung along the curved street past the entrance to the Bowl, and on over Cahuenga Pass. Beyond Universal City, the cab turned right on Tuluca Road.

Lennox said: "I like the country, but I wasn't plannning on a ride tonight."

The man at his side chuckled without mirth. "Getting sensible, are you? Rather thought that you would."

Lennox squinted into the darkness. "Maybe if you'd tell me what it's all about I'd get a general idea. Surely no one supposes that Sol would pay money to get *me* back?"

The man at his side laughed. "I never met Spurck, but from what I've heard, he isn't good at paying out dough. All we want is a little information." The voice hardened. "What did you do with that Schultz broad?"

Lennox's eyes narrowed into the darkness. He wished that he could see the other's face, wished that he had some idea who it was, but all he knew was that the gun was pressing harder into his side.

"Never heard of her."

The gun pressed harder. The husky voice said: "Don't lie, Lennox. You're not in such a good spot yourself. We know that she worked in that *Footlights Revue* that General is releasing next month."

Lennox said: "For —— sake, you don't expect me to know every extra that works on our lot? Hell, I can't even remember my girl's birthday."

The man said, softly: "But you know Schultz. You were at her house this morning. A man came with a truck and an empty piano box. I wonder what he took away?"

"You seem to know everything."

"Almost everything—except where the dame is and what happened to the twenty grand that Bert Rose had. It might interest you to know that the money belonged to me."

Lennox hid his surprise. "If Rose had twenty grand, the cops must have got it. Do you think that I'd roll a stiff?"

"What you'd do doesn't interest me." The voice had an edge now. "I want to know where that dame is. My men trailed her to the General gate this afternoon. She didn't come out."

Lennox grinned in spite of the gun against his side. Marian Delaine had gone to her new home in a town car, borrowed from Spurck for the occasion. The shadow hadn't expected that, had not looked closely at the car, evidently.

"I'll tell you," he said, with apparent candor. "I did go to Schultz' place this morning, but I didn't get a slant at anyone's twenty grand, and if the girl isn't around, she must have blown town. You can rod me, of course, but I can't see the percentage."

The man said: "Hell!" under his breath.

Lennox sensed that he was hesitating. The car swayed left into a side road, graveled and rough. They bumped across a wash and ground to a sliding stop. Lennox peered through the gloom and saw a shack, a crazy, tumbled down affair. The gun prodded him harder. "Get out!"

He got the door open and obeyed. The driver was on the ground to receive him. The driver said: "In there," and pushed him towards the broken wooden porch. Lennox swung for the man's chin and missed. Something hard crashed into the side of his head, and he went down.

ONSCIOUSNESS came back slowly. He lay where he was for several minutes without moving, aware of the open door through which light came faintly, of the stale smoke-laden air, and the mussed, dirty bed. Then he swung his feet to the floor and started gingerly towards the door.

There was a man in the other room, seated in a chair, tilted against the opposite wall. A kerosene lamp burned smokily upon a rickety table. Lennox recognized the man as the cab-driver, not from his face, but from the semi-uniform that he wore. The man held a newspaper in his hands, but he wasn't reading it! He was staring at the door. "Awake, huh?"

Lennox stepped through into the other room, feeling the side of his head tenderly. The driver grinned, showing stained teeth. "Little boys shouldn't go round, striking at people."

Lennox said: "How long do I stay here?"

"That depends on you," the driver told him, tossing the newspaper to the floor. "When you get ready to talk, then we'll think about that. The boss is coming back at noon. You should have a swell story by that time."

Lennox shrugged and sat down. There was a whiskey bottle and a soiled glass on the table beside the lamp. He picked up the bottle, ignoring the glass, and took a long drink. It was lousy, but it sent warm fingers through his chilled body.

The driver said: "No use shoving over the lamp. We're four miles from the nearest place, and I'd find you in the dark. I'm like a cat."

Lennox didn't say anything. He returned the bottle to the table, found a cigarette, and lit it. The driver seemed to want to talk. "This is a hell of a hole to be stuck in," he said. "I had a date tonight."

Lennox said: "I'm sobbing for you," and stared moodily at his cigarette.

The driver grinned. "Better save your sobs for yourself. The boss likes to hear them squawk. He'll probably heat your feet if you don't spring the dope on that broad. He'd as soon lose twenty grand as his right eye."

Lennox looked at the man and started to say something, then he stopped, for the door at the driver's side had moved ever so slightly. The taxi man took no notice. "I don't see why you couldn't have kept out of this," he complained. "We had things coming our way when you stuck your schnozzle into the play. What the hell do you want with that broad, anyway? A guy with your job should be able to pick and choose."

"That's what you think," Lennox said, watching the door from the corner of his eye. "Besides, I haven't said that I know where she is." He was talking to cover any sound from the door, saying things at random. The crack was wider now. Air came through it, blowing against the lamp. The taxi man turned in his chair. The door came wide. He said: "What the—" and grabbed for his pocket; then stopped. There was a man in the doorway, a man with a gun.

"Go easy." The voice sounded excited, not certain. The newcomer stepped into the room.

Lennox called: "Keep back. Don't get too close to him."

The other's eyes wavered, went towards Bill. Lennox swore. He saw the taxi man move sidewise in his chair, his hand clawing at his coat pocket. Even as he saw—he sprang forward. His fingers closed on the man's wrist, forcing him backward, holding the hand. The chair went over sidewise with a splintering crash, and they went to the floor, Lennox on top. They rolled over twice, legs thrashing, fighting for control of the gun.

Lennox knew that it was only a matter of time. The other was too strong. His free hand was at Lennox's throat, forcing Bill's head back, slowly backwards. Then the newcomer moved. He had stood as one paralyzed for a minute, gaping at the twisted bodies. Now he stepped in and slammed the barrel of his gun against the taxi-man's head.

The fingers at Lennox's throat relaxed suddenly, the man went back on to the floor. Lennox rolled free and came slowly to his feet. For a moment

he shook his head to clear it, then he got the gun from the unconscious man's pocket and dropped it into his own. His rescuer said:

"Don't try anything, Lennox."

Bill swung about to see the gun level with his belt. He said: "You too? What is this? Open season on me?"

The other had black hair and eyes. He was very young and not too sure of himself. He said: "I want to know where Irene is?"

Lennox swore softly. Ignoring the gun, he walked to the table and took another drink. It burned his throat but cleared his head; then he looked at the black-haired one. "What's the idea, Kid? Where do you come into this?"

The man with the gun, hoarsely: "Where's Irene? Don't try to stall me, Mister, I mean to find out."

"Try guessing." There was an edge of contempt in Lennox's voice. He stared at the unmoving figure on the floor, then muttered: "I suppose I've got a long walk ahead—" Suddenly an idea hit him. He looked at the black-haired boy. "Say, punk. How'd you happen to blow in here?"

He said: "I followed you, Lennox. I was parked in a car half a block from the restaurant when you came out. I followed you there, then I followed your cab. My car's down the road a ways."

Lennox laughed softly. "Maybe you'll tell me why you're trailing me."

The boy said, angrily: "I have told you. I saw Irene leave her house this morning and go with you to the studio. She didn't come out. I asked the gateman, but he wouldn't tell me anything. Then I went looking for you. I saw you on the Boulevard, followed you until you went into *Sardi's;* then I went back and got the car and parked it where I wouldn't miss you when you came out. Lucky thing for me that I did, or I'd have lost you when you got into that cab."

"Lucky thing for me," Lennox told him, without humor. "Let's get your car and get out of here before Oswald's friends come back." He looked at the unconscious man on the floor.

The boy threatened: "I'm going to drive you straight to the police station unless you tell me where Irene is. Don't think that I don't know how your type turns girls' heads." He sounded very young. Lennox shrugged, his brows drawing together in a frown.

"Listen, you! You've got the wrong angle, but I can't have you gumming things up. Gimme your name and telephone number and I'll have Irene call you as soon as I can get in touch with her."

They eyed each other in silence for a moment. The boy uncertain, Lennox impatient. "What's the name?"

"Rose, Wilbur Rose. Irene knows my number, but I don't—"

Lennox stared at him with lidded eyes. "Rose? Any relation to Bert Rose?"

Surprise showed in the boy's face. "I've a brother named Bert."

"Have you seen tonight's papers?"

"No—What are you talking about?"

Lennox said, soberly: "He's dead. They found him in a ditch this morning."

The black-haired one seemed stunned. "Why—I— saw him last night. He— he was all right then."

Lennox's voice sharpened with interest. "Where'd you see him? What time?"

Rose's eyes were suspicion laden. "What's it to you?"

Lennox shrugged. "Nothing, except the cops are trying to learn who put him on the spot. I thought you might know something."

Rose said, hoarsely: "If I did, I wouldn't tell you. Bert and I weren't very close. He's done things that weren't so nice, but I'd like to find out who killed him."

Lennox looked at the quiet taxidriver, started to say something, shrugged, and changed his mind. After all, he couldn't accuse anyone without having questions asked, questions which

he did not care to answer. "Let's go to town," he grunted.

IT was fifteen after twelve when they reached the corner of Hollywood Boulevard and Highland. Lennox unlatched the door on his side and stepped to the pavement.

"Go on home, Kid, and stick by the phone. I'll have Schultz call you in a couple of hours and tell you that she hasn't been manhandled, but I'm warning you; try to see the Kid and you'll gum things up for her plenty."

He slammed the door on the threat which Rose uttered, and strode across the intersection with the light. On the other corner he took a cab and gave the driver an address. They rode five minutes, then the taxi pulled to the curb and Lennox got out. He paid the driver and watched him pull away, then turned around and looked at the building. A large sign across the front said, "Boyton Tile Company." Lennox grinned.

The windows were dark, as was the front door, but he paid no attention to that. He went around the corner, stepped between the building and a signboard, crossed a parking lot half-filled with cars, and knocked twice at the side door. The door opened, held in place by a short chain. The door closed, the chain rattled. Then it opened again and a black-browed, one-eyed man said: "Hello, Bill! Long time, no see."

Lennox grinned. "Hello, One-eye. How's things?"

"Not good, not bad." The one-eyed man shut the door and refastened the chain. Lennox watched him with amusement. "What's the big idea of all the caution? The cops aren't bothering with liquor now, and the Feds are too busy clearing their dockets to make more arrests."

The one-eyed man grinned. "Gotta

give the customers' some thrills." He winked his single optic. "If we didn't, they'd go down to the nearest barbecue joint and buy beer."

Lennox nodded and went on into a large room. A long bar extended the full length of the far wall, five bartenders working busily. The room was crowded with the after-theatre gathering. Lennox swept the place with his eyes, nodded to Ham Robbins and Duke Smith, and then went into a phone booth. He dropped a nickel and called the number of the girl's apartment house. "Miss Delaine, eight-o-two," he told the switchboard operator.

A sleepy voice said, uncertainly: "Who is it, please?"

"Lennox," Bill told her. "Listen, Kid! I just met a friend of yours, Wilbur Rose. Know him?"

He heard her draw her breath sharply, then: "Well?" She tried to make her voice sound normal and failed.

"He's hot and bothered," Lennox told her. "Got the idea that I'm a wolf and that your name is Red Riding Hood. I told him that I'd have you call him up and assure him that my intentions are honorable."

She said, uncertainly: "All right. Should I call him now?"

Lennox's tone sharpened. "Listen, Kid! How well do you know this Rose?"

"Not so well."

"Stop lying." His voice was cold. "He knows you plenty."

"Well," her voice was stubborn, resentful, "we grew up in the same town."

Lennox swore under his breath. "What's the punk doing out here?"

"He isn't a punk."

"I didn't ask you what he was. What's he doing out here?"

"I don't know. Nothing, I guess. He's —he's just out here on a trip, or something."

"Or something—" Lennox repeated, in disgust. "So you lied to me this morning when you said that you didn't know Bert Rose very well."

"But I don't." Her voice had taken on a note of fear. "He was older. I don't know how he came to be—"

Lennox's voice rasped: "Shut up, you little fool! Someone may be listening. Now you get this: Call up Wilbur; tell him that you are okey. Tell him anything you like, but don't tell him where you are, what you're doing, or anything about his brother. Get me?"

She said: "Yes," in a very weak voice.

"And further. Get him to scram, to go back home, anywhere. We can't have him hanging about, recognizing Marion Delaine as Irene Schultz. Use your head, Kid. You'll never get another break like this."

He hung up, giving her no time to answer, and walked towards the bar.

Duke Smith turned around and waved a glass at him. Lennox said: "What's new in the Fourth Estate?"

Duke shrugged, "I wouldn't know," he countered. "I'm only a leg-man."

Lennox said, idly: "Anything new on that killing up in the valley, Ross or something like that?"

"Bert Rose, you mean?"

"Yeah, that's the one. Did the cops get anything?"

Smith shrugged. "Not much, and Rose wasn't much loss, but there are funny rumors going around town."

"What kind of rumors?"

"Well—I don't know. Rose wasn't such a nice boy. He'd done a stretch, and then he'd been working on one of the gambling barges at Long Beach. I heard downtown tonight there was some movie extra in the picture, but we haven't got hold of her yet."

Lennox swore to himself. "Know which boat Rose was working on?"

Smith raised an eyebrow. "You're curious as the devil."

Lennox shrugged. "Thought maybe there might be a story in it. Which barge was he on?"

"The *Palace*. Speed boats leave from Seventh Street. I think I'll go with you."

Lennox stared at him; then he

laughed suddenly and looked at his watch. "Almost one. We can drive it in an hour. Is that too late?"

The newspaper man said: "It's never too late until it's morning. My car's outside."

They went out and crawled into a Chevy coupé. Smith said, as he stepped on the starter: "Wouldn't want to tell me what it's all about?"

Lennox shrugged. "You wouldn't believe me if I told you."

He lit a cigarette and watched the speedometer climb past sixty. A cop swung in beside them and Smith brought the coupé to the side of the road. He listened in a bored fashion to the other's angry questions, found his press card, and passed it over. The cop looked at it, then went on with his lecture. "You newspaper guys think you own the world."

He passed back the card and climbed on to his machine. "The next time, I take you in," and he whirled away.

Lennox grunted: "The power of the press! Come on, fella. We're wasting time."

The coupé went on, cutting through the darkness. They came into Pedro, went through Wilmington, and along Harbor Boulevard. Ten minutes later they were cutting across the dark water in a speedboat.

Somewhere, muffled by intervening doors or distance, an orchestra still played as Lennox went up the swaying ladder to the deck above. Smith joined him a moment later, and they stood looking about.

"Nice layout," Bill commented.

The newspaper man said: "Swell, There's Harry Rossi. He runs the joint."

Lennox looked and saw a short, heavy-featured man standing beneath one of the deck lamps. He was talking to two women in white and they were laughing at something that the gambler had said. Smith grinned.

"Harry's quite a ladies' man. That's Madge Edmonds and Sally Barbeur. Wonder what they're doing this far

south. Santa Barbara is their hangout."

As he spoke, two men in evening clothes appeared, their white shirts gleaming beneath the light. They nodded to Rossi and moved towards Lennox. Bill stepped back and waited while they descended into the bobbing speedboat. Rossi turned towards them, and Smith said: "Want you to meet a friend of mine, Harry. Bill Lennox, of General-Consolidated."

Bill felt the man's fingers close about his hand, heard Rossi say: "This is an honor, Mr. Lennox," in a voice that he knew. It was the voice that he had heard earlier in the cab. There was no surprise on Rossi's face, nothing. His heavy lips smiled faintly as he took Bill's arm, led him towards the companionway. "We've got a nice play here, Mr. Lennox. I've been hoping for some time that you'd pay us a visit."

Bill, conscious of Smith at his heels, smiled also. "That's swell, Rossi. I suppose that dealer of yours getting killed last night will hurt business. That kind of publicity won't help you."

The gambler smiled faintly. "I think you're wrong there, Lennox. Of course, we don't seek that type of publicity, but since it came—well, we have a bigger crowd here tonight than we've had in months."

He led the way into a crowded room. Three roulette wheels occupied the middle, while two crap layouts and blackjack tables were ranged about the sides. At one end, a spacious bar served beer.

Rossi said: "We don't serve anything but beer at the bar, but if you care to come into my private office—"

Smith said: "We sure do. I haven't had a good drink since the last time I was on this barge."

Rossi's white teeth flashed in his dark face. "Thanks, my friend. You are very kind."

He led the way down a short companionway and opened a white door, stepping aside for them to enter. The office was heavy with massive furniture. Smith and Lennox found seats on

52

a cushioned locker at the right. Rossi opened a small barette and produced bottles and glasses. He looked inquiringly at his visitors.

Smith said: "The scotch is too good to spoil it with outside ingredients. I'll take mine straight, thanks."

Rossi looked inquiringly at Lennox, and Bill nodded. The gambler filled the short glasses, poured some water into tall tumblers, and carried the small metal tray to the locker; then he shot some soda into his own glass and raised it. "You'll pardon me, but I never drink during working hours."

Smith tossed off his drink. "With whiskey like that, I'd pardon you anything—even murder."

The full lids drooped slightly above the gambler's black eyes. His glance went to Lennox's face, but Bill gave no sign that he had heard. He raised his glass and drank it slowly. "You're spoiled," he told the reporter. "That's no way to drink good liquor."

The tension in the room lessened. Rossi said: "How's the picture business, Mr. Lennox? I hear that General has a good musical ready to release?"

Bill nodded. "As good as most," he said, indifferently. "Think I'll take a shot at your wheels."

Rossi smiled. "We expect that, of course. We hardly run this as a sightseeing station; yet I do not want you to feel obligated simply because I have given you a drink."

"And what a drink!" Smith's voice was hopeful. "Think I'll hang around down here a while if you don't mind, Harry. I want some dope on that dealer of yours that they found in the valley."

ENNOX went up the passage to the gambling-room. He regretted having brought Smith. He wanted to see Rossi, to see him alone. For perhaps five minutes he watched one of the wheels, then put a dollar on seventeen

and lost. Then Smith came up to him, stopped at his side and stared at the board. "Any luck?"

Lennox shook his head. "None. Think I'll try black-jack." He moved away and saw the reporter slide into the place which he had vacated. He paused at a black-jack table and lost five dollars, then moved around the room, keeping an eye on Smith. The reporter was winning and seemed engrossed in the game. Rossi was nowhere in sight.

Lennox went along the companionway and knocked at the office door. The gambler's voice bade him enter, and he pushed open the door. Rossi looked up from the desk, a faint trace of smile curving the thick lips. "Thought you'd be down."

Lennox closed the door and hunted for a cigarette. His hand touched the cold metal of the gun which he had taken from the taxi-driver. It gave him assurance. He found a cigarette and held his lighter to the tip, then put the lighter back into his pocket and looked at the gambler.

"Let's put our cards on the table, Rossi."

The other's only answer was a shrug and a gesture of his hands. Lennox took it for acceptance. "I know that you killed Rose," he stated, flatly. "Oh, I can't prove it," as the man at the desk started to speak, "but I can have some unpleasant questions asked."

Rossi said: "Has it occurred to you that you might have to answer some yourself? Some mouthpiece once told me that it wasn't strictly according to law to move a stiff before the cops got to look at it."

Lennox smiled thinly. "Okey, Rossi. You can't prove that I did that, either. You know it, but you can't prove it. So far we're even. Let's stay that way. I'll forget that I knew anything about a killing and you'll forget that a certain girl used to live at a certain number."

The man at the desk said: "But my twenty grand?"

Lennox shrugged. "I don't know anything about that dough and neither does the broad."

The gambler's eyes were very narrow. "How do you know that she doesn't?"

"Because she wasn't there when Rose was knifed. She spent the night with another girl. I checked that, and you can be sure that I know. She didn't find the body until a few minutes before I got there. Your men were watching the house. They can tell you that she hadn't been there long."

"What does that prove?" Lennox thought that Rossi sounded uncertain, but he couldn't be sure.

"It proves plenty," Lennox said, with disgust. "Didn't your hoods frisk Rose after they knifed him?"

"I haven't admitted," Rossi began, but Lennox cut him short.

"Leave that. You know that they did, that they didn't find the dough. How would the girl find it?"

Rossi said, stubbornly: "Maybe he hid it somewhere, somewhere where she would look."

"You're screwy. She went out with me. She didn't have it with her and she hasn't been back to that dump since. What's more, she's not going back. Get this, wop, and get it straight. Lay off that girl. Search the house all you please, but stay clear of her. I've written out a statement of what I know and planted it with a friend. If anything happens to me, you'll burn." He pushed out the cigarette in the metal ash-tray and, stepping forward, leaned across the desk. "I'm not trying to act tough, but better guys than you have tried to buck me in this town and they aren't here any more. Think it over."

Rossi said, slowly: "If I lay off the girl, what?"

Lennox shrugged. "I'm not a cop. As I see it, Rose wasn't such a swell citizen that I should waste tears on him. I never saw him alive and I'm not bowed down by grief, but so help me, if so much as a whisper about the Schultz broad gets out, you're going to move and move fast."

Hate looked at him from the dark eyes; hate, and a trace of fear. Rossi started to speak, stopped, took a long breath, then said: "It's a deal." He extended his long-fingered hand. Lennox ignored it, and looked at the gambler's face, which was darkening with gathered blood.

"I don't like you, Rossi. I'm not shaking hands."

The man at the desk managed a laugh, a choking sound, as he rose. "Okey, Lennox, if that's the way you want it."

"That's exactly—"

A white light winked on the corner of Rossi's desk. The gambler's oath was a startled sound. The blood drained from his face, leaving the skin sallow, almost yellow looking. Heavy feet came along the companionway. Lennox swung about as the door opened and men seemed to pour into the room. He saw Smith in the background, a sobered, curious Smith. The man in the lead swept Lennox with his eyes, then looked at Rossi.

"Hello, Harry!"

Rossi said, tonelessly: "Hello, Hampton. What's the idea?"

Hampton said: "This is a pinch; a rap that you won't beat, Harry. It's murder."

The man behind the desk did not move. He said, tonelessly: "You're screwy. Besides, you haven't any jurisdiction here."

The man laughed. "We thought of that, too. We've got a Federal man with us and a deputy from Orange. One of us has jurisdiction. We don't care which so long as we take you in."

Rossi smiled. "Who am I supposed to have killed?"

"Rose, Bert Rose. Get your hands out." He shook the cuffs so that they rattled.

Rossi's eyes flamed. "You rat," he stared across at Lennox. "You double-crossing rat. So you'd make a deal with me you—"

Lennox said: "Shut up, you fool! I

54

don't know what this is all about."

Hampton snapped the cuffs on Rossi and looked at Lennox. "Guess I'll take you along, too."

Lennox said: "Try it."

A man came up behind him and ran quick hands over his coat. "He's got a rod, Chief."

"And a permit." Bill's voice was unhurried, serene, but his mind was busy and he cursed silently. This was a tough break, a break he hadn't expected. Smith was at his elbow, grinning at the deputy from the sheriff's office.

"This is Bill Lennox of General films," he explained. "He isn't going to run anywhere."

The deputy looked at Lennox uncertainly, then at Rossi. "You'll have to come over to the sub-station and do some explaining," he said, finally.

Bill nodded, a trifle wearily. "Mind telling me how you happened to pick up Rossi?"

The man shrugged. "Sheriff's office got a call from someone who said that he was Rose's brother."

"Rose's brother?"

"Yeah. He told us to go out into the valley and pick up a taxi-driver; said that the driver knew something about his brother's death. We sent out the flash to the radio cars and they picked this guy up in a shack out there. Someone had bumped his head plenty, and he wasn't feeling so hot. The boys got him to talk and he named Rossi. That's all I know."

Bill said: "Thanks," and swore to himself.

If the cabman had talked, the chances were that he had spilled the whole works. Bill felt very tired, but, he wasn't beaten yet. If he could get to the man in time— He stepped aside as they led Rossi past. The gambler's black eyes glowed like coals as he looked at Lennox. Bill thought for a moment that he was going to speak, then he went on.

They walked up the short companionway and through the gambling room. The place was already deserted. Lennox

smiled. A lot of people in that crowd didn't want publicity. They were there with wives, but not with their own. The attendants were grouped forward on the deck, held back by two officers. Rossi's eyes swept the crowd; then, with a slight shrug, he moved towards the ladder.

The police boat was alongside the float, but at the far end was one of the water-taxis. Rossi went down first, using his manacled hands to steady himself. Suddenly, as if from a pre-arranged signal, the engine of the water-taxi raced. Rossi leaped across the float and jumped into the boat. It was already in motion, cutting away from the barge in a wide circle. Guns spat from the rail of the gambling ship. The police boat went forward and Lennox, standing beside Smith, saw Rossi stagger suddenly, then plunge headlong from the water-taxi into the dark sea.

5

MITH said: "Come on, Bill. Gimme the story."

Lennox looked at him. "Honest, fella, I would if there was any to give. Rossi's dead. He was dead when he hit the water. The cops are going to ask questions that I can't answer, and I've got to make a phone call. It's up to you to help."

The reporter grinned. "Just a pal. You drag me all over Southern California and then don't spill the dope. Supposing I print that Bill Lennox was mixed up with Rossi in the killing. What do you think that would get me?"

"A swell libel suit," Lennox told him. "You know these guys. Get them to let me ride into town with you. I'll show up at the sheriff's office and spin them a yarn when we get in."

Smith said: "Do I get the real story?"

"Listen," Lennox's voice was harsh. "If you hadn't been with me, you'd have missed all this. See your friend the deputy; then call your paper."

Smith nodded. "Okey. But when I get washed up with the City Editor, you give me a job in the General publicity department."

Lennox said: "I'll give you the whole damn' studio. Come on! Snap it up!"

Ten minutes later he was in a telephone booth of an all-night drug-store. He called Sam Marx and waited impatiently until the lawyer answered.

Marx said: "This is a hell of an hour to get a man out of bed. What kind of jam are you in now?"

Lennox grinned without mirth. "Listen, Shyster! The sheriff's office is holding a cab-driver named Krouch, Ed Krouch. He's being held as a material witness on that Rose killing."

Marx's voice sharpened. "What about it?"

"He accused Harry Rossi, of the *Palace* gambling ship, of the killing. Rossi is dead, killed half an hour ago, trying to escape. Now get this: I want you to get to Krouch, find out how much he's talked and get him to keep quiet. Get him out on bail as soon as you can. Then tell him to jump it. With Rossi dead, the cops aren't going to care much."

Marx said: "What's the idea? Tell me what's up?"

"No time. Every minute counts. Krouch might spill something that would gum the works. You get him out and I'll stand the bail."

"Just a big-hearted boy." The lawyer's voice was mocking.

"Sure, but for —— sake, get the lead out of your pants and move. I'm in Long Beach now. As soon as I get back to town I'll go to your place and wait until you show up."

He replaced the receiver and left the booth. Smith was still talking on another phone. Lennox bought a coke and sat down at the fountain. The reporter came out of his booth and sat down at his side. He eyed the coke with disgust and ordered beer.

"What did Marx have to say?"

Lennox swore. "I've known nosey guys that got their schnozzles busted."

"You shouldn't talk so loud," the reporter told him. "Those booth walls aren't too thick."

He finished his beer and they went out to the car. The street looked pale, dirty in the uncertain light. In the east, a streak of crimson gave promise of a hot day. Lennox yawned as he climbed into the car.

"Sheriff's station, James."

Smith grunted and put the Chevy into gear. They went out Atlantic and swung towards town.

After his session with the sheriff they started on again.

At the corner of Broadway and Ninth Lennox got out of the coupé. There was a red-top in the cab rack. Lennox shook the driver awake and gave him Marx's address, then he climbed in. He was very tired, his head felt woozy and his mouth tasted of too many cigarettes. Half an hour later they pulled up before the lawyer's house. Lennox paid the man and, going up the walk, rang the bell.

Marx himself answered. He shut the door and led the way into his study. "You need sleep."

Lennox grinned wryly. "You're telling me. I thought I'd never get away from the sheriff's office. Did you see Krouch?"

"Yeah. He's over at Lincoln Heights. They haven't booked him yet, so I can't bail him out until after sunrise court. I've got a man over there, waiting. It'll be a couple of hours before they get here. Do you want to wait?"

"If you've got a spare bed."

For answer Marx led him upstairs and into a room with yellow bed covers. Lennox looked at the covers, grinned. "Shame to sleep in those alone." Marx went out without answering and, three minutes later, Lennox was asleep.

He was awakened by Marx's Chinese boy, who indicated a dressing-gown. "Boss, he say, you come."

Lennox shrugged himself awake, put

on the gown, and followed the boy down
the stairs. Three men were in Marx's
study. Krouch, standing beside the window, looked around as Lennox entered.
The taxi-man was hollow-eyed; his
clothes were mussed, and a thick, dirty
stubble covered his chin. He looked
nervous, uncertain. Marx was talking to
a big man who, Lennox judged, was the
one that had attended to Krouch's
bail.

The taxi-man said: "Marx told me
you want to see me."

Lennox said: "Yeah! How much
did you spill to the cops last night?"

The man said: "I told them that
Harry Rossi did it. I hear he's dead."

Lennox said: "He is."

The man seemed relieved by the
words. "I wouldn't have spilled that
much, but they were sweating me."

"You didn't—say anything about
where the body was—I mean at first?"

Krouch shook his head. "Why should
I?"

Lennox's relief did not show in his
face. He said: "How well do you like
this town?"

The man shrugged. "I've seen ones
that I liked as well."

"Then my advice is for you to scram."

"You mean for me to jump bail?"

"That shouldn't worry you. It isn't
your dough."

Krouch's eyes got crafty. "Want tuh
get rid of me pretty bad, don't you?
Well, Mister, I'm not in any hurry. The
cops haven't got a thing on me. I'll
hang around until you make it worth my
while. I didn't move any bodies—"

Lennox rasped: "Ever hear of a kidnaping rap? Think I've forgotten that
you dragged me out into the valley? I
figured you for sense." He swung about
and looked at Marx. "You guys heard
him try to blackmail me?"

Marx nodded, as did the big man at
his side. Krouch looked at them uncertainly. "Trying to frame me, huh?"

Lennox said: "You framed yourself.
Take him back and throw him in the can,
Sam. I'm washed up. Then see the

D.A. and tell him about the snatching
and the little blackmail."

Krouch said, hurriedly: "I didn't
mean anything. Honest, I didn't mean
a thing. I'll scram, but I ain't got a
dime. Gimme enough to eat on till I
get located."

Marx looked at Lennox, who apparently had not heard. "Okey!" he said,
suddenly. "Get a confession signed by
him, Sam; then get him out of town.
If he ever lands in this State again, give
the confession to the D.A."

"Do I get dough to eat on?" Krouch's
voice was a whine.

"Give him fifty," Lennox said. "I'll
settle with you when I settle the bail.
Now get him out of here."

He watched while the big man led the
taxi-man into the next room, followed
by Marx. In fifteen minutes, the lawyer
returned to find Lennox asleep in the
chair. He was about to tiptoe out when
Bill suddenly opened his eyes. "Is
Krouch gone?"

Marx nodded. "My man's riding him
as far as San Berdoo. He'll get a rat-
tler there."

Lennox yawned, stretched, and asked
what time it was.

"Almost nine," Marx told him. "You
want to sleep some more?"

Bill shook his head and reached for
the phone. He called Nancy Hobbs'
number and after a little wait, said:

"Hello, Nance! How's the brat this
morning? Listen! Wantta do something for me? You don't?" He grinned.
"Well do it anyway. I want you to
interview a newcomer, and, boy! is she a
comer? . . . Now, listen! She has a
bit in *The Footlights Revue*—name,
Marian Delaine. Yeah. I know you
never heard of her, but I'll have that
name in lights yet. Listen, Kid!
You're going up there with me, then
you're going to get your boss to run it.
I'll get you some pictures this afternoon.
Where are you? . . . Swell! I'll pick
you up there in three-quarters of an
hour."

He hung up and looked at Marx. "Let

me borrow your razor and a shirt," he said; "then call me a cab."

6

COLD shower drove the sleep from Lennox's eyes. As he rode across town in the cab, his active mind was already framing the interview which Marian Delaine was to give Nancy Hobbs. "A convent?" He considered the idea and discarded it as being trite, overdone. "I've got it," he said, so loudly that the driver turned to look at him. "She traveled with her father. He was—a—a mining engineer. Swell! He was killed—in China, by bandits. Yeah, that ought to go."

The cab swung towards the curb before Nancy's house, and he saw her smiling at him from the sidewalk.

"You look swell," he told her, as the cab started again.

"And you look like the devil," she said, frankly. "Give me the low-down, Bill. Tell me who this Delaine really is."

He grinned at her. "Wait until you see her, sweetheart." The cab went down Franklyn and turned right, stopping before the apartment house.

Nancy said: "Some class. Is she spending her own dough?"

Bill didn't bother to answer. He went in and asked at the desk for Miss Delaine. The switchboard operator rang her apartment, rang again. "Miss Delaine does not answer," she said.

Bill swore softly. "I told her not to leave the joint," he muttered to Nancy. "Come on up and we'll have a look."

They rode up in the automatic elevator and walked along the heavy rug of the corridor. Before the apartment door, Lennox paused and drew a key from his pocket. Nancy Hobbs watched him with amused eyes. He caught the look and flushed slightly. "Don't go getting ideas, Brat. This is business."

He fitted the key into the lock and opened the door, then swore. The apartment was in disorder. Drawers were half open, doors swung ajar. Lennox went through the rooms rapidly, then returned to the front. Nancy Hobbs stood beside a small end table, fingering a large square envelope.

"This is for you, Bill."

He took it, read his name in a large, feminine hand, and tore it open. Looking across his shoulder, Nancy read:

Dear Mr. Lennox:

Sorry to run out on you this way, but Wilbur and I are going to be married; then we're going back to Topeka, Kansas. We have loved each other a long time, but did not have money to marry. Last night, Wilbur got a letter from his brother, one that Bert mailed before he was killed. There was twenty thousand dollars in it. Think of it—twenty thousand.

It was swell of you to want to help me, but Wilbur says that he does not want me to be an actress, as he thinks that actresses aren't very nice, so you just get another girl in my place. If you should ever come to Topeka, be sure and come to see us.

Your friend,
Irene Schultz (Rose pretty soon).

Bill dropped the letter and looked at Nancy. She was laughing, laughing so that her eyes were wet. He started to swear, stopped, and grinned a bit wryly. Slowly he drew an envelope from his pocket.

"Ever see anyone tear up a million-dollar bill, honey?"

She said, still laughing: "You're silly. They don't make them that large."

Solemnly he took from his billfold an oblong-folded paper and put it with letter and envelope, then put the halves together and tore them. The contract, signed by Marian Delaine, dropped to the carpet.

Gamblers Don't Win

By W. T. BALLARD

Not even when a murder fixes the bet

BILL LENNOX, trouble-shooter for General-Consolidated studio, stared thoughtfully at his program. The third race was just coming up. The horses were already on parade, the bright silks of their riders making color splotches against the gray-green background of the distant hills.

Nancy Hobbs, pert and chic, plainly pleased with Lennox, said, "It's a nice place."

Lennox nodded as he looked around the clubhouse lawn. "Nice, and all the movie bunch are here, to be taken." His voice was cynical.

She smiled slightly. "You're here, too, aren't you?"

He said: "I had to be here, Honey. Spurck decided that what he needed was a racing stable. He's got one, and one of his horses starts in the feature this afternoon. If I hadn't been here to see the nag perform, Sol would never have recovered. There he is now." He pointed with his program to where Sol Spurck, head of the West Coast studios of General Consolidated, was standing in one of the front row boxes. "Look at him. He's having the time of his life."

The girl looked in that direction, shielding her eyes with one hand. "Next you'll be telling me that you don't like races."

"Sure I like them," Lennox told her. "I think the horses are swell. It's the people I object to, the chiselers, the touts, the gamblers."

She said: "But they aren't going to have any out here. They're being very careful to keep them off."

Lennox' lips twisted slightly. "I'll admit they're being careful, Honey. I'll admit they've got a better class of horses here than they ever had on the Coast before. I'll admit that this track is run on the level and that the racing commission is making every effort to keep the sport on the highest plane possible, but there's easy money connected with racing, and you're bound to have some chiselers. Come on. Let's walk around and have a look. This is a nice plant."

He linked his arm through hers and they crossed the lawn towards the grandstand entrance. Several people spoke to them, others waved. It seemed to Lennox that Hollywood had moved *en masse* to the track. Movie capital had helped build it. Movie capital had helped bring racing back to California after some twenty years, and the picture people were entering the new sport with enthusiasm. Spurck was not the only producer to buy horses, and any number of actors had followed suit.

They left the clubhouse and threaded their way through the thronged betting shed. A tall, well-dressed man with black hair and a hawk's nose stopped Lennox. "Hello, Bill."

Lennox let his surprise show. "Hello, Claude. Long time, no see."

The man's white teeth flashed. "I heard you were out here. How's every little thing?"

"Not bad. What do you think of the plant?"

"As nice as any I've seen." The

crowd carried them apart and the girl asked, with interest,

"Who was that?"

Lennox gave her a twisted smile. "That was one of the boys I've just been talking about. That's Claude Custis. He used to be a big-shot New York bookie. He's a bigger shot gambler now, and bad."

She said: "He doesn't look bad. He looks like a gentleman."

"Claude's a gentleman." Lennox' grin was sour. "I doubt if he ever said ain't in his life, but he's bad, any way you take him. I wonder what he's doing out here."

"Probably came out for the climate."

"More likely the easy money. Claude doesn't know there is a climate. There's no percentage in climate, and Claude plays percentages. Well, it's not my lookout." He pushed on through the crowd to be stopped a few minutes later by a heavy, red-faced figure. "Hello, Floyd! Looks like old-home week."

Detective Captain Floyd Spellman grinned. "Hello, Nancy! You're in bad company."

"She is since you came," Lennox told him. "What are you doing out this way?"

Spellman moved heavy shoulders. "Looking around. It's a swell joint."

"I'll guess it burns you up to see them betting legally," Lennox suggested.

"Yeah." Spellman grinned. "Well, I gotta be getting back to town. I just came out to give it the once-over."

Nancy asked: "Could I bum a ride? I've got a story to finish, and Bill can't leave until after Spurck's horse runs."

Spellman said: "Sure. I'll take good care of her, Bill."

"You can't take good care of yourself," Lennox told him, "but Nance can take care of both of you. See you tonight, Kid."

He watched them move away through the crowd, then turned and walked slowly back towards the clubhouse.

PURCK'S horse was in the fifth race, a gelding with powerful shoulders and beautiful stride, a distance horse. Lennox watched him through glasses as they paraded to the post. The horse had a good record at Chicago and Detroit, no Derby winner, but certainly not a plater; he should win from this field without much trouble. The field was small, only seven, and they were at post hardly a minute.

Lennox watched as they broke from the gate, picked them up with his glasses as they hit the first turn and followed Spurck's entry, his brows drawing into a scowl. The boy had taken the horse wide going into the back stretch and had dropped from third to fifth, holding him there, the four leaders drawing away ever so slightly.

There was nothing in the ride that the judges could call, but Lennox knew that the kid wasn't trying, that he was holding the horse out of it until too late. They came around the far turn; the field strung along the fence, and thundered into the stretch, with Spurck's horse on the extreme outside. He had no chance, and the boy was driving him now to finish a badly beaten fifth.

Lennox slid his glasses into the case and, turning, stared towards Spurck's box. He saw the producer slumped in his chair, disappointment showing on his heavy features. The boys were weighing in, the official sign went up, and the horses were being led towards the barns. Lennox glanced at his program. Spurck had another horse in the seventh, a good plater that he had picked up in Kentucky.

The horse had a good chance to win, should be at least second favorite. Lennox knew Spurck's orders, had heard the producer tell the trainer that he wanted to win today if possible. Bill's mouth set grimly as he waited. It was grimmer yet as Spurck's horse finished a bad seventh.

Without going near the producer's box, he went out to the parking place and got a cab. It dropped him downtown, and he went directly to the hotel where the rider was staying. He'd been seated in the lobby twenty minutes when he saw the boy come in and go to the desk for his key. Bill crossed to the elevators and rode up in the same car with the jockey, followed him down the hall and waited until he unlocked the door, then crowded into the room after him and shut the door.

The boy stared at him with startled eyes. "Say, what's the idea?" He looked young, very small. Lennox judged that he weighed about ninety pounds. Bill stood there, staring at him for a moment, and a flush of anger crept up into the jockey's cheeks. "I asked you what the big idea was?"

Lennox said, softly, "I'm a friend of Spurck's. I don't like the way you ride his horses."

The color faded from the boy's cheeks, but he tried to bluster. "I don't know what you're talking about."

"Sure you do." Something that Pop Henry had told him in New Orleans five years before came to Lennox' mind. Pop had been a good trainer, and he'd developed good riders. "Most of them are kids," Pop had said. "You can't talk to them, but you can use a bat on them. Whale hell out of them. That's the way."

The boy was staring at Lennox, his fingers twisting nervously. "What right have you to crash in here and talk this way? You ain't got a thing on me." He sounded nervous, ill at ease.

Lennox smiled coldly. "Listen, Kid. Spurck doesn't know anything about racing, about horses. He got stung plenty when he bought them, but he did get some good horses. That gelding in the fifth could have come close to winning with a decent ride. He didn't get it and I'm up here, asking you why. I know that Spurck would make a swell front for a gambling stable. He'd never know what was going on, and if there was a blow-off, he'd be the goat. He'd probably be ruled off every track in the country. Not that that would matter, but it wouldn't be the kind of publicity he'd want. *He* may be dumb when it comes to racing, but *I* know what it's all about. Get this: I'm watching you from now on, and if you pull another horse, I'll make it my business to see that you don't ride again on any association track in the country. Do you get me?"

It was clear that the boy understood. His lips worked, and there was fear in his dark eyes. "Who are you?"

Bill said: "My name is Lennox. If you kids think you can pull a fast one on Spurck, think again."

He opened the door and, stepping backward into the hall, closed it behind him. As he rode down in the elevator he thought it over. The obvious thing was to go to Spurck, to get the producer to change riders. But would it do any good to change jockeys? It might be a jockey ring, banded together for betting purposes. If so, the track officials would break it up in time, but Spurck's reputation might suffer, and Lennox did not want that.

He had an affection for the little producer, one that he refused to admit even to himself. He decided to wait and see what happened. He left the hotel, got a cab, and drove to his apartment. He'd hardly reached it when the phone on the night stand beside the bed shrilled.

A voice said, "Is this Mr. Lennox, the man who was talking to Frank Jarney half an hour ago?"

Bill said, "Yes." The jockey's name was Jarney, but he wondered—

The voice said, hurriedly, "Please, Mr. Lennox. This is Frank Jarney. Will you do me a favor? Will you ask Mr. Spurck to get another boy?"

Lennox swore with surprise. "Will I— Say, what is this? You aren't under contract to Spurck. You don't have to accept mounts from him unless you want to, do you? Refuse to ride for him if you don't want to; but I'm

warning you. If you do ride, ride to win."

"But I'm afraid to refuse, I—" Suddenly there was a click at the other end of the wire. For a moment Lennox stared at the silent phone, then with a shrug he hung up. He turned away and pulled off his coat, wondering what the boy was afraid of. Maybe it was a gag, an out, an excuse for pulling Spurck's horses. His mouth set as he went into the bathroom and put a fresh blade into his razor. If the kid thought he could pull another horse and get away with it, he'd better think again.

IT was almost twelve-thirty that night when Lennox returned to his apartment hotel, entered the lobby and started across towards the elevator. The night clerk's voice stopped him as he passed the desk. "Oh, Mr. Lennox!"

Bill stopped, turned. "What is it, Tom?"

The clerk said: "Some girl's been calling you every half hour since nine o'clock. She left a number, wants you to call as soon as you came in."

Lennox glanced at the clock behind the desk. "It's pretty late."

The clerk said: "She wanted you to call no matter how late it was. I think it's important. She sounded very worried. The number is Rochester 50845."

"Didn't she leave a name?"

The clerk shook his head. "She didn't, but she seemed terribly anxious to reach you."

Lennox hesitated, still looking at the clock. "Okey! Ring it for me, will you? I'll take it in the booth." He turned and, crossing the lobby, entered the telephone booth.

A woman's voice said, "Yes?" inquiringly.

"This is Bill Lennox," he told her. "Someone from this number left a call for me."

"Oh, Mr. Lennox," relief flooded the

voice. "This is Betty Donovan. I don't suppose you remember me?"

He said, "Donovan, Donovan?" over to himself. "I'm afraid I don't."

"I'm Bert's sister."

"Oh." He remembered her then, a fourteen-year-old kid with long black curls and a pretty Irish face. "How are you?"

She said: "I hate to bother you, but I've got to see you at once. It's frightfully important."

"Can't it wait until morning?"

"I'm afraid to wait. Won't you please meet me tonight?"

He said: "Okey. Where are you?" He was tired, very tired, and he had a hard day coming up, but he couldn't refuse Bert Donovan's sister.

She said: "I don't want you to come here. I'll meet you any place you say. A public restaurant would be best, I think."

He hesitated for a moment, then named one on the Boulevard. "Know where that is?"

She said: "I'll take a cab. I'll meet you there in half an hour," and hung up.

Lennox left the booth, lighted a cigarette, and stood for a moment, thinking it over. He hadn't seen Bert Donovan for six years, hadn't heard of him for three. He wondered what the girl was doing in Hollywood, hoped that she hadn't come out here with an idea of getting into pictures. Too many did that, too many with pretty faces and no ability.

"Better call me a cab, Tom," he said finally, and went out to meet it. The cab took him across to the Boulevard and turned west. It was cold, with a chilling wind blowing directly from the ocean. It would probably rain before morning, he thought, as he stepped from the cab before the restaurant, paid the driver, and went in.

A man at the bar spoke to him and Bill nodded in return, without stopping. He went towards the back of the long room, passed the screen which separated the beer bar from the tables at the rear,

and looked around. He had no idea that he would recognize her. She'd probably changed in six years. Six years, that would make her about twenty, no, nearer twenty-one.

The room was not crowded. An orchestra on a raised platform played fitfully, and there were perhaps fifty people at the tables clustered about the small dance-floor. Lennox nodded as one of the proprietors, an ex-picture heavy, came up to him. "How's things, Fred?"

The man said: "Not good, not bad." His face was flat, with a broken nose and bushy eyebrows. He grinned and led Lennox towards one of the leather-upholstered wall booths. "Alone?"

Bill said: "I'm meeting a girl here. She'll probably ask for me."

The man nodded and moved away as a waiter came forward. Lennox ordered beer, took a long pull at the glass, and looked around. A leading comedian was at a corner table with four women. Lennox knew that he was a little drunk, that he was always a little drunk; but, drunk or sober, he was funny, and Bill grinned in spite of himself as the man raised a hand in salute. Then someone touched his shoulder and he came to his feet to see a dark-haired girl facing him.

She wore a suit of heavy tweed, fur trimmed, with a little hat that perched above one ear. There was something about her that spoke of assurance, capability and of a seriousness that wasn't lost even when she smiled. "Bill Lennox. I'd have known you anywhere."

He smiled and pulled the table aside so that she could enter the booth. "I should say the same, Betty, but it wouldn't be true. Still, you do look like Bert."

Color stained her cheeks slightly and was gone. Lennox said: "How is Bert?"

Her eyes widened. "Didn't you know? He was killed in an automobile accident two years ago."

Lennox swore to himself. "I'm

sorry, Kid. He was a swell pal."

"It means a lot to hear you say that," she told him. "Bert liked you."

"And what happened to the stable?" Lennox asked, when he had finished ordering beer for her, and sandwiches.

"I'm running it." Her lips twisted slightly. "I've got eight horses out here. Al Hinds is training for me. Remember him?"

Lennox nodded. "Not very clearly, but he was tall and thin, without much hair."

She said, "Right," and was silent while the waiter served the orders, then her face got serious. "Listen, Bill! I'm going to ask you a favor. I've no right to ask it, except that I know you thought a lot of my brother, and this is pretty important to me. I talked to Frank Jarney tonight. I want to ask you to leave him alone."

Lennox stiffened. "You talked to Jarney? What did he have to say?"

She was twisting her glass in her fingers, making wet rings on the bare table top. "Only that you threatened him."

Lennox' smile held no mirth. "I'd hardly call it a threat. I told him that he wasn't riding Spurck's horses the way they should be ridden, and that if he didn't change, I'd do something about it."

She said, tensely: "He's riding to orders."

Lennox stared at her. "Not Spurck's orders?"

She shook her head slowly. "No—"

"Then whose?"

"I don't know."

"Now, listen." Lennox was leaning across the table, his voice so low that it barely reached her ears. "Spurck bought that stable against my advice. It's not his game. He doesn't know a thing about it, and he got hooked plenty on the purchase, but I'm not going to have a bunch of cheap gamblers run his horses out of the money until they get a price built up and then win with them. I don't know who's giving Jarney or-

ders, but I do know that if he tries any more funny business, I'll have him put on the ground and he'll stay there the rest of his life. I'll see that he never gets a leg up on another horse."

HER face had a white, pinched look. "Listen, Bill, I'm asking you this, not because you were a friend of Bert's, but because I need help. If Frank were to listen to you, he wouldn't live twenty-four hours. He's got to ride according to orders, not only on Spurck's horses, but on others, and I'm telling you this; he's not the only rider that's taking orders. There are others, not because they want to, but because they're afraid not to."

Lennox stared at her. "You've either said too much, Kid, or not enough. Who's giving these orders?" he asked again.

She shook her head.

His voice gained a harsher note. "Meaning you don't know, or merely that you won't tell?"

She said: "Don't ask me; please don't. There's a reason why I won't—can't answer you."

"Are you in love with Jarney?" His tone was blunt.

She shook her head. "Please, won't you please do what I ask?"

Lennox shook his head slowly. "I tell you what I will do. If Jarney is afraid to refuse to ride Spurck's horses, I'll see that he doesn't have to. I'll have him fired."

Her eyes darkened. "Don't do that."

Surprise made him silent for the moment. "Now, listen. Tonight over the phone Jarney asked me to do just that. What's the idea? Just what are you trying to pull?"

She said, desperately: "Nothing. Please believe me, but it's too late for you to do that. They heard him talking to you tonight. If he were fired, they'd still do something to him. Why can't you leave things as they are? What does it matter to Spurck whether he wins a few races or not? He's got plenty of money. He has everything."

Lennox' lips were twisted. "I'm a funny guy, I guess. It isn't the purses he loses that I'm thinking about; it's the public, the betting public. I can't use a roulette wheel that's wired, Kid, and crooked dice burn me. It's the same with this. Thousands of people go out to the track and bet their dough. They bet on Spurck's horses, not because they really know anything about the nags, but because they know who Spurck is; they know he's on the level, and they figure that his stable will be run that way." He broke off, embarrassed. He wasn't used to expressing his feelings so frankly.

Betty Donovan was staring at him, her fingers working with the edge of the napkin. "And you'd get a boy killed for that?"

He narrowed his eyes. "Listen, Kid. If you know something, the thing for you to do is to go to the cops, or better, to the track officials. Gamblers can't win. They will go along swell for a while, but in the end, the judges will catch up with them. Come on, I know the chief steward, where he's living. We'll go over there—" He started to rise, but she stopped him.

"Please, you'll—you don't know what you're doing." There was fear in her voice, more than fear.

He dropped back heavily into his seat. "Listen, Betty. Your brother was a swell pal of mine. I want to help you, but I can't if you don't come clean with me, I—"

Her voice changed. "You aren't a reformer, are you, Bill?"

He shook his head. "I'm not."

"Then wait. I can't tell you anything now. All I ask is that you don't interfere."

"Well, I'll talk to Jarney."

She hesitated. "I don't know—"

He said: "I won't play any other way, Kid."

The girl seemed to come to a sudden decision. "All right. Come on."

She rose, and Lennox motioned for the check. In the cab, riding downtown, neither spoke. Fine drops of rain sprayed across the cab's windows, driven by the wind, and the girl shivered. Lennox said, finally, "Looks like a muddy track in the morning."

She did not answer and, after a moment, he lit a cigarette and stared out at the wet, glistening sidewalk. The cab drew up before the hotel and they got out. Lennox paid the man and followed the girl across the wide lobby to the elevators. They rode up to Jarney's floor in silence and went along the corridor to the door of the jockey's room. The girl knocked, three quick taps, then a heavier one, and waited. There was no response, and after a minute's hesitation, she pulled a key from her bag and, sliding it into the lock, opened the door.

Lennox watched her without comment, his eyes thoughtful. She looked across her shoulder, met his gaze, and red crept up into her cheeks, but she offered no explanation, and, pushing the door open, stepped into the room, with Lennox at her heels. She stopped so suddenly that he almost ran into her, and a little toneless cry, more like a moan, came from her throat. Then Lennox, staring across her shoulder, saw Jarney stretched across the bed, his head hanging over the edge.

Lennox pushed her aside and crossed the room quickly, bending over the bed. Then he straightened and went back to the door, shutting it and shooting the night lock into place. The girl stood where she had first stopped, her widened eyes on the still figure, the back of her left hand pressed tightly against her lips. Slowly her eyes came away from the bed, met Lennox', appealing, yet uncertain.

He said, softly: "Hadn't you better tell me about it, Kid?"

She stared at him. "You think—you think I killed him?"

Lennox watched her. "I'm not thinking, but the time's come to talk, Honey. You can't afford to stall any longer. If you didn't kill him, someone else did; someone who thought he had a reason. You may know that reason." He waited for her to speak, but her eyes had switched back to the bed. Slowly she went forward until he said, sharply, "Don't touch anything."

She stiffened at his words, then turned. "What are you going to do?"

He said: "Call the police. There isn't anything else to do. Any other way, we'd just be hunting trouble for ourselves."

Fear came back into her eyes, fear, and a look that he could not understand. "Please, I can't be found here. I'm not ready for the police, yet."

He stared at her. Did she mean that she had killed Jarney? It didn't make sense. If she had killed the jockey, why had she brought him here; what did she mean by saying that she was not ready for the police, yet?

The girl seemed to read his thoughts. "I didn't kill him." Her voice was low, yet so intense that it was convincing. "You don't think that I would lie to you, do you, Bill Lennox?"

Her eyes met his squarely, and the conviction crept over him that she was telling the truth; yet he knew that the cops would not share his belief. The fact that she had known Jarney, had had a key to his room, would bear heavily against her. He said, suddenly, "Give me that key."

Her voice was uncertain. "What are you going to do?"

His voice was grim, almost sardonic. "Play the fool, probably. Give me the key and get out of here."

Relief flashed into her eyes. "But won't you get into trouble?"

"Probably. Come on." His tone was urgent. "We haven't got all night. And you'd better use the stairway, going down. We've already ridden in the elevator too much tonight."

Hesitantly she opened her bag and handed him the key. "I—I can't tell you how much this means to me, Bill. I—I wish I could do something to repay you."

He said: "You can. You can tell me what you know."

"I will, sometime." She was moving towards the door.

He said, "Wait," harshly, opened the door, and peered out into the hall. It was empty, and he stood back. "All right, Kid. What's your address?"

She murmured it as she passed him and hurried down the hall. He went inside the room, shut the door, took the key from his pocket and, wiping it with his handkerchief, tossed it on to the desk; then he crossed and stared down at the still figure on the bed. Someone had driven a knife, hard, just below the heart.

He wondered if the girl could have struck the blow, decided that she could have. He looked around and, walking to the phone, called Spellman, at home. The sleepy, irritable voice of the detective captain reached him. Lennox said, "I've just found a body. I thought you ought to know."

Spellman swore. "Don't you think I'm ever off duty?"

"You're never on," Lennox said, and gave the hotel and room number. "You'd better come yourself, and don't bring too many cops. The management wouldn't appreciate it." He hung up, and wandered about; then he lit a cigarette and sat down to wait.

 PELLMAN was puffing slightly as he came into the room. Lennox said: "You're getting soft on that desk job. They ought to put you back into harness where you'd have work to do."

The detective captain ignored him. He crossed the room and stood staring down at the body, then he turned around. "Who was he?"

"Jockey. His name was Jarney, Frank Jarney."

Spellman's voice dripped sarcasm. "I suppose it would be too much to ask what you're doing here?"

Lennox regarded the smoke which curled slowly upward from the tip of his cigarette. "I came up to see Jarney. He's riding Spurck's horses, and I didn't think he was getting the most out of them. I was going to offer a couple of suggestions."

"Yeah, and what?" It was obvious that Spellman wasn't impressed by the story.

"He was dead when I walked in."

"And just why did you walk in?"

Lennox shrugged. "Well, the door was unlocked. I thought it was funny that Jarney didn't answer my knock, so I came in to see why, and found him." He indicated the still figure with a slight motion of his hand. "Then I called you."

Spellman stared at him. "Which elevator did you come up in?"

Lennox had been dreading the question. "Now listen, Floyd. Just because I happen to walk into this mess is no reason why you should get suspicious. What earthly reason would I have for killing Jarney?"

Spellman moved heavy shoulders. "I wouldn't know," he admitted, "but it happens that the city pays me a salary to ask questions and there's nothing said about your being an exception. I can easy enough find out. Hey, Harker."

"Yeah, Captain!" A big plain-clothes-man removed his shoulders from against the wall and stood erect.

"Trot down and bring along the boys from the elevators. I want to see if one of them remembers Lennox."

The big dick opened the door and an excited little man came bursting through. "What's going on here, what's going—?"

Harker said: "Who the hell are you?"

The little man drew himself up coldly. "I'm the assistant manager. You have no right to disturb my guests."

"Your guests shouldn't get themselves bumped off." Harker stood aside so that the manager could see the still figure on the bed.

The manager's mouth dropped, then he closed it slowly. "Why wasn't this reported to the house officer?"

"Probably asleep," Spellman said, curtly. "Go on, Harker."

The manager flushed angrily. "Who's in charge?"

"I am." Spellman turned his back on the man and was looking about the room.

"Well, Lieutenant?"

"Captain," Spellman's voice cut at him, and Lennox laughed.

The manager said, with not quite so much assurance, "Please be as quiet as you can. This is terrible, terrible. If the papers get—"

No one paid any attention to him. Harker came back leading five boys whom he lined up against the wall. Spellman looked at them. "Any of you kids ever see this guy before?"

The boy at the right end nodded. "I brought him up about forty minutes ago."

"Sure?"

"Positive. I remember thinking how pretty the girl with him was."

"Girl? What girl?" Spellman spun around to face Lennox. "Who was with you?"

Cursing under his breath, Bill kept his eyes on the cigarette in his hand. He'd been afraid of this, but, after all, she was Bert Donovan's sister, and he did not think she was guilty. "The kid's mistaken, Floyd," he lied. "I remember there was a girl in the car, that she got off at this floor; but she wasn't with me."

Spellman's red face gained a deeper shade and his little eyes got very narrow. For a moment he stared at Lennox, then swung back to the elevator boy. "You sure the dame was with this guy?"

The boy looked uncertain. "Well, Chief, I ain't sure. Come to think of it, I didn't see them speak, but she got in the car right ahead of him, and they got out at the same floor. I just kinda thought—"

"You kinda thought—" Spellman's voice was sarcastic. "Get his name and address, Harker." He swung back to Bill as the man from the coroner's office came in. "Sure that dame wasn't with you?"

Lennox shrugged. "I ought to know."

"Sure, you know." Spellman sounded mad. "The question is, are you telling? Where were you tonight?"

"A number of places." Lennox named half a dozen restaurants and clubs. Nance and I were seeing the town."

"Yeah? Sure she didn't come up here with you?"

"Certain. We met Mary Barker at the last joint we made and Nance went home with her for the night. You can check if you want to."

"Don't worry. I'll check. Then after you left her—what?"

"I stopped in Fred Logram's place on the Boulevard, had a glass of beer, and came down here."

"Talk to any people there?"

"Sure, several. Are you going to run me in for that?"

Spellman spread his hands. "Dammit! I'd like to get you in a place where you'd have to talk, just once. You've got too much drag."

Lennox said, pleasantly, "You never learn, Floyd. Every time you tangle with me, you get it in the neck. I'm not going to skip town. I'll be around, and you know it. What about letting me go home."

Spellman hesitated. "Who'll I report this to?" He indicated Jarney's body.

Lennox shrugged. "I don't know. Spurck's trainer probably would. His name's Hopkins, but I don't know where you'd reach him tonight." He rose. "Still want to hold me?"

Spellman said: "You'd better come in and talk to the D.A. in the morning. I still think you're not telling all you know. Hey! Hold on! Supposing you wait until I can check your alibi

with Nancy Hobbs. What's Mary Baker's number?"

Lennox smiled as he gave it, but not from mirth. He was wondering just how long it would take Spellman to learn that he had been with Betty Donovan in Fred Logram's place, how long it would take the police to find the cabman who had driven him to the hotel.

He heard Spellman talking on the phone, then saw him cross the room and confer with the coroner's man. Finally the detective captain turned around. "Okey! I guess you can go. Both Nancy Hobbs and the Baker dame say you were with them from ten-thirty until twelve, and Doc tells me that Jarney died around eleven, as near as he can judge, but listen, Bill. Why don't you help a guy? Why do you always have to play dirty?"

Lennox shrugged and turned towards the door. "See you in the morning."

"You'd better." Spellman's voice followed him into the hall.

Bill rode down in the elevator with the boy who had identified him, conscious of the lad's curious glances and, crossing the lobby, stepped out to the sidewalk. As he climbed into a cab he looked around and saw Harker loafing just inside the doorway. He smiled grimly as he gave the driver his apartment address. Evidently Spellman wasn't as satisfied as he had appeared. Lennox debated trying to throw the trailer off the track and decided against it. After all, it was hardly worth while.

He settled back on the seat and stared at the rain-clouded windows. It was raining steadily now, not a pouring deluge, but a steady fall which slanted against the windshield. He closed his eyes and, leaning back, thought it over. The more he thought, the greater the puzzle grew. He decided that the girl had not killed Jarney, but he could not figure out the reason for her actions. He had assumed that she was in love with the rider, but certainly she had given no indication of it on finding his body. Grief, yes, surprise, but certainly not the

68

grief of love. What then? Lennox gave it up as the cab stopped before his apartment hotel. He paid the driver and sprinted across the wet walk to the doorway.

Here he paused for a moment and stared up the dark street to where another cab had stopped, halfway up the block. Harker would have a wet night for watching, he thought, as he went on to the desk and paused for a moment. "Listen, Tom. Will you do something for me?"

The clerk said, eagerly. "Sure, Mr. Lennox. Anything."

"Just forget that phone call and number, will you? I don't think they'll bother, but the cops might be asking questions, and it would gum up a swell girl. You can take my word that there's nothing to that call that—"

The clerk winked, and Lennox turned towards the elevator. If the clerk wanted to think things, let him, as long as he kept his mouth shut.

ILL LENNOX was up and dressed, ready to go downtown, when the phone rang. He wondered if it were Betty Donovan, and hoped that it wasn't. It might be possible that Spellman had got ambitious and put a man on the switchboard below. He crossed the room and picked up the instrument. A man's voice said, "Is this Lennox, William Lennox?"

Bill's brows drew together. The voice sounded familiar. He had a good memory for voices, yet— He said: "Yeah. What is it?"

The voice said: "This is a friendly tip to stick by your own racket. No one ever got hurt, playing his own game."

"I don't get you." Lennox wanted to keep the man talking, wanted a chance to listen, to place the voice.

The man laughed shortly. "You're a wise guy, Lennox. From what I hear, you come damn' near running this town, but don't try to run the race track.

Someone might not like it. Someone might do something about it."

Lennox almost cried out with surprise. His mind had been groping, trying to connect the voice with something, and mention of the race track did it. He almost said, "Claude Custis," and didn't. Instead, he said, "I think that you must have made a mistake."

"No mistakes," Custis' voice told him. "We don't make mistakes. We bury them." There was a click at the other end of the wire, and Lennox hung up slowly, stared for a moment at the silent instrument, then went downstairs and got a cab.

DISTRICT ATTORNEY PIKE looked up from his desk as Lennox came into the office and nodded. "How are you, Bill?"

Lennox settled himself into a chair. "I'll live." He found a cigarette and rolled it thoughtfully between his fingers. "Thought I'd better come down and have a little talk. Spellman suggested it."

Pike's face got grave. "Listen, Bill. This office has always been on the level with you, hasn't it?"

Lennox moved his shoulders slightly. The D.A. wasn't a bad guy. A politician, yes, with his eye on the main chance, but fairly honest, fairly smart. Ordinarily, Lennox would have told him what he knew, but he couldn't tell him in this case, couldn't talk, yet. Betty Donovan was Bert's sister, and if he told what he knew, she'd be picked up, questioned, probably held. He didn't want that, not until he knew more about the affair.

She might be guilty, of course, but Lennox had played his hunches for years, and his hunch said she wasn't. If that were true, it would merely block the trail to the real murderer if the cops got her. He said: "Sure, you've been a good guy, Pike, aside from a little unpleasantness now and then."

"Well," the D.A. was leaning forward, "why don't you play the game with us then? Why don't you come clean, Bill? There was a girl with you at the hotel last night. We found that she met you in Hollywood, that she rode downtown with you in a cab, and that she rode up to Jarney's floor in the same elevator. At least the descriptions we get from the cabman and the elevator boy tally. Who was she? What did she have to do with Jarney's death?"

Lennox hesitated for just a moment. He was used to thinking fast, to making quick decisions. He said: "Okey. There was a girl with me, but she didn't have a thing to do with Jarney's death and there's no use in dragging her into this mess and get a load of bad publicity."

Pike tried to make his eyes hard, to match his tone. "Now listen, Lennox. It's for us to decide whether she's tied up with this jockey's death. That's what we're here for. If I give you my word that the papers won't learn anything about it until after we've investigated her story, will you tell me who she is?"

"No."

Surprise crept into the District Attorney's eyes, buried a moment later by anger. He was not used to being defied. Years of office had given him the habit of authority. His anger showed in his voice when he said, "Do you know what concealing evidence in a murder rap means?"

Lennox' voice was bored. "Don't read the law to me, Pike. I know it as well as you do. I should. I've heard you fellows talk about it often enough. Okey, I'm not going to answer until I'm convinced in my own mind that telling you will help find Jarney's killer. So what are you going to do about it?"

"I'll, by—" Pike was on his feet. "I'll hold you. I'll make you talk."

Lennox stared up at him. "Listen, Pike. You don't have to get hard with me. You can't make me talk, and you know it. Pick me up on any charge you want to name, short of murder, and

I'll be out in half an hour. I called Sam Marx before I came down here."

The District Attorney sat down slowly. "All right, Bill." He had gained control of himself. "I guess you're right, but it's not playing the game."

Lennox said: "Since when did you ever play the game? If I told you the girl's name, it would be on page one of every paper in town. I didn't kill Jarney. I don't know who did; but the girl we're talking about didn't, and there's no use dragging her into the mess. She happened to be with me when we found the body. It was a lousy break, but I could stand the publicity, and she couldn't."

"An actress, huh?" Pike almost licked his lips, and Lennox stared at him with disgust. He'd been feeling like a heel, not coming clean, but now he didn't. Jarney's death meant publicity to Pike, nothing more. He rose and stared down at the man at the desk.

"Am I free to go?"

The District Attorney managed a smile. "Sure, Bill, but listen. If you learn anything—"

Lennox went out. In the hall he stopped for a moment. He knew that he wasn't clear yet, that the cops and the D.A. investigators would tail him if they could. He knew that Pike hadn't released him because he wanted to. He was free because Pike was politically ambitious, and behind Lennox was the squat, rounded figure of Sol Spurck, head of the State Central Committee. Bill's mouth twisted grimly as he rode down to street level and stepped out on to the sunlit street. He wondered what the telephone call that morning had meant. Had Custis killed Jarney? Or, rather, had the gambler had the rider killed? Custis wasn't the type to take chances in cold blood if he could find someone else to do it for him.

For seconds Lennox stood there, thinking it over. His impulse was to face Custis, to have a showdown; then he shrugged. He couldn't do that, yet.

He had to know where Betty Donovan fitted into the picture. He didn't want the girl hurt. She seemed a swell kid, and she was Bert's sister.

His next impulse was to talk to her, but that was what Pike would expect him to do. Instead, he flagged a cab and told the man to take him out to the studio.

The noon papers carried banners. *Police Hunt Mystery Girl. Studio Executive Questioned in Jockey's Death.* Lennox read them as he lunched at the Vine Street *Brown Derby*. As he was leaving the restaurant, two reporters stopped him on the sidewalk. He refused to comment, and took a cab back to the studio. Spurck's secretary said that the producer wanted to see him. Lennox grinned sourly and went into the thickly carpeted room to find Spurck behind the enormous desk.

"What's on your mind, Sol?"

Spurck spread his hands. "He asks me what's on my mind? Honest, Bill, a minute's peace I ain't had this morning, y'understand. First it is the D.A.'s office, then the papers, then the D.A.'s office. Can't they have one good murder in this town without your mixing in?"

Lennox didn't laugh. "Take it easy, Sol."

"He wants I should take it easy?" Spurck appealed to the ceiling. "Honest, Bill. How much publicity like this can the studio stand?"

"Now, listen. I don't see where the studio comes into it."

Spurck seemed suddenly short of breath. "You don't see? Look once, what the *Star* has, the *schlemiels.*" He pulled forth a folded paper and tossed it on to the desk.

Boxed on the center of page one was a list of General's female stars with an enormous question mark and a caption, *Is One of These the Mystery Woman?*

Lennox stared at it, his eyes narrowing. The *Star* was more or less of a scandal sheet, willing to go to almost any length for a sensation. He said, slowly, "I don't know what we can do about it."

Spurck's chubby finger indicated the list. "Is it one of them?"

Lennox shook his head. "She isn't in pictures, Sol."

"Then tell who she is. Honest, Bill, I'm telling you, we can't afford nothing like this now. You gotta tell."

Bill's mouth set. "Listen, Sol. I'll have to play this the way I see it."

For a moment it seemed that Spurck would have a stroke. "Is that your loyalty?" he demanded, finally. "After all I have done for you—I find I am nursing a—a coyote to my bosom."

Lennox rose. "This isn't getting us anywhere," he said, looking at his watch. "Think I'll go out to the races."

"Go!" Spurck was on his feet. "Go, and don't come back, and when you see my secretary, tell her she should call the papers and say that you are fired." He sank heavily into his chair and scowled at the paper on his desk.

 ENNOX left the office and relayed the message to the secretary. She grinned at him uncertainly. "Suppose it's safe for me to send it out? He'll probably change his mind in half an hour."

Lennox shrugged. "That's up to you, Honey. Billy doesn't work here any more." He slapped on his sun-faded felt and closed the door.

At the track he ducked the clubhouse and went directly to the grandstand. There was less chance of meeting anyone he knew, and he did not feel like talking. His eyes ran down the list of entries for the second race, stopped at the fifth horse as he noted, "Miss Elizabeth Donovan, owner."

He'd come to the track in the hope of seeing her, and looked around the crowded stand, searching for sight of her face, but without success. Then he settled back to watch the race. It was a six-furlong event with nine starters; the girl's horse, a black colt, was in fifth post position. Lennox trained his glasses on the gate, saw the starter's flag drop, saw the horses break. It was an almost perfect start. For ten lengths the field held their positions, then the horse on the extreme outside pulled ahead and started to cut over towards the rail.

The girl's horse was third on the rail, then fourth, as another horse passed him, going into the far turn. Lennox swore softly to himself. He couldn't be sure, but it looked as if the rider was holding the horse out of it. And the colt was fast. Lennox had seen that in a brief flash of speed on the back stretch.

But colt and rider were fifth coming into the stretch, sixth at the finish.

His mouth grim, Lennox pulled a copy of the *Racing Form* from his pocket and examined it. The horse had won once at Detroit and had a second and third at Chicago, with better horses. In the three starts he had made on the Coast, he had been badly beaten. It might be, of course, that the long trip out had knocked him out of training. Some horses, Lennox knew, did not ship well, but on the other hand, it had looked as if the boy wasn't trying.

Bill rose and went down towards the betting shed. As he came down the stairway he saw a man and girl standing near a post across the crowded room. His brows drew together above his narrowed eyes as he recognized Betty Donovan and Claude Custis. For an instant he hesitated, then pushed towards them. He had almost reached them, was partially behind the post, when he heard Custis say, in a low voice which was barely audible to him,

"That was a nice ride Gentry gave last race. We'll win next time out."

The girl did not answer. Her eyes were on the program in her hand, but Lennox saw her lips twist into a little smile, and anger flooded through him. This was the girl he was protecting, this was Bert Donovan's sister. He almost stepped forward, then didn't. He

wanted a chance to talk to her, to talk to her alone, when Custis wasn't around. Carefully he retreated through the crowd to the stairs. From this point of vantage he waited until he saw the gambler turn and disappear towards the paddock.

For a moment the girl stayed where she was, staring down at the program in her hand, then came towards the stairs. The betting shed was emptying rapidly. It was almost time for the next race. The warning bell sounded, indicating that the horses were at the post, and still Lennox held his place. Betty did not see him until only a few feet separated them. Then she stopped, color flooding up into her face, her eyes widening.

Bill said, in a low voice, "I want to talk to you."

"But—not—we'll miss the race." It was evident that she did not want to stop.

His right arm shot out, his fingers closing about her slender wrist. "Better talk to me, Kid. A couple of words, and the cops will be looking for you." They were almost alone now. Outside, the roar of the crowd told that the race was being run.

Her face lost color until it was almost chalk-like. "You, you wouldn't do that?"

He said: "Wouldn't I? Listen. I tried to play fair, I tried to help you, and what do I find? I find that you're running a gambling stable, that you're purposely running them cold, losing until you get a price on your horse. I find you playing with the tough boys, with Claude Custis. You'll either promise me now to quit, or I'll turn you up on that Jarney killing."

She said: "I didn't do that. I swear that I didn't, Bill. Please don't turn me up yet, I've—" She was so pretty, so appealing, that he almost weakened.

"No sale, Kid." His voice was harsh. "You're going to promise me now to cut loose from Custis. Think of your brother. Think—"

She said, miserably, "I can't, Bill,

I—" Her eyes widened as she looked across his shoulder and, swinging around, Lennox found Custis not five feet behind him. The gambler's thin lips parted in a little mocking smile.

"Hello, Bill!"

Surprise held Lennox silent for the moment. He had no way of knowing how long Custis had been standing there, how much he had heard. Bill had been too intent on what he was saying to the girl to notice anything. The race was evidently run. People were drifting back across the betting shed, lines forming before the payoff windows. He said, "Hello, Claude!" and watched the gambler narrowly.

Custis looked towards the girl, his eyes seeming to ask a question, then they switched back to Lennox, cold, hard, like two gray flames. His lips still smiled, but there was no mirth in his face. His eyes went back to the girl. "Coming?" It was a command.

Lennox looked at her also, saw her hesitate, then without a word, turn and follow Custis. He swore softly under his breath, trying to decide, then with a shrug turned and climbed the stairs. He found a seat in the stand and sat down to think it over. His first impulse was to tell the D.A. what he knew. The girl would be picked up for questioning, and then—Lennox couldn't think what would happen then. In spite of her evident connection with Custis, it was impossible to think that she had had any part in Jarney's murder. After several minutes he rose, still undecided, and walked towards the exit. In the large parking place he crossed towards a cab, climbed in, and told the man to take him to town. They swung out on to Huntington Drive and started in. Lennox, his hat pulled low over his eyes, leaned back into the corner of the seat.

A big, black car left the parking place and tailed them, its speed moderate. He peered back at it a couple of times, then grinned sourly. That would be some of the D.A.'s men, following him. He wondered if they had seen him talking to the girl. He'd forgotten about being tailed, had not noticed anyone since leaving the studio. The big car gained speed, creeping closer. Finally its horn sounded and it swung out to go around the cab. Lennox frowned. Maybe he'd made a mistake. Maybe they weren't tailing him, maybe they'd just—then he swore suddenly and tugged at the gun in his shoulder-clip, for the car had swung in, crowding the slower cab towards the curb until the driver was forced to jam his brakes. Two men leaped from the other car. One shoved a gun though the half-open window towards Lennox. "Easy punk," and to the driver, "Keep your eyes front."

Lennox stopped, his gun half clear of the clip. He said: "What is this?"

The man did not bother to answer. He had the door open, the gun still steady on Lennox. "Out with you."

Bill got out slowly, wondering if he dared try for his gun, and decided against it. The man caught his wrist, pulled his hand away from the coat empty, had the gun from the clip in a moment, and dropped it into his coat pocket. The second man tied a handkerchief over the taxi-driver's eyes, bound his wrists behind his back. A third raised the cab's hood and pulled the wires loose from the plugs with one sweeping jerk. Then they shoved Lennox into the big car and it swung into motion.

The whole thing had taken less than three minutes. The big car moved fast, swung away from the usual lines of traffic and made a detour. They were ducking pursuit. As they crossed Sunset, Bill asked: "Why's Custis having me brought to town? We've passed some swell ditches."

He tried to make his voice light and almost failed. He knew Custis. The man killed or had his killings done if it suited his purpose, and Lennox could think of no reason why the gambler should wish him to live.

The man on his left said, "Custis who?" and Bill gave it up.

The car continued along the wide, concrete street until it reached Beverly, then turned right and went west. The gun against his side pressed harder as the traffic increased, but the men made no effort to blindfold him, no move to prevent his knowing where he was being taken. At Vermont they went south, slowing now. They passed policemen at almost every corner, and Lennox grinned sourly. He hadn't wanted to help them, and now he couldn't ask their aid. They turned west again at Ninth, covered several blocks, and swung into a side street, then into the driveway of a rambling, shingled bungalow.

HE yard was large, screened by neglected shrubbery. The car went around to the back, stopped before a double garage which looked as if it had been a carriage-house at one time. On order, Lennox stepped to the ground, followed closely by the man with the gun. They stood waiting while one of the other men unlocked the back door of the house, led the way across a screened porch and into a long, wood-paneled front room. The house was very large and at one time had been a show place. Lennox looked around curiously. It wasn't the type of place he would have expected Custis to choose, yet it offered an excellent hideout, well back from the little-used street, with an empty house next door.

What puzzled him was why they had bothered to bring him here. He couldn't imagine his being released alive, after Custis' threat over the phone, but why take all this trouble? Shrugging, he sat down on the big couch and picked up a morning paper he found there. The man with the gun grinned.

"You're pretty cool, guy." There was a note of admiration in his voice.

Lennox looked at him. "It wouldn't buy me much to get excited."

The man grinned. "It wouldn't buy you a thing. The boss' orders were to keep you here, to leave you loose if you acted smart, to tie you if you got funny. Take your choice."

Lennox masked his surprise. "I'll act nice," he said. "What about the radio?"

The man said, "Help yourself," and sat down on a chair beside the door.

Lennox rose and turned it on; then crossed the room to the row of bookshelves beside the fireplace and examined the titles. Someone, he saw, had good taste. Was it Custis, or had they rented the house furnished? He helped himself to one of Dumas' and returned to his place on the couch.

About six, another man appeared with a tray which he set upon the low table beside Lennox' elbow; then relieved the man at the door. Bill ate in silence, wondering how long this would last.

He was still wondering on the third morning after, when he rolled over on the couch bed and stared at the guard in his regular place beside the door. "Has anyone in this joint got a razor?"

The man grinned. "Why worry about your looks? You ain't going anywhere."

Lennox ran his hand across the stubble on his chin. "It itches," he complained.

The man shrugged. "All right, Sport. As soon as Bob comes, we'll see about digging up a razor. There's the paper." He tossed it across the room. Bill carried it to the fireplace and sat down before the blaze. It was chilly and he shivered. He opened the paper to the sport page, after a brief glance at the banner head which read, *"Film Man Still Missing. Police Hunt Lennox as Murder Witness."*

The man by the door said, "You're getting a lot of swell publicity," but Bill paid no attention. His eyes went to the race column. He looked at the results for the preceding day and finally at the entries. Suddenly he stiffened. The girl's horse, the same black colt, was entered in the sixth race. He whistled under his breath, remembering Custis' words. "We'll win the next time out." That would mean today. He looked towards the man beside the door, but the guard had turned his head and was apparently listening.

Sound reached Lennox. A car had come into the driveway. The back door opened and closed, and in another minute the man called Bob appeared in the doorway. The guard rose and grinned at his pal.

"Lennox is getting particular. He wants to shave."

The newcomer looked towards the fireplace. "A shave wouldn't hurt him. I'll go out and dig up a razor. There's the food." He laid three well-filled sacks on the chair, and, turning, disappeared. The guard laid his gun beside the sacks and drew out a cardboard container of coffee, some rolls, and a glass of jelly. "Come and get it." He picked up the gun and backed away.

Lennox crossed the room, picked up the chair, and carried it with its burden to the couch. He sat down and ate quickly, thinking things over as he did so. He was still puzzled that he was alive. He couldn't imagine any reason why Custis hadn't had him killed before this, but evidently he was to continue to live, at least for the time being. Certainly otherwise his guards would not take the trouble to get him a razor. What mattered whether or not a man about to die shaved?

It was almost half an hour later when the other guard returned and tossed a small, paper-wrapped package on to the couch. "There you are. You know where the bath is."

Lennox nodded and, picking up the package, unwrapped it. There was a new safety razor, a package of blades, and a tube of shaving cream.

He said, "Thanks. I'll remember this when you're in jail."

The man laughed. "When I am, brother. You might as well go eat, Charley, while Lennox cleans up."

The other man nodded, and, handing over his gun, disappeared. Lennox went towards the door, saw his guard back into the hall ahead of him, the gun ready. They weren't taking any chances, but they weren't being as cautious as they had been. He went along the hall to the bath and went in, not troubling to close the door. The room was small, dark, opening off of what had evidently been the maid's room, its single window giving on to an air shaft. There was no chance of escape that way. He switched on the light, turned on the hot water, then pulled off his shirt and rubbed lather into his face with the tips of his fingers.

"You might have brought me a clean shirt," he suggested. "This one could stand alone."

The guard was leaning against the wall in the hallway. He said, "You won't be needing one after today—" and stopped suddenly.

Lennox stiffened, half turned, then didn't. With fingers which he kept steady by effort he adjusted the razor. "Meaning what?"

The other was silent for a moment, then he laughed. "I'll let you figure that out yourself."

Lennox was doing just that, and he didn't like the answer his mind evolved. He drew the razor cautiously along one cheek, staring in the mirror at the guard, measuring his chances. He could slam the door and shoot the bolt into place before the man could stop him, but what then? Even if the window had opened on to the yard instead of the air shaft it was too small to permit the passage of his shoulders. He continued his shaving, still unable to figure out why they had kept him alive for three days only to kill him now. There could be only one answer.

Maybe the girl wouldn't stand for his death. Maybe Custis had kept him alive in an effort to hold the girl in line until after today's race. He finished his shaving and returned to the other room, just as the regular guard came in at the kitchen door.

Lennox looked at the clock above the

fireplace and saw that it was almost eleven-thirty. The sixth race would go to post in about four and a half hours. It would be at post three or four minutes perhaps, and it would take another minute or two to run. If he were right in his surmise that it was to hold the girl in line that Custis was keeping him alive, he had something like five hours to live. His mouth was a grim line as he saw the regular guard take up his place beside the door, saw the other leave, and heard his car back out of the driveway.

They were alone in the enormous house, alone, two men, one with a gun. Lennox eyed the gun. He wished that he could get close enough to grab it, to have a chance to fight it out; still, he wasn't sure that he'd make it, even then. The man was powerful, with wide shoulders and a heavy frame. He did not look like a gangster, a gunman. His face was tanned, and the knuckles of his long-fingered hands were knobbed as if from work.

Lennox decided that he must have been a track roustabout whom Custis had picked up somewhere. He said, "Shame we can't see the horses run today."

The man yawned. "I'd rather sleep. You got it easy, Sport. All you have to do is lie down and snooze. I've got to keep my eyes open."

Lennox grinned sourly. "It would be okey with me if you closed them. What's Custis paying you for this job?"

The man shrugged, his leather-like face not changing. Bill said: "I might be able to dig up ten grand. That would be pretty nice for you, all alone, no cuts, and no danger. If you're caught, there's a kidnaping rap against you, and it's tough for kidnapers in this state. They catch them."

The man said, "No sale. Forget it, Sport."

Lennox walked restlessly about the room. The clock above the mantle struck, twelve times. He said finally, "How about a little two-handed stud? I've got to do something or go nuts."

The guard hesitated for a moment. "Okey. You can deal them on the low table. Bring it over, but not too close."

Lennox obeyed. He got a deck of cards from the shelves beside the mantel and carried the table across to a spot a couple of feet in front of the guard's chair.

"What'll we play for? Let's make it a dollar a card with five on the last if you want to draw."

The man shook his head. "That's too steep for me. Better make it a quarter with a dollar on the last."

Lennox peered at him, then shrugged. "What difference," he thought, "did it make what they played for if he were going to die that night. His captor would never have to pay off; still, the man might have funny ideas." He said, "Okey," and dealt.

The man looked at his hole card and kicked in a match in place of a chip. Lennox stayed and was beaten by a pair of fours, back to back. He played on, steadily, the matches drifting across the table one by one. He thought, grimly, "It's lucky we aren't playing for dollars. I never could pay off." From time to time he glanced at the clock, saw the hand creep to two, to three, to quarter after, then to half-past. Once he threw down the cards in disgust and, looking up, saw the guard grinning at him.

The man was not so careful now. His gun rested on his knees, his eyes dropped to the cards, stayed there. Lennox lost again, had a pair of kings beaten by three deuces. Cursing, he gathered up the deck, started to shuffle it, and suddenly scaled the loose cards into the man's face. They struck him directly in the eyes. Instinctively his hands went up, but Lennox jumped forward across the low table, his shoulder striking the man's chest, carrying him and the chair over backwards, the gun flying half across the room, the man's head thudding heavily on the floor.

The guard groaned once and lay still, his head rolling sidewise, his big body tangled in the wreckage of the chair.

For an instant Lennox thought that the man was dead as he rolled over and got slowly to his feet; then he saw the guard was breathing, that he was merely out.

Bill shot a glance at the clock. It was almost twenty minutes of four. The race would go to post about four-thirty. He looked at the man again, then dived towards the hall, raced along it and out the rear door. A black coupé stood in the graveled parking place. He hesitated for an instant, then leaped towards it. The keys were in the lock and, jerking the door open, he slid beneath the wheel.

The motor was cold and he wasted seconds getting it started. Then he swung about the driveway and out into the street. He smiled grimly. It seemed such a simple getaway, but he knew it had been built on three days of careful acting that had dulled the guard's alert watchfulness and finally given him his chance.

HE coupé, a '31 Ford, had evidently had excellent care. Lennox drove it across town, using the side streets to avoid traffic, hit Beverly just west of Vermont, and went over to Silver Lake. It was four twenty-seven as he turned into the parking place at the track, drove down the long lane, and stopped almost at the gate. An attendant came running. "You can't park here," he growled, but Lennox did not hear him. He was already out of the car and sprinting for the gate.

The horses were already at the post when he reached the lawn before the grandstand. He paused, hesitated for a moment. He didn't know what to do, how to proceed. He'd intended to reach the track, to get hold of the girl, and force her to withdraw the horse from the race, but it was too late for that now. He could go to the judges, of course, but could he prove anything, could he—? He stiffened as he saw Custis across the lawn, near the fence.

Betty Donovan was not in sight, anywhere that he could see. The crowd was milling forward and he went with it, forcing his way until he was within twenty feet of the gambler. Then there was a cry, "They're off!"

Lennox did not have his glasses. Without them, he saw the horses break from the gate and come up the back stretch in a bunch. It was hard to pick out the black colt without glasses, hard; then Lennox saw him, third on the rail, running easily. His hands tightened as he watched. The boy was riding a canny race, holding his position. No. He was pulling out farther towards the middle of the track. Lennox stared. Was he trying to go round the leaders? He didn't seem to be. The horse was still under wraps, and two others had passed it on the inside.

Bill stole a glance at Custis. The gambler was leaning forward, his eyes glued to his glasses. Something about his shoulders spoke of anger as the field hit the far turn. The black colt was sixth now, still coming wide, on the outside. It was evident to Lennox that he couldn't get up, that he hadn't a chance. The race thundered into the stretch, the black colt still on the outside. Then the boy went to bat. The horse was creeping up, running over slower horses, but the two leaders had him by twenty lengths. He hadn't a chance, and barely got up to beat a staggering horse for third.

Lennox' mouth was a thin line, as he stared at the numbers. What had happened? Had there been a change of plans? This was the day the horse was supposed to win. Then he looked towards Custis. The gambler was also staring at the track, his face dead white, his long fingers nervously twitching at the strap which held his glasses. He turned and passed within three feet of Lennox without seeing him, and went towards the betting shed.

Lennox turned and followed. It was evident from Custis' face that whatever had. happened had not been part of the original plan. Lennox tried to think it out as he threaded his way through the crowd. That the horse could have won with a better ride was obvious. He had had much more speed at the finish than the leaders. They had both been ridden out with just enough left to come down under the wire. The black colt had lost plenty of ground by that swerve in the back stretch, and more by coming wide at the turn. It might have been an accident, of course, but it looked deliberate to Lennox.

He followed Custis across the betting shed, saw the man grab a hurrying stable boy by the arm, and pressed close in an effort to hear what the gambler said. Custis' voice was low, contained, yet with a strident note which reached Lennox' ears.

"Have you seen Miss Donovan?"

The boy grinned. He was freckle-faced, fifteen or sixteen; then, as he saw the gambler's face, his smile vanished. "She was out at the barn a little while ago."

Custis nodded and turned away. He went across the shed with Lennox following, and walked rapidly towards the distant barns. Lennox saw a plain-clothesman in the crowd and ducked behind a post. The man might not recognize him, but with every cop in town looking for him, there was a chance, and he did not want to be stopped now. He waited until the man moved on, then hurried after Custis.

The gambler had disappeared when Bill reached the barns and he stopped a hurrying swipe. "Where's the Donovan barn?"

The man turned and pointed, white teeth flashing in his dark face.

Lennox slid a quarter into the man's palm and went on. He reached the corner of the barn, got close to an open door, when he heard voices, Custis', level, cold with suppressed anger. "Did you see the race?"

Then the girl's answer. It held a flat note, a note of finality which Lennox had not heard there before. "I saw it."

"Wait until I get my hands on Gentry. I thought that kid knew how to ride. He let the colt go out in the back stretch and then took him wide. If I thought he'd done it on purpose—"

"He did." The girl's words seemed to hang in the silence like some suspended thing.

"What?"

"I said," her voice was measured now, slow, "that Gentry did it on purpose. He rode to orders, to my orders. I told him to lose the race."

"You told him?" It seemed that Custis' collar was suddenly too tight. "You told him. Why?"

She said: "Because you had money bet on that horse, Custis. Because I knew you had flooded every handbook in the country, that you had swamped the bookie clearing-houses in Syracuse and Akron. Because I knew all your friends had bet on him, bet on him at your say-so. They'll be looking for you, Custis, the boys you play with, the wise boys, the gamblers. They'll think you crossed them, lied to them, that you didn't bet your own money. You know what that means, don't you?"

Custis knew what it meant. Lennox could tell by his very silence that he knew. The man sounded strangled when he said, "You did that? You ruined me, took every nickel I had, put me on the spot? Why?"

"Because," her voice was very clear, very steady, "you killed my brother. You didn't know that I knew, that I suspected, did you? I couldn't prove it. I hadn't a chance to do anything, but the man that loosened that steering gear the night Bert was killed, told me when he was dying. I hadn't anything but his word. I had no proof that you paid him for the job. I couldn't even prove that you wanted Bert out of the way because he wouldn't play your game, because he was protecting the riders from you. All I could do was to take over the stable, to wait, to throw in with you when I got the chance and play your game, waiting for a time when you had all your money bet, when you had tipped your friends.

"I was set to do it once last summer in the East; then something happened and I had to wait. The boys helped me, the riders that had been loyal to Bert, the ones that were riding to your orders. I didn't expect you to kill Jarney. I might have gone to the police then, but I couldn't prove anything, and you had too much money, too much power. You haven't got it now. I've stripped it from you, and your own friends, your own kind, will be yapping—no, don't move." Her voice had sharpened, and Lennox stepped quickly forward to the open door.

Custis stood with his back to the door, facing the girl. He was leaning forward, his shoulders hunched. Something in her hand glittered. "Keep back!" It was a small gun.

Even as Lennox reached the door, he saw Custis spring forward, saw the little gun speak once, the bullet just missing his ear as Custis, with the litheness of a cat, sprang in, caught her wrist, twisted it until the gun dropped to the floor of the "tack" room, his other hand closing over her mouth.

"So you framed me." Something in the man seemed to have snapped his power of control. Lennox sensed it as he leaped in, sensed that in another instant the girl might be dead. His arm locked about Custis' neck, pulling his head back sharply, breaking his grip on the girl.

The gambler twisted with the swift movement of a snake, drove his elbow into the stomach, just above Lennox' belt, broke Bill's grip and backed away, his jade-like eyes flaming, his right hand, concealed for a moment in his coat. Then it appeared, holding a short, squat gun.

Lennox leaped at him, felt something burn his side, heard an explosion almost in his ear; then his arms were locked about Custis and they went over

on to the floor together. The gambler was trying to bring up his gun, Lennox, his fingers locked about the man's wrist, attempting to keep it down. His breath was short and Custis' shoulder against his nose made it harder. His lungs seemed to be bursting, yet he knew that if he once released his grip it meant death, death not only for himself, but also for the girl.

Tiny black spots danced before his eyes. Custis was strong, surprisingly so. His arm was like a coiled band of steel, coming up, slowly, ever so slowly, despite all Lennox could do. Inch by inch the gun moved. Lennox sank his teeth in his lower lip as he hung on, then he suddenly released his grip with his left hand on the man's back and rolled over, feeling Custis' arm, the gun beneath him. He lashed out with his left fist, heard the man's muffled curse, rolled clear, and kicked hard at the wrist. His shoe hit the gun instead, sending it spinning half across the room to strike the girl's side, but Lennox never saw it.

He was on his knees, then his feet, swaying there for an instant. Then he jumped at the gambler, storming through the blows raining upon him, his shoulder striking the man's chest, his fingers searching for the white throat as they went over again. Confusedly he knew there were other people in the room, but he had no idea who they were, did not in the least care. He was tired, too tired to be certain of things.

THEN big hands had his shoulders and were hauling him to his feet and a voice he knew said,

"What the hell's going on here?"

With the back of his left hand Lennox wiped the sweat from his eyes and stared at Spellman. He tried to grin, but his upper lip was puffed, swollen. "I never thought the day would come I'd be glad to see you, Copper."

"So you're glad to see me?" Spellman's heavy voice held sarcasm. "Well, I'm kinda glad to see you. I've been looking for you for only three days."

"Swell." Lennox was trying to straighten his coat. "It's nice to know I've been missed. How'd you happen to blow in so opportunely, Floyd?"

The city detective shrugged. "I saw you hiding behind a post in the betting shed a few minutes ago and thought I'd tail you and see just what the idea was."

"For once in your life," Lennox told him, "you did right. If you'd grabbed me then, this gentleman," he indicated the silent Custis, who was being held by a couple of barn men, "might have got rough."

Spellman looked at Custis. "Who is he? His face is familiar."

Lennox said: "Just a gambler. You probably saw a circular on him sometime. Besides that, he's the killer who got that rider at the hotel the other night."

"The hell you say!" Spellman was looking at Custis with renewed interest. "Can you prove it?"

"Of course not." Custis had regained his self-control. "The idea's absurd, Captain. I had a little personal trouble with Lennox, and this is his way of paying me back."

Spellman looked questioningly at Lennox, who hesitated. After all, he had no proof that Custis had had Jarney killed. But Betty Donovan said, suddenly, "I can prove it. At least I can get six jockeys to swear that he threatened them, that they heard him make threats against Jarney. I can prove that he's been framing races for a year."

Spellman looked at her. He said to Lennox, suddenly, "Is this the girl that was with you at the hotel?"

She answered before Bill had a chance. "Yes, I'm the one. I was with him when he found Frank Jarney's body."

Spellman scratched his head. "I guess you'd all better come downtown. The D.A. will have to straighten this out."

IN the police car, riding towards town, Lennox could not talk to Betty because of Spellman's presence. Custis was in a car ahead in the custody of two of Spellman's men. Bill watched her set face, thinking how pretty she was. And her gameness. The thought of it made him wince. She had played the game with one of the country's smartest gamblers, played without asking favors, and won. He wanted to tell her about it, what he thought of her carrying on for Bert, and that he was sorry he had doubted her, but Spellman's hulking shoulders beside the driver were half turned, and he knew that the detective captain would be listening.

The District Attorney heard their story and questioned them for almost an hour, then let them go with orders to report to his office in the morning. Lennox gave the address of her hotel to the cab driver and hesitated. "I'd like to come up and talk to you for a little while, if you're not too tired."

She said, "It's you that should be tired. That wound in your side—"

He grinned. "Forget it, Kid. That wasn't much more than a burn, and the doc out at the track fixed it up swell."

"Then come on." He got in, settling himself on the seat gingerly. "What I can't understand," he said, when the cab was in motion, "is why Custis didn't have me killed when he had me. I don't get why he kept me alive for three days."

Betty Donovan stared at him, her expression changing. "You thought it was Custis that—that held you in that house? It wasn't, it was I."

"You?" He stared at her and she nodded.

"Yes, I. You see, after the way you spoke to me at the track the other day, I was afraid that you'd do something to spoil my plan. I almost told you what I was doing. Then Custis came up behind us and I was afraid, so I had three of my barn men kidnap you. The house where they held you is one that I've been living in this winter. I moved to the hotel that night. But you're not going to make a charge against me—are you, Bill?"

Lennox chuckled softly. "You're swell, Kid." Then he sobered. "I'm sorry about Bert. It's tough, and I'm afraid they won't get Custis on a murder for Jarney. They'll get him, yes, on a gambling charge of some kind, but murder—" He shook his head. "I talked to the D.A. after you were through. They haven't enough evidence. They'll probably let him make a plea of some kind."

The girl's face set and he feared for a moment that she was going to cry, but no tears came. He said: "If I can help you, Kid—"

One of her small hands closed over his. "You can, Bill. Have dinner with me tonight. I feel so terribly alone."

He said, "Sure," and opened the door as the cab stopped in front of the hotel. Half an hour later, over coffee in one corner of the large dining-room, he asked, "What will you do now?"

She moved her shoulders. "Sell the stable. I'm sick of it, Bill. It killed Bert because he was too honest. I hung on, hoping for a chance to even things up. There's a boy in New York. He didn't understand why I kept on and I couldn't explain. I was afraid he'd get mixed up in things."

Lennox nodded. He was liking her better all the time. "So what?"

She said: "I'm going to sell out and go East. I want to see if it's too late."

"It won't be," he told her, "not if—" He turned as a page came into the dining-room, his voice sounding clearly above the chatter:

"Calling Mr. Lennox. Calling Mr. William Lennox."

Bill said, "Here, boy," and raised his finger.

The page turned and came to the table. "You're wanted on the phone."

Lennox slipped a quarter into his hand and rose. "Excuse me a moment." He left the dining-room and walked to the row of phone booths. Spellman's voice reached him over the wire.

"Thought I'd catch you there. Saw you getting into the cab with the jane. She's not bad looking."

Lennox said sourly, "Did you call me up to say that?"

The detective captain laughed dryly. "I called you to tell you that your boy friend isn't any more. They got him as he came out of the building, got one of the guards in the shoulder at the same time. Thought you'd . like to know."

Lennox said, "Custis?" with surprise.

"Who do you think I'm talking about? Santa Claus? You wouldn't have any idea who got him, would you?"

Lennox' voice was flat, final. "I wouldn't."

"Now, now," Spellman began, but Lennox hung up. Before he got back to the dining-room he heard, behind him, the bellboy calling again:

"Mr. Lennox. Paging Mr. Lennox."

That would be Spellman, calling back, Bill knew, and paid no attention. Betty Donovan looked up inquiringly as he reached the table.

"What was it?" Her voice was nervous.

He said, softly, "Someone shot Custis as he was leaving the D.A.'s office. You can forget him, Kid. Your brother's debt is paid."

She was silent a long time, said finally, "I wonder who got him?"

Lennox shrugged. "I wouldn't know, and I don't care. One of the boys he'd been playing with, probably, one of those he told to bet on your horse. They probably figured he'd crossed them."

"I wish," her voice broke, "I wish it hadn't happened that way. I wish the law had got him."

Lennox bent forward. "Listen, Kid; don't cry, don't feel bad. It wasn't you that got Custis. It was the way he lived. If it hadn't happened now, it would have some time." He was silent, thinking of what he had said to her earlier, "Gamblers Don't Win."

SCARS of MURDER

A movie star kill and a strangely elusive girl send Bill Lennox on his trickiest Hollywood hunt

BILL LENNOX, trouble-shooter for General Consolidated Studios, turned into the Vine Street Brown Derby. It was late, a little after eleven, and he was tired. He pushed his gray summer felt back on his head and stared around the room, wondering whether to stay or go home. Then his straying gray eyes narrowed as he saw two people seated toward the rear.

He hid his start of surprise, moving slowly forward, ignoring the waiter who called him by name. Ben Fields turned and, seeing Lennox, smiled, but Bill's eyes were not on the lawyer, they were centered on the small figure across the table from Fields.

The boy looked like Frank Hayes, but Lennox knew that it couldn't be Hayes, that Hayes was dead, that Hayes had been murdered in his dressing room on the General lot four weeks before.

Fields saw the intent look on Lennox's face and spoke hurriedly. He was a short man, heavy through the shoulders, with a thick neck and a round,

By W. T. BALLARD

bullet-like head. His black hair grew in tight curls, making a dark skull cap which matched the blackness of his eyes.

"Hello, Bill."

Lennox pulled his eyes away from the boy's face and looked at the lawyer. Fields didn't look very intelligent. Lennox knew that he was, knew that Fields was one of the smartest men in Hollywood.

He said, "Hello, Ben" and then let his eyes switch back across the table to the small figure as he took a step closer. He stopped there, stayed by surprise, for he saw something which he had not noticed before. Fields' companion wasn't a boy. She was a girl.

Her hair was cut short, combed back with a part on the right. Her suit was cut along the lines of a man's, not like a woman's slacks. Her breasts, now that he noticed them, were small, little mounds under the white silk of the man's shirt which she wore. A four-in-hand tie completed the picture. Even in a town where the women frequently wore mannish clothes, she looked as if she had set out consciously to dress like a man.

Lennox had reached the table, was staring down at her, making no effort to conceal his interest.

Ben Fields had risen. For an instant he seemed ill at ease, then he said, "Bill, I want you to meet June Hayes."

He turned and smiled down at the girl. "June, Lennox works for the studio which employed your brother."

"Brother!" Lennox started again. This was his night for surprises. His long suntanned, good looking face seldom altered expression, but for just an instant it mirrored his surprise.

There was a tiny smile on the girl's lips as she looked up to acknowledge the introduction, then it vanished.

Lennox, completely master of himself, sat down, waving Fields back into his seat. He smiled as he said, "You gave me quite a start, Miss Hayes. Your resemblance to your brother is startling."

She was nervous, ill at ease, as she glanced twice at her watch, then looked toward Fields. "I'm afraid that it's later than I realized and that I'll have to go."

Fields started to rise, but she was on her feet before either man could move. "I'm glad to have met you, Mr. Lennox. I trust that we'll meet again. Don't bother. The doorman will get me a cab. I'll be perfectly all right." She was gone, leaving them staring after her.

Bill's eyes were narrow, his mouth tight. "Who is she, Ben?"

Fields looked at him, then his eyes turned toward the door through which the girl had vanished. "She claims to be Frank's sister."

Lennox's mouth was tight. "Yeah, I heard you before, but Hayes' sister is dead. Wait a minute. I know the story. I was working on the *Tribune* in Chicago at the time and they sent me down to St. Louis to cover the killings.

"Frank's father came from southern Missouri. He moved to St. Louis, and married a wealthy woman. They had two children and the mother died. A couple of years after her death he married again, a dancer this time. You know her as Charl Hayes.

"The second marriage didn't turn out so well. One night Hayes came home plastered. There was an argument. He pulled a gun, shot the two kids and then himself.

"The little girl died, or was supposed to have. Charl nursed the boy back to health, and brought him out here. She got him a job in pictures and he became General's leading juvenile. He died last week from an — accident." Lennox's mouth tightened.

Only he suspected that Frank Hayes' death was no accident, but murder, and he was keeping that suspicion to himself. There was no use in dragging the studio into a mess of bad publicity when he had no proof.

Fields was drumming in the table thoughtfully. "You're sure the little girl died?"

Lennox shrugged. "I couldn't go into court and swear it but . . . " he let his voice trail off.

Fields said, "All I know about it is that this girl showed up yesterday, claiming to be Frank's sister. Her story is that she wasn't killed, merely wounded; that her uncle, her father's brother, spirited her away from St. Louis, took her down to the Ozarks and raised her as his own child. That the doctor was bribed to swear that she was dead."

Lennox shook his head. "That's a stupid story. Why the hell would her uncle do that?"

Fields shrugged again. "The girl claims that they were all afraid of her stepmother, afraid of what Charl might do if she found out that the girl was still alive. She claims that her father didn't shoot her brother and her and then kill himself. Her story is that Charl did the shooting. That her father was murdered."

Lennox's voice was tight. "If that's true, why did Charl nurse the boy back to health? Why didn't she just let him die?"

Fields said, "I'm just repeating what that girl told me, but I know this part is true. There's a trust fund, set up for those kids by Hayes' first wife. If the boy had died, while a minor, that fund would have reverted to the first wife's family. As long as the boy lived, Charl had the use of the income from it. Another thing, Frank Hayes was twenty-one just a week before his accident. According to his will the trust fund is left to his stepmother, along with all the money he made in pictures."

Lennox whistled softly. "Frank's death really meant something to Charl, didn't it?"

Fields nodded. "It certainly did, and if everyone wasn't so sure that Frank's death was an accident, I'd think—well, skip that part, but the girl's story interests me, and she certainly looks like Frank.

"She sure does," Lennox's voice was thoughtful. "Have you tried to get in touch with the doctor, the one who said that the little sister died?"

Fields' voice was tense. "He's dead. I'm in a funny position, Bill. I'm the lawyer for Frank's estate. I have to investigate this girl's claim from all angles, but personally I can't help but believe that there's something to her story."

Lennox was thinking the same thing. If his suspicions were right, if Frank Hayes had been murdered, this might well tie into it, might well provide the motive. He wasn't ready to tell Fields his suspicions, yet he had to have some reason to explain his interest, and he invented one.

He said, "This is interesting. The studio would like to know who Frank's real heir is. You see, Frank came up in pictures so fast that he was worth a lot more to us than his contract called for.

"But that was before the Coogan law was passed and the minors in pictures were taking an awful beating, most of their earnings being spent by parents or guardians.

"For that reason, Spurck kept Frank at his old contract, and put the rest of what we might have paid him into a fund, which we meant to turn over to him later. The fund is still being held by the studio. Legally we don't owe it to anyone, but if we turn it over to anyone, we'll want to be sure that it is Frank's real heir. I'd like to talk to that girl again. Can you give me her address?"

Fields hesitated. "Why don't you meet her at my office?"

Lennox said, "I'd rather talk to her alone. Don't you know her address?"

The lawyer hesitated a moment longer. "Why certainly. She's staying at the Hotel Vincent, on the Boulevard. I just thought it would be easier if you met her at my office."

Lennox looked at him sharply, but Fields was staring at the glass which he was twisting in his hand.

ALTHOUGH he had seen her at the restaurant, it still gave Lennox a start when the girl stepped from the elevator. He had the same sensation as if he were seeing a ghost as she crossed the lobby toward the street door.

She certainly did look like Frank Hayes. Instinctively he stepped backward behind a row of sheltering potted palms, wondering as he did so where she was headed. The wall clock showed that it was well after one.

He hadn't expected to see her again that night. After leaving Fields at the restaurant, he had stopped in at the hotel on his way home, merely to make sure that she was registered and here she was—still wearing the slacks, looking more like a boy than ever.

The swell of her breasts was concealed by her coat. Only the extra width of her lips and her walk gave her away.

Still wondering, he followed her through the street door, saw her take a cab, and on impulse got one and followed.

It was the dead hour. Watchmen had killed the window lights, and the city, saving power, had turned off every second street lamp.

The Boulevard was almost empty of traffic. They crossed La Brea, slid past the row of darkened apartments, and turned right into Laurel Canyon. The shell of a sickle moon lay on its back above the dark fringe of somber hills.

Here and there a single light broke the dull, drab monotony of the brush-covered slopes as Lennox's cab went into second and ground up the tortuous curves of the winding road.

The girl's taxi was out of sight, above them, as it climbed through the dark chill of the steep canyon. The fog thickened, threatened to cut out the distant moon. Already it was a hood above the city, which, like some giant inverted mirror, caught the glow of the neons and sent it back downward to bath the buildings in a red haze.

As his cab rounded the last curve and pulled up the steep straight of way, Lennox saw the girl's cab swing left onto Mulholland Drive and disappear around the first curve.

His own taxi followed, and they rounded three curves without sighting the girl. To their right, the lights of San Fernando valley made a twisting checkerboard. They rounded another curve and their head lamps picked up the girl just as she stepped from her cab. Lennox leaned forward, ordered his driver to pull around the next bend and stop.

He was tense as he left the taxi and started back, for the white hillside home before which the girl had stopped belonged to Charl Hayes, Frank Hayes' stepmother.

As he reached the hedge the girl was barely distinguishable as she moved across the dark lawn between the rows of shrubbery.

He followed, realizing that she was not headed for the front door, but rather for the dark French windows at the side of the house.

He saw her pause, fumble with the lock, then push the glass doors open and slip through. Lennox moved quickly forward to a point where he could see into the house.

There was a little light in the room, put there by the distant moon. He saw movement in the bed, then someone sat up and suddenly turned on the bed lamp.

Lennox saw a woman, saw the lacy negligée which she drew about her shoulders, saw that she was beautiful, and heard her gasp as she stared at the intruder.

For a moment the woman in the bed was rigid, then she laughed, the sound reaching Lennox faintly. She spoke, and there was a harsh note in the soft voice, but no fear or panic.

"You startled me for a moment. I thought that you were a boy, that you

were someone. . . ." Her voice trailed off. "You do look like him."

The girl's voice was low, intense. "Like Frank Hayes?"

Charl Hayes started. "You do look a little like Frank."

The girl said, "I should. I'm his sister."

The woman in the bed stirred. "Ah, so that's it. Well, young lady, I don't know what your plan is, but I can make a guess. You want money, and you hope to get it from me."

The girl said, steadily, "I think I will. I think that you'd better listen. I came out here at this hour because I thought that you wouldn't want publicity. I gave you a chance to play fair. I am June Hayes and I have some rights."

The woman was laughing without sound. "You did a foolish thing, coming here at this hour, alone."

The girl said, "I don't think so." A little gun had appeared in her hand. "I can take care of myself, Charl Hayes."

The woman did not answer. Lennox could see her hand pressing hard on what he supposed was an electric buzzer by the bed, but the girl wasn't looking at her hand.

After a couple of minutes, the bedroom door behind the girl was opening. He wanted to cry out, to warn her, but he knew that it was better if he kept out of this. The door was wide now and two men moved through it.

They caught the girl from behind, caught her roughly as she struggled in their grasp. Her shirt was ripped open in front and one of the small breasts showed clearly in the light from the bed lamp as she was pushed into a chair.

One of the men held her. The other stared, then turned. "Jeez, she sure looks like Frank."

Charl Hayes laughed. "That's what she counted on. She claims to be the sister, the one who died. She wanted money. We'll keep her until we find out who she is, who is behind this . . ." she broke off as there was the sound of pounding from the front door.

Her eyes glittered. "Find out who that is and be careful."

One of the men left the room. He came back in a few minutes and there were two uniformed policemen behind him. A little frown drew Charl Hayes' brows together.

Lennox shrank closer to the shadows. He'd been so intent on what was taking place in the room that he had not heard the police car.

One of the uniformed men said, "Sorry to bother you, but a hack driver called in to say that he'd delivered a girl out here, a girl in boy's clothes and that she'd acted suspicious." He glanced toward the small figure in the chair.

Charl Hayes smiled. "Thank you for your vigilance, but it's not needed. This girl is a friend of mine. She's been to a costume party and—"

The girl wrenched free of the man who had a hand on her arm and came to her feet. "Don't believe her! Please don't leave me here! She'll murder me, kill me like she killed my father and my brother."

The cops jerked around to stare at her. Charl Hayes showed no surprise, nothing, but her voice was grave. "I lied to you, officer. This girl suffers from hallucinations. They will pass in a little while but while they last she dresses up as nearly like a man as possible and had the idea that someone is trying to kill her."

The uniformed man's hand had been close to his holstered gun. "You mean that she's screwy?"

The girl jumped forward, clutching her torn shirt with one hand, grasping his Sam Browne belt with the other. "She's a murderess, I tell you. Don't let her fool you! They were getting ready to kill me when you came. Take me to the police station, take me anywhere, only don't leave me here."

The cop's big hands closed on her narrow shoulders. "Easy, kid," his big voice was kind. "No one will hurt you. Why, a nice lady like Mrs. Hayes would

do anything for you. Everyone in town knows who she is."

The girl had pressed her face against his uniformed chest and was crying desperately. He looked around for help, found none, hesitated, then said, helplessly, "I guess I'll have to take her in, madam. It will be simpler that way. You can some down in the morning and explain to the captain."

For an instant Charl Hayes' eyes were like twin dark coals. Lennox half expected her to pull a gun, but after an instant the glitter died, and she said, "Perhaps that would be better. Naturally I wanted to avoid publicity if I could, but she's worse tonight than she's ever been."

The cop said, "Sure." He had an Irish voice. "You just come down in the morning. The captain's a right guy and maybe it won't even get into the papers. O. K., Joe," he looked toward his partner. "Come on, let's take this kid with us."

Charl Hayes watched them go, her body outlined plainly under the single sheet. Not until she heard the front door close did she speak, then her voice was sharp. "Get the touring car. I don't want anyone talking to that kid until I find out who she really is."

One of the men said, "But they know she was here. They'll be back to ask questions."

"I'll handle that. Get moving!"

He turned without another word and disappeared. Lennox backed away from the house, his mouth a tight line as he circled the grounds. He reached the driveway just as the touring car came drifting along it, moving without lights.

The car was big, powerful, an old model. He saw that there was a spare tire and trunk rack on the rear but no trunk. He stared at the rack. He didn't like the idea, but there seemed no other way.

He stepped out into the drive, took half a dozen running steps, thankful that the fog had settled down so that it blocked out all light from the rim of the moon. He caught the tire and swung up onto the rack.

They turned from the drive into Mulholland in time to see the tail light of the police car disappear around the first curve.

THE DRIVER of the touring car cut on the lights and started after it, increasing his speed until they pulled abreast of the police sedan. One of the men was on the touring car's running-board, a heavy gun in his hand.

His tight voice cut harshly through the foggy night. "Pull over, copper, or your wife will collect your pension."

The brakes of the police car squealed protestingly as the foot brake was shoved down. The tires skidded on the fog-moist pavement. The touring car came to an abrupt stop, ramming Lennox's head against the back of the car body. He lost his grip and sat down heavily in the road, his ears ringing from the force of the blow, unable to move for an instant.

In a confused sort of way, he saw the two police officers herded from their car, forced to the edge of the steep bank, and pushed over.

The bank dropped a good hundred feet of brush-covered earth. He could hear the crash as their heavy bodies rolled helplessly down it toward the bottom of the canyon. He knew that the fall wouldn't kill them, but that they would never be able to climb back to the roadway in time to help.

He dragged himself to his feet, stood swaying. One of the men grabbed the girl, dragged her from the police car and shoved her into the touring.

Lennox fumbled inside his coat, loosened the gun from his shoulder clip and stepped around the car. His head still hurt. His neck felt as if it had been shortened an inch, but the gun in his hand was steady. The two men, both masked, saw him at the same instant.

Their hands jumped toward their guns, stopped as Lennox said, "Hold it!"

Slowly their hands went shoulder high. Lennox ordered them to turn around and walk to the edge of the bank. "Now, jump!"

One of them snarled something under his breath. Lennox put his free hand in the middle of the man's back and pushed. The man disappeared over the edge, clawing desperately at the air in an effort to regain his balance.

His partner spun around and made a grab for Lennox, his nails drawing two lines across the trouble-shooter's cheek as he all but missed.

Bill's left fist came up in an upper cut and caught the man on the side of the mouth, sending him backward over the edge of the bank to disappear in the darkness of the brush-covered slope.

Lennox spun about in time to see the girl leap from the car and start running down the winding pavement. He caught her before she had traveled fifty feet, picked her up, and carried her, struggling, back to the car.

"Behave!" His tone was short. His head still hurt and his knuckles were raw where they had crashed against the man's teeth. He thrust her into the front seat, climbed under the touring car's wheel.

He had almost reached the stop sign at the bottom of the canyon before the girl spoke.

"Who are you? Where are you taking me?" There was fear in the voice and Lennox realized that she hadn't recognized him in the darkness.

He said, "The name is Lennox. I met you at the Derby with Fields."

She caught her breath. "From the studios."

He nodded. "What were you trying to pull at Charl Hayes' tonight?"

She was silent for several minutes, then she said, "I wanted to talk to my stepmother while no one was around. I wanted to see if she wouldn't make a settlement, to save my taking her into court." There was a hardness under the tone which Lennox had not heard there before. The girl was small, but there was certainly nothing weak about her.

"Where are you taking me? How'd you happen to be there? Are you a friend of my stepmother?"

Lennox shook his head. "No. I just happened along at the right time." It sounded weak, but he didn't care and he wanted to try an experiment. "Care for a drink?"

She hesitated, and he said, "You need one after what happened." He drove across to Sunset and turned right onto the Strip.

HE Three Stars Club was almost to the Beverly Hills line. Lennox turned the car over to the attendant, and walked toward the entrance with the girl at his side.

The check-room girl caught her breath when she saw Lennox's companion, then relaxed slightly as she realized that it was a girl.

As they walked onto the supper room the girl whispered, "What was the matter with her?"

Lennox said, "Frank Hayes used to give this spot a heavy play, and you look like him, you know."

She didn't answer and they crossed the foyer. At the supper room door they were met by Rubell, the manager. Rubell showed surprise at sight of the girl, but only for an instant. Then he put his smile back into place, letting it light up his dark, lean face.

"Evening, Mr. Lennox."

"Hello, Rubell. A quiet table over by the wall somewhere."

The man hesitated. "We're very full tonight. Perhaps at the bar."

"Anything will do us. That table over by the wall will be oke." He was already moving toward it.

For seconds Rubell stared after them, then, with a tiny shrug, he motioned a waiter and turned away. Lennox had

reached the table and was holding a chair for the little figure in boy's clothes when the waiter came up.

There was a tall girl, swinging a piece in the middle of the little dance platform, while the orchestra cut it wide as they hit the upbeats. The tall girl could sing and she could put it over, but Lennox was not listening at the moment. He drew a card from his pocket, scribbled something on it and, with a dollar, slid it into the waiter's hand.

"Give it to Carmen."

The waiter moved away and, as the tall girl finished her number, slid Lennox's card into her hand.

She glanced at it as she left the stand, hesitated, then came toward their table. Lennox rose and pushed out a chair for her as she came up. "Hello, Carmen."

She said, "Hello, Bill," but her eyes were on the girl at the far side of the table. "Who—who is this?" The words stumbled over each other, her cheeks whitened under her make-up, and she sank weakly into the chair. Lennox pushed a glass of water toward her and she touched it to her lips mechanically without shifting her stare.

"I thought for a minute—"

Lennox said, "Carmen, meet Frank's sister. At least she claims to be."

"Oh." It was almost a gasp. "How do you do?" Then: "I—I've got to go now, Bill." She'd risen and moved away. He excused himself and followed, catching her just outside of the door which led back to the dressing rooms.

"Listen, Carmen. I knew how you felt about Frank. That's why I came here. I want you to take this kid home with you tonight, and find out what you can. She just went up to see Charl Hayes, and ran into a jam."

The singer turned on him. "Then this was a bum place to bring her—knowing Rubell's Charl's brother! You should know better. Be careful."

He said, "I always am. Will you help, Carmen?"

She shook her head. "No." Without another word she turned and disappeared. He shrugged and went back to the table. The girl stirred, looked at him. "Well?"

Lennox said, "A swell kid. It was bad to give her that shock. She used to go around with your brother Frank. Guess it was a silly idea to come here."

The girl offered no objection, and they moved toward the exit. Rubell was waiting for them in the foyer. "Leaving so soon?"

Lennox nodded. "C h a n g e d our minds." He got his hat from the checkroom and moved through the door. But he didn't turn toward the parking lot where he had left the touring car. He moved, instead, toward the cab rack. He was just about to help the girl into the first one when he heard his name called. He saw a hand waving toward him from the last cab in the line.

He went toward it cautiously, his hand not far from his gun, then he relaxed as he saw Carmen peering out at him through the open door. "Get in, quick."

He pushed the little girl ahead of him and followed. The cab moved as if the driver already had his orders.

Bill leaned forward. "What's the matter, kid?"

Carmen said: "It's Rubell. He saw me talking to you, saw the girl. He wanted to know what you were up to. It scared me so I sneaked out the back way. I'll take her home with me like you suggested."

Lennox said, "I don't like this. I don't want to get you into a jam with Rubell. He's tough."

Carmen shrugged. "To hell with Rubell. You can't take this kid back to wherever she's staying. Somebody may be watching. I'm going to take her with me." She winked at him across the girl's head.

"I'll handle things, and you can forget Rubell."

Lennox told her. "You can't forget Rubell. Remember, he's Charl Hayes' brother, although it's not generally known around town. And he *is* tough. I knew him when he was running a spot

in South Chicago and Charl was dancing in the joint.

"That was some time back. I was not much more than a copy boy on the old *Tribune* and prohibition was running high, wide and handsome.

"Even in those days he was tough, and from what I understand he's tougher now. I'm not going to let you into this, Carmen. I made a mistake. coming over to the club. I wish now that I hadn't."

But the girl said nothing, seeming not to care about their plans for her. The singer was stubborn. "You let me run my business. If this kid *is* a sister of Frank's, she's a pal of mine, and Rubell, nor a thousand chiselers like him, is big enough to take her away from me. And if she's out after Charl Hayes, that's right up my alley. I never liked that dame and I never will. She's too smooth and too good looking for my taste. We'll drop you in Hollywood and I'll call you in the morning." Her tone had a flat note that booked no argument.

ENNOX had been asleep. How long he'd been asleep, he had no way of judging. He turned over, hoping that the knocking on his apartment door would cease. It didn't. Only half awake, he threw back the blankets, found robe and slippers and shuffled toward the door.

He unlocked it and pulled it partly open, but the knob was jerked from his hand, and the door slammed back against the wall as Rubell pushed in.

Behind the night-club man's shoulder Lennox had a confused glimpse of Charl Hayes. There was a tall man behind her and he guessed that this was one of the men who had been in the touring car. There was a long scratch across the lean jaw which might well have been put there by the brush of the steep hillside.

Lennox backed down the hall as Rubell came after him. The night-club man's face was tight, his mouth a thin line, his hands both deep in his coat pockets.

"Easy, Lennox. I never liked you much, anyway."

Bill's lips felt stiff when he smiled. He wasn't kidding himself. He knew that Rubell was dangerous. The man had gotten out of Chicago because he had to, and it had been rumored that his departure was speeded by the syndicate which had gradually taken over the town.

Rubell said, "Watch yourself and you won't get hurt, but don't get the idea that because you're an important onion in this berg we won't step on you, because we will."

Lennox didn't answer. He'd backed into the apartment's living room.

Rubell reached around and clicked on the light. Lennox picked up a small, tooled-leather cigarette box, lit a thin Turkish cigarete and let smoke dribble from his thin-walled nostrils. When he spoke it was to Charl Hayes, not to her brother.

"You're making a mistake, Charl."

Rubell said, "You're the one that's making the mistake, Bill! You didn't have to pick up that little tramp, just because she happened to look like Frank. Think what Charl did for Frank! She saved his life, mothered him, got him into pictures, and fought agents and producers until he got somewhere."

Lennox nodded. He was still watching the woman. It gave him a start to look at her. It always gave him a start every time he saw her. Charl Hayes was very beautiful. He knew that she was about his age, that she had been very young, back in the Chicago days, but she looked not much older now. She could have passed easily for twenty-two or-three.

She was master of the situation too. She flashed a look at her brother which silenced him, then stepped forward until she had to look up into Lennox's face. Her tone was soft, deceptive. Bill knew that it was deceptive. He knew her for what she was, but he still felt the pull of her personality, the danger of her charm.

She said, softly, "There's no use getting tough with Bill, Rubell. It's just that he doesn't understand. You and Slim go on back down to the car. I want to talk to Bill for a couple of minutes."

Rubell said, "But—"

Her lips tightened. Her voice was still soft, but there was steel beneath the velvet of her manner. "I think it would be wise if you went back down to the car."

They turned and went. Lennox took another drag on his cigarette as the door closed, then he grinned at the woman. "Nobody in town would believe it if I told them what I've just seen."

She smiled at him, her lips curving upward in a slow, sleepy gesture. "Might I have one of those cigarettes?"

He extended the open box to her, held the flame of his lighter steady, closed the box and watched her blow out smoke between carmined lips. She said:

"You and I have known each other a long time, Bill. I put on a front around this town, but I'm not trying to put on a front with you. I come from the rougher part of Chicago; I know it, and I know that you know it."

He waited, on guard, not deceived by the indirectness of her attack.

She said, "You're smart. I'd make a play for you if you weren't. I could go for you, William, and that isn't all conversation. I like men who can count to nine without using their fingers, but it wouldn't go over and I know it, so I'm asking as a matter of fair play. Lay off. Don't pull cards in this game. This little girl you saw tonight isn't Frank's sister. Without you, she won't get to first base."

He said, "Is that the reason your men tried to take her away from the cops? That wasn't a smart trick, Charl. You really slipped on that one. The cops are funny. They'll ask questions in the morning."

She shook her head. "I don't think so, not those two. They're having a purge

Page 91 detective prose

of the police department at the moment, and I happen to have friends."

He didn't argue. The point in itself wasn't of great importance. He said, "You've got it wrong. I'm not backing this girl. I'm not even taking a hand in the game. It's none of my business."

Her eyes showed that she did not believe him. She said, "If that's true, where is she? Where have you hidden her?"

He shook his head. "You're wrong again. I haven't hidden her."

The woman's face hardened. "Look, Bill, I'm no child. I'm not going to sit by and see everything that I've worked for washed away. You're either with me, or against me. If you're with me, you can write your own ticket. I mean that, money or anything else."

He shook his head, still smiling. "Sorry."

She said, viciously, "You're a fool."

"Probably." He still held the box of cigarettes, loosely in his left hand. He saw her reach into her purse, but she wasn't fast enough. With a little flip of his wrist he sent the box directly at her face. Her hand came up to protect her eyes. Cigarettes jumped from the box to shower over her. He caught her purse with his other hand, jerking it from her surprised fingers.

He delved into it and brought out the little gun. He slid it into his dressing-gown pocket. extending the bag. "Hadn't you better go?"

Her dark eyes had narrowed, were hating him. "I should have let my brother and Slim—"

"You should have. You rather over-estimated your abilities. Good night, Charl."

Her poise did not desert her, even in retreat. "I think," she told him from the door, "that you'll be very sorry for this night's work." The door closed.

Lennox took a dozen strides forward and shot the night bolt into place, then he brought his hand up and drew it across his forehead. It came away wet. He smiled, but there was no mirth in the

twisted lips. He wasn't kidding himself, Charl Hayes was dangerous.

IELDS was ushered into Lennox's office at the Studio early in the morning. The lawyer folded his short legs over the edge of the chair and ran one hand through his hair.

"That gal calling herself June Hayes has disappeared, Bill. She didn't come back to her hotel last night."

Lennox looked up. "Oh, she's all right. She's staying at Carmen's apartment."

Fields looked startled. "With Carmen? You mean that singer at Rubell's club? What are you trying to do, get that kid killed? Didn't you know that Rubell is Charl Hayes' brother?"

Lennox nodded. "I also know that Carmen was in love with Frank. She'll find out whether that kid is June Hayes or not. Don't worry about that."

Fields pulled his lower lip thoughtfully. "I hope that you're right, but I don't trust either Charl or Rubell, and I wouldn't give a dime for that kid's life if they get their fingers on her." He rose, moved toward the door. "Hell, I'm only the lawyer for the estate and—"

"When you talk to Carmen, tell her to bring the kid over to my office."

Lennox stared at the closed door, then he called the long distance operator and put in a call to Ted Donovan of the *Dispatch* in St. Louis.

It took twenty minutes to complete the call. When he had his connection he said. "Donny, this is Bill Lennox of General. How are you, fellow? Yeah, now listen. Do you remember the old Hayes murder? That's the one. We covered it together, remember? It was my first big job.

"Now listen. Donny. Both kids were supposed to have been shot. the boy recovered. the girl died. Well, they had an uncle and aunt living down in the

Ozarks somewhere. I want you to find them if you can."

Donovan's voice was getting excited. "Has this anything to do with Frank Hayes who was killed accidentally on the General lot?"

Lennox hesitated. "Look, Donny. I can't explain now, just find those people, question them, get them to tell you all they know and especially establish the fact of whether the little girl died or not. Call me as soon as you get anything."

He cut short Donovan's flow of questions by hanging up. Then he dialed Carmen's number. She answered almost at once and she sounded excited.

"I was just going to call you, Bill. The girl's gone."

"Gone?"

"Yeah, gone. She slipped out without waking me, and I don't like it. But, Bill, I found out something, something that she told me and I don't think she realized what she'd said. I don't want to tell you over the phone and you won't believe it when I do tell you."

"What are you talking about?"

Carmen said, "I'll tell you when I see you but, Bill, you'd better try and find that kid first."

He caught the note of worry in her voice. "I'll check her hotel, Fields' office and such, and then call you back." He hung up, hesitated, then rose and went down the hall and into Spurck's office.

The vice president in charge of production for General Consolidated's West Coast Studios was short, inclined toward flesh, with a round, moon-like face and horn-rimmed glasses which accentuated the roundness of his blue eyes.

He looked up as Lennox stepped into the cathedral-like office and smiled slowly. "Bill, I have just seen the dailies on the college picture, and this Buddy Ames, who is taking Frank Hayes' place, gives a colossal performance. Never have I seen such acting, y'understand."

He thumped his big desk, and a diamond caught a streak of sunlight and

sent it flashing out into Lennox's eyes.

Bill nodded. "Yeah? I came up here to talk about Frank."

Spurck's good spirits vanished and a look of intense pain clouded his eyes. "Frank was a good boy, and I feel lousy we gotta put someone else in his picture, but business is life, ain't it, and life goes forward?"

Lennox nodded. "Sure, Sol. I understand. It wasn't that I meant. A girl showed up last night. A girl who claims that she's Frank's sister."

Spurck stared at him. "A sister, is it? Are you crazy or didn't Frank tell me once that his sister got shot or something?"

"He probably told you that," Lennox admitted. "I didn't say that she was his sister. I said that she claimed to be."

"Pff!" Spurck dismissed it with a wave of his hand. "She ain't his sister. If she was she'd have shown up years ago. Can you imagine a girl which is a sister of a movie star, hiding herself under a bushel or something?"

Lennox knew better than to argue with his chief, but as briefly as he could, he told Spurck what had happened, and what he had told Fields about the bonus due the estate of Frank Hayes from the studio.

Spurck winced when it was mentioned and shook his head. "Me, I think you are crazy. Why should we be interested in this dame from nowhere or maybe Missouri?"

Lennox leaned forward and said in a low voice, "Because I don't think that Frank was killed accidentally. I think he was murdered. I think someone *let* that steel girder crush him."

Spurck gaped at him. "Now I know that you are crazy."

Lennox shook his head wearily. "I wish I were, but there are too many things that weren't right about that death. I talked to the guy that handled the machinery. Afterwards I tried to talk to him again. I can't. He's vanished. So has Frank's valet, the one that had the portable dressing-room placed under that steel girder. The chauffeur tells me that the valet insisted on the dressing-room being placed in that exact spot. The chain that broke and dropped the girder had been fooled with, and the coffee in the thermos was doped.

"No!" Spruck yelped.

"Yes! Frank was asleep when it happened. I suppose they wanted to make certain that he'd be there."

Spruck's eyes looked larger than usual behind the thick lenses. "Why was it that the police—"

Lennox said, "On the face of it, it was an accident. No one made any protest, and cops are like anyone. They jump at conclusions."

Spruck was rigid. "Who is it you have told?"

"No one, yet."

The breath went out of Spruck slowly. "Honest, Bill, for a minute I could see headlines. 'Actor Killed on General Lot. Murder in the Studio.' We can't have that. We got this new financing coming up, and with business what it is the pictures aren't grossing, y'understand. Positively, you can't do nothing about it—unless," his eyes were smaller, "unless you find the murderer. Then, you have a free hand, y'understand. To get the schliemiehl which would kill a fine boy like Frank I would wreck the whole industry.

"Now get out of here so I can tell them wolves from the East why they ain't making twenty per cent even on their money."

THE HOTEL VINCENT looked shabbier by daylight than it had the night before. Lennox rode the elevator to the floor on which June Hayes had been living, and knocked on her door. There was no answer.

A maid came along the hall, and Lennox's eyes settled speculatively on the ring of keys which hung from her waist. She went past him and on down the hall to the linen room, opened the door and stuck her head inside.

Lennox followed her, cat-footed, his feet making no noise on the hall runner as he came up behind her. He suddenly clapped his right hand over her mouth and pushed her into the large linen room. He grabbed a towel from one of the shelves and gagged her.

"Sorry, sorry as hell," he said to the pop-eyed, stunned woman.

Then he grabbed her flailing hands and twisted them together with a bath towel. He did this as gently as he could. He tied her feet, and took her ring of keys.

"Take a rest, lady. You won't be hurt."

He peered out, shot a quick look up and down the hall, saw no one. He shut the door, locked it, and hurried back to June Hayes' door. The lock yielded to the third key he tried, and a moment later he was inside.

He searched the room with quick efficiency, finding nothing that would help him solve the mystery of the girl's identity, and was just coming out of the bedroom when he saw the hall door swinging inward.

For an instant he thought it was the girl returning, then he saw that it was a man and that there was a squat, ugly automatic in his hand.

The man was almost as surprised as Lennox was, but he had been ready for anything when he came through the door. His voice cracked as Bill's hand jumped toward the gun in his clip: "Hold it!"

Lennox was motionless, his hands came up slowly until they were shoulder high, palms out. The man came in and shut the door.

"Where's that little Hayes dame?"

Lennox recognized the newcomer as one of Rubell's men, and felt suddenly easier. If Rubell didn't know where the kid was, the chances were that she was safe. His relief showed in his voice. "I'm looking for her myself."

The man grunted. "Look, Lennox.

Charl isn't here to save you this time, and I don't like you, so stop stalling. For your own sake the girl had better be here, and you'd better dig her out quick."

Lennox stared at him. The man wasn't fooling and he knew it. He pretended to hesitate, then he said. "O. K., you win. She's locked in the closet in the bedroom."

The man grinned. "Get her."

Bill turned, still keeping his hands raised, and walked into the bedroom, knowing that the gunman was close behind him. As he opened the closet door, his body blocked the man's view. He reached in, got an armload of the dresses as if he were pulling out the girl.

The man with the gun moved in closer. Lennox backed toward him. Suddenly he dropped onto his hands and kicked out, his left foot smashing solidly into the man's stomach, knocking him backward across the room.

The man lost his gun as he fell, and Bill whirled, jumping in. But the fallen man was already rolling toward his gun, his fingers closing over it.

Bill dived for the door instead, gained the hall and raced for the stairs. He made the pavement safely, and from the corner drugstore called the hotel. surprising them greatly when he told them where to look for one of their maids.

The clerk was so astounded, he foolishly said, "Thank you."

Lennox got a cab at the corner and told the driver to take him to Whitley Terrace. At the corner he paid the cab and started along the street.

Carmen's apartment house was of yellow stucco. He went in, found that there was no desk, and went back along the hall without seeing anyone.

Her door was on the second floor, the third on the right. He knocked, his knuckles making hollow sound, but nothing happened, and he tried it again, frowning down at the worn carpet at his feet.

Suddenly he stooped as he noticed the dark spot just outside the door. He put out inquiring fingers and found it damp, a little sticky. He held his fingers to his nose, and got the unmistakable odor of drying blood.

With a curse he grasped the knob, expecting to find the door locked. It wasn't and the force of his charge would have thrown him half across the room, had not the swinging door struck something which kept it from going wide.

Lennox pushed again, then shoved his shoulders through the crack and peered down to see what the obstruction was.

Carmen lay half against the door, half on the floor. Her eyes were closed, her face dead white. She wore a red housecoat, but the red of the coat was not as dark as the blackening blood.

The housecoat was fastened up the front by a long zipper, but the cloth to the right of the zipper was ripped as if someone had tried to drag her across the floor by the coat's collar. Her left breast protruded, and Lennox felt sick when he saw the bullet hole in it.

He pushed his way in and bent over her, hoping against hope for signs of life. There were none, and he sucked his breath sharply as he realized that the girl had been horribly beaten. A trail of blood spots showed across the carpet. Despite the beating, there had been enough life left in the tortured body for her to drag herself to the door.

Rage burned up through him. She'd been a nice kid, playing the game straight as she could in a town which had little patience with straightness.

He turned, shot a quick look around the disordered room. Someone had searched it. He wondered what they had been looking for. The telephone had been ripped from its cord. and he realized that he couldn't call the police from the apartment.

He took a last look at Carmen, then left the room, shutting the door softly behind him. As he reached the entrance and stepped out, something made him look quickly up and down the street.

Subconsciously he saw a car beginning to move at the end of the block.

He paid no attention until it had almost reached him, then the squeal of its brakes jerked his head around. Pure reaction made him dive behind the big pottery jars which lined the yard. Bullets stung the pottery, breaking the jars with smashing sound which mingled with the explosive sound of the guns.

Then the car leaped ahead down the grade, taking the corner sharply, its rubber screaming as it made the turn. Lennox did not move for seconds, then he rose slowly, shaking off the broken fragments of pottery.

Windows had been thrust open, heads appeared, but he ignored them as he moved toward the drugstore at the corner.

His knees seemed to have the consistency of rubber, and there was a sinking feeling at the pit of his stomach as he moved toward the phone booth. He called the downtown police station and was lucky to find Spellman.

"Listen, Floyd. Bill Lennox. There's a little singer been killed in her apartment. No, someone beat her to death. Come on," he gave the address and hung up. Then he walked to the soda fountain and asked for water. When he emptied the glass he moved to the street door and stepped out onto the sidewalk.

A voice at his side said, "Easy, lug, or you get it behind the wishbone," and something was pressing tightly against Lennox's ribs.

He twisted his head to stare into dark, malignant eyes. The voice said, "Walk down the block. I'll be right behind you."

Lennox walked. There was nothing else to do. The short hairs at the back of his neck felt stiff, electric. At the entrance of the alley, he was ordered to turn. He obeyed, and saw the dark car parked a quarter of a block down.

The car was a sedan. He didn't realize that there was anyone in it until he reached it and the rear door swung open, then he saw Charl Hayes smiling at him coldly.

"Get in, Bill." She was all in black,

the somberness of her costume accentuating the blondness of her hair. The dress was tight, but her body could stand it.

He got in and sat down, staring at her without speaking. Her crimsoned lips were parted, still with their tiny smile. "Listen, Bill. I don't know what you're thinking of me. Maybe I shouldn't care, but I do. You're one of the few people in this town whose opinion I value. I want you to know that that girl isn't Frank's sister. She can't be. Who she is I don't know, but I do know that Frank's sister is dead."

"Yeah?" Lennox snarled.

"I'm not putting on any act for you. I married Hayes for his money, and I was sore as hell when I found out that it had all belonged to his first wife and had been left in trust for the children. We had a lot of battles and he finally tried to kill the kids and then shot himself. I did what I could for Frank, and it wasn't easy. Now I want what is mine, and I'm going to have it. No little tramp is going to cut in."

Lennox' face was hard. "Why tell me?"

She said, "Because without your Studio behind her, this kid wouldn't have a chance, and as far as this goes, you are the firm. Spurck will be governed by what you say. I've always liked you, Bill. I've always wanted a chance to know you better, to give you some of the things that a man like you deserves."

His tone was dry. "Like being shot at from a car?"

Her eyes got startled. "Shot at from a car?"

He said, "Look, Charl, stop playing dumb. You had your boys take a crack at me a few minutes ago. Don't deny it."

Her dark eyes were filmed with something he did not understand. "You fool! Get out! Get out, I say."

He got out of the car slowly, turned to look at her, but she slammed the door and, leaning forward, gave the driver an order. Lennox stood there, watching as the car pulled away. He frowned, then turning walked back slowly toward the street.

 E GOT back to the front of the apartment just as the squad car pulled to the curb. Spellman came bouncing out of it, his thick legs threatening to shake the sidewalk as he hit it, his broad, flat face looking redder than usual.

"Who's the dame? How'd she get killed?"

Lennox told him, turned and led the way into the apartment. There were three men with Spellman, and their heavy feet made the old stairs creak as they mounted to the second floor.

The Detective Captain swore when he saw the girl. "Geez, what a hell of a thing to do to a wren like that. Nice looking kid, and they beat the very devil out of her! Who the devil did it?"

Lennox moved his shoulders. "How would I know?"

"You found her, didn't you? How'd you happen to find her?"

Bill motioned him across the room, away from the others. He told Spellman about the girl, about her visit to Charl Hayes, and the rest.

The Detective Captain stared at him. "You mean that that's the kid the two cops lost? I saw a report on it. Why the devil didn't you call Headquarters then?"

"Because the Studio had already had enough publicity on Frank Hayes' death, and I thought I could handle it."

Spellman swore. "So this girl gets killed, and God knows what else will happen!"

Lennox nodded. "That's right." His voice was tight. He was feeling rotten about Carmen's death. "What are you going to do now?"

Spellman said, "Pick up Charl Hayes and her brother, then try and locate this mystery girl."

Lennox had a memory of Charl Hayes as he had seen her a little while before.

"I don't think you'll get anything out of them. They'll be in the clear somehow. Well, there's nothing else I can do here. I'm going back to the Studio. You can reach me there if you want me." He turned and left before Spellman would have a chance to tell him not to.

At the Studio, the telephone operator stopped him as he passed her desk. "St. Louis had been trying to reach you, Mr. Lennox."

"Put the call through now. I'll be in my office." He went on down the hall and sank wearily into the chair behind his desk. Five minutes later his phone rang. He picked up the receiver and heard Donovan's voice.

"Listen, Bill. As far as I can get from checking the records the little Hayes girl died ten years ago. I've tried to locate where the body was buried, but relatives took it away. I phoned our man in the little mountain town where the aunt and uncle live, but they aren't there."

"Where are they?"

Donovan said. "They're on their way out to Hollywood."

"What!" Lennox had jerked erect. "They are? When did they start?"

"I'm not sure. I think they're flying out. Our local correspondent talked to the telegraph operator down there and found out that they sent a wire to Miss June Hayes at the Hotel Vincent before they left."

Lennox said, "Thanks," and started to hang up. Donovan shouted:

"Hey, remember I work for a newspaper. What's this all about anyhow?"

Lennox's voice was impatient. "I don't know anything yet. When I do, I'll see you get the story, Donny." He hung up, dialed the office of the telegraph company, got hold of a high official and told him what he wanted. He had to put on some pressure but, inside of five minutes, he had scribbled a message on his desk pad.

It read:

"WILL ARRIVE LOS ANGELES FOUR-THIRTY PLANE ON TUES-

DAY. PLEASE MEET US. UNCLE."

He used the phone again to order a cab and hurriedly left his office. The driver grinned when Lennox offered him ten dollars if they made the airport before four thirty.

But they failed to make it. Neither of them had counted on the flat tire. As it was, when Lennox dashed into the air depot and asked if the plane from St. Louis had arrived, he was told that it had been in for ten minutes.

Lennox swore, turned and left the building. He paused for a moment, then walked toward a group of cab drivers who were loafing in the shade. He paused before them, waited until they looked up.

"Any of you fellows here when the St. Louis plane came in?"

Several nodded. One said, "So what?"

Lennox said. "There was an old couple on the plane. looked like farm people, were probably met by a good looking, dark-haired girl. Any of you see them?"

A short driver nodded. "Yeah, I saw them. The girl was a honey."

A dollar bill materialized in Lennox's hand. "Did they take a hack? Do you know the driver or the cab number?"

The short man grinned. "I can do better than that. I was standing by Jake's cab when they got in. They wanted to be taken to the Anson Hotel. It's on Hollywood Boulevard, three or four blocks west of Western."

Lennox handed him the bill. "There's an extra five if you get me there in twenty minutes."

The driver was on his feet smiling. "Cinch!"

HEN Hollywood was a separate town, before it was absorbed by the sprawling boundaries of Greater Los Angeles, the Anson had been a commercial hotel. As the cab pulled up before it, the driver said:

"Those people must be important. You're the second person to ask us drivers about them."

Lennox was already half out of the cab. He stopped, stared. "The second? Who else?"

The driver said. "A little guy with funny eyes. I didn't like his looks."

Lennox paid the man, turned toward the hotel. It had been remodeled since the old days, but it still looked pretty shabby as Lennox crossed to the desk.

The clerk looked up inquiringly. Lennox said: "Some friends of mine came in less than fifteen minutes ago. The name is Hayes."

"They're in 210, shall I ring?"

Lennox breathed a sigh of relief. "Never mind. They're expecting me." He turned and walked toward the rattle-trap elevator.

Bill stepped out at the second. looked to see which way the numbers ran, and turned right. The room numbers were of nickel, big, unmistakable. He paused and knocked.

His ear detected movement beyond the panel. but no one came to the door. He knocked again, then dropped his hand to the knob.

The door wasn't locked and he pushed it open. There was a little man in the exact center of the floor, a little man with his hand filled by a big gun. Aside from the little man, the room was empty.

He stared at Lennox with oddly shaped purple eyes, eyes which threw back light like dull mirrors. His voice rasped as he said, "Come in, and shut the door."

The window behind the little man was open, the curtains gently bellowing in with the wind. There was no sign of the girl. her uncle, or aunt.

The little man watched Lennox close the door, then he said, "Where are they?"

Lennox didn't try to stall. He shook his head. "I don't know. I missed them at the airport the same as you did."

The little man smiled thinly without

mirth. "How do you know I was at the airport?"

"One of the taxi drivers told me." Lennox was keeping his voice carefully level. He knew that this man was a little crazy. It showed in his eyes, in the way he moved around. He wasn't crazy in the ordinary sense, but something was bothering him.

The little man said, "I'm going to find her, see? I'm going to take her back." He had an odd way of putting words together as if he wasn't used to speaking often.

Lennox said, quickly. "Back where?"

The man stared at him, then suddenly there was a knock at the door. The man with the gun shot a quick, startled look at Lennox. He jerked his gun in a gesture which told louder than words his intent, then he backed toward the window, and stepped backward onto the fire escape.

Lennox did not move. The sound of the knock came again. Then Bill jumped backward, half expecting to draw fire from outside the window, but none came, His hand closed on the knob, and he ripped the door wide to expose Ben Fields standing in the hall.

The lawyer stared at him in surprise. "What the devil!" Lennox had turned and jumped toward the window, jerking his gun as he went, but the fire escape outside was empty. There was no sign of the little man.

He turned back to the room to find that Fields had paused just inside the door, his brows drawn together into a straight line.

Lennox told him, "There was a little guy here with a gun."

"A guy with a gun?" Fields looked almost stupid. "Who was he, what the devil was he doing here? For that matter what are you doing here?"

Lennox put the gun back into his pocket. "That question could go both ways, Len."

The lawyer shrugged. "Sorry, I guess I'm upset. I got a phone call from June

Hayes to meet her here. I didn't expect to run into anything like this."

Lennox lied. "I came to meet June Hayes too. I can't understand why she isn't here."

The lawyer looked startled. "To meet June? You mean she sent for you?"

Lennox smiled thinly. "In a way." He thought for a minute before speaking further. "I think she's going to make some kind of a deal with Charl, a deal out of court."

Fields said, "That's funny. You'd think that they would consult me. After all, I'm the lawyer for the estate."

Lennox said, "That's probably why she sent for you; then maybe she couldn't wait. But I wish I knew who the little guy with the gun was."

Fields didn't seem to hear. He was backing toward the door. "Well, there's nothing here. I've got to go. Coming?"

Lennox followed him into the hall. "I think I'd better get back to the studio." He walked with the lawyer through the lobby and out to the cab stand, got into the taxi and gave the driver the studio address. The cab pulled away, turned left at the first corner.

Lennox leaned forward. "Swing around into that driveway."

The hackman looked at him over his shoulder, but there was something in Lennox's face which stopped all argument. The cab swung around, backed out, headed the other way just as a second taxi went along the Boulevard toward the west. Lennox had a glimpse of Fields in the second cab. He told his driver to follow and they turned back into the Boulevard.

It was beginning to get dark as the cabs went through the Hollywood business section and turned up Laurel Canyon. Fields' cab was a full block ahead but Lennox did not worry. He was sure where the lawyer was headed — to Charl's.

The cab driver shifted into second as the winding grade steepened, and the old motor was laboring long before they reached the crest and turned left into

Mullholland. They rounded the curve, and Lennox saw that there were lights in the windows of Charl Hayes' hillside home.

He told his driver to stop, got out and paid the man, then he walked forward, sheltered by the hedge. There was a taxi in the drive, Fields beside it, paying the man. Lennox had a clear view of the lawyer in the lights from the house. The cab pulled away, and Fields climbed the three steps to the wide porch.

Lennox waited until the lawyer's taxi had passed, then he stepped into the darkened drive and moved rapidly toward the house.

A butler had opened the door to admit Fields, and closed it again. Lennox did not go near the porch but moved toward one of the open French windows.

Charl Hayes was sitting behind a small coffee table. The soft light from the wall bracket lamps was very kind to her. The girl was across the room from her, looking young, very pretty in a white dress. It was the first time Lennox had seen her in a dress and he caught his breath, sharply.

Age was the only difference between the two, but, he thought, given his choice he might have chosen the older one.

There were two other people in the room, a man and a woman. The man's face was heavily tanned as if most of his life had been spent out of doors. His skin looked like seamy, worn leather. The woman was a small, stooped figure with traces of faded beauty about her tired old eyes.

 HARL spoke without moving. "Your claim is absurd, but I don't want any trouble. I'll give you one third of the estate and that's my last word." She broke off as one of the servants appeared in the doorway to announce Fields.

The lawyer shot a quick look around the room, then came down the two steps which separated the living-room from the hall. "Evening, Charl."

The woman on the couch was not pleased to see him, and she made no effort to conceal her displeasure. "What the devil do you want?" Lennox plainly heard the anger in her voice from his post on the terrace.

Fields ignored Charl. He looked around, then took a chair beside the fireplace. "It won't hurt to have me here, will it, Charl?"

She opened her mouth to answer, seemed to change her mind and was silent, but Lennox saw her hand go out and press a bell, set in the framework of the little table. Then she sat back, a tiny, mirthless smile tugging at one corner of her mouth.

There was movement in the doorway, and the butler appeared with Rubell at his heels. Fields started to rise, then sank slowly back into his seat.

"What is this?" He tried to sound assured and failed.

Rubell looked at his sister. The little smile had widened. "I'm talking business with these people. Take this shyster down the hall and lock him in the back room until I get through." Her voice was soft.

Rubell jerked his thumb. "On your feet, mouth-piece."

Fields tried to bluster. "Hey, wait a minute. After all, I'm the attorney for the—"

Rubell took three stiff-legged steps forward, grasped Fields by the slack part of his coat, just under the collar and jerked him upright. The big butler caught the lawyer expertly from Rubell's grasp and shoved him toward the door. "Scram!"

Rubell started to follow. Charl said: "Take the girl along, too, and put her in the small sitting room. I can talk to her uncle better if she isn't here."

Rubell said, "And how do I know that she'll stay there?"

Charl smiled. "She'll stay. If she doesn't, something will happen to these two which she won't like." She indicated the man and woman. "Take her out."

The girl was going to object, then she didn't. With a sharp glance toward the old man and woman, she rose and moved toward the hall door.

Lennox hesitated for a minute, then he turned and moved along the terrace in the shadows. The small sitting room had French windows, too. He reached the first and peered in. The girl was pacing back and forth, smoking a cigarette nervously. Lennox reached down, tried the little brass knob, found that the window was unlocked, and pushed the French door open.

She turned at the sound, terror leaping into her dark eyes, then giving way slowly to surprised relief. "Mr. Lennox!" A smile started to wipe the surprise from her eyes, then faded as there was no answering one to relax the stiff mask of Lennox's face.

"What—what's the matter?" she asked.

He closed the door softly behind him, glanced around. The room was small, expensively furnished and, except for the two of them, obviously empty. He went slowly toward her and something in his eyes made her back away, repeating her question as she went: "What's the matter?"

He told her, and his voice was tighter than he intended. "It's time for a showdown June, if that's your name. You are June Hayes? You are Frank's sister?"

She said, "Yes," sharply, but it didn't sound convincing somehow. There were two large buttons on each shoulder, holding the narrow straps of her dress. Before she could guess his intent he had reached out, caught her shoulders. His fingers undid the buttons and her dress was already falling before she knew that the straps were unfastened. Her hands went up to catch it, but he caught her wrists, held them as the dress slid down.

The dress caught for a moment on her hips and he held both hands with one of his while he helped its downward progress. She wore lacy underthings but no slip.

Color came up into her cheeks as his eyes swept downward. He saw the rounding flatness of her stomach above the line of the panties, but there was no break in the white skin, no sign of scars.

He stepped back, leaving her standing there, a statue of pink and white. Her shoulders were wide, her flanks slim, her legs well formed.

She recovered from surprise, and anger glinted in her dark eyes. "I've heard of Hollywood, but I didn't expect a direct attack like this."

He looked at her, unconscious for the moment of her body. "No scars."

She didn't get the meaning for the moment. She said, sharply. "If that's a compliment—"

He shook his head. "Wrong, kid. I'm sorry, but I had to know. June Hayes was shot twice in the stomach. She might by a thousand to one chance have recovered, but nothing in this world or in hell could have healed those scars. You're not June Hayes. Who are you?"

The words struck the girl with the impact of a sledge hammer. She winced, then tried to gather her scattered wits. "I—I—"

Lennox said, harshly. "The game's played out. Stop stalling. You don't think that Charl will split the estate with you now? You can be prosecuted. You've only got one chance. Who are you? Who put you up to this? Tell me that, and maybe I'll help you."

She stared at him. "You—you can help?"

He shrugged. "I don't know. Perhaps."

She took a step forward, leaving the white dress a crumpled mass where it had fallen about her feet. "Please, you've got to. I'll do anything you want—give you anything you ask, only don't expose me."

Her meaning was perfectly clear, it showed in her eyes, in every movement of her body. The palms of Lennox's hands were suddenly damp and there was a dryness which threatened to crack his lips. Her mouth was partly open, inviting, one hand extended to touch his arm. For just an instant an impulse to take her in his arms and crush her to him was almost overpowering, then he laughed and the sound broke the spell.

"No go, kid. You're not expert enough to play that game. Last chance. Who put you up to this?"

She stepped back, silent, sullen.

He shrugged. "O. K." He stepped forward, picked up her dress. "I guess you won't go far without this," and turning, went toward the door.

She watched him with eyes which smoldered, but he paid no attention. He shut the door and moved rapidly down the hall toward the front room. It was empty. He stopped to stare around. He hadn't expected this. He'd expected that at least Charl Hayes would be in the room. His forehead creased with thought for a moment, then he crossed to the small serving table and punched the bell in the coffee table frame.

He turned to face the door, wondering who would answer. He waited, getting no response punched it again, twice.

Heavy feet came along the hall and the big butler was in the doorway, staring at him, surprise drawing the bushy eyebrows down into an almost straight line above the small, pig-like eyes.

"What the hell?" His hand was moving toward his left arm pit.

Lennox said. "Hold it," sharply. "Where's Charl?"

The man's hand had halted half-way toward the gun. "What do you want with her? How the hell did you get in here?"

Lennox' voice rasped. "Never mind that. Where is she?"

The big man did not answer. Instead he turned his head and looked up and down the hall. As he did so there was a shot from somewhere in the rear part of the house, the explosion seeming to come right through the thin plaster walls.

Lennox swore and jumped for the door. The big butler was in the way and his shoulder struck the man squarely in the chest, knocking him backward out of the way.

The man swore and tried to grab him as he went by, but Bill managed to elude the grasping ham-like hands, and raced along the hall toward the door of the small sitting room.

He didn't know from where the shot had come, but he feared that it had come from the room he had left only a short time before. He threw the door open and jumped in, then he stopped.

There hadn't been any scars on the girl's white body before, but there was one now—a bluish hole just under the left shoulder blade from which a little blood was seeping.

He didn't turn her over. He didn't need to know what the heavy slug had done to her. He knelt at her side, felt for pulse, rolled the head so that he could raise the eyelids, then he rose. The girl was dead. Whoever she was, she would never get any of Frank Hayes' money.

He straightened, his lips tight, and turned to find that the big butler was watching him from the doorway. The man's face was impassive, unreadable.

The girl had been shot in the back, shot evidently as she'd run toward the hall door. That meant that the killer had stood on the terrace. Lennox walked across the room, pushed open the French door. Outside everything was dark and still. Even the night insects had hushed their cries.

He turned back and again asked for Charl, but at that moment, Charl herself pushed the butler to one side and stood staring at him. She kept her eyes on his face for a full moment, then dropped them to the girl's still form. She screamed.

He watched her. She might easily have killed the girl herself, killed her to keep from dividing the estate, but he did not think so.

He said, "Listen, Charl. I think that the play is about over and that the curtain is about ready to come down."

Her eyes were still on the girl's bare back. "Who killed June?"

He said, "That isn't June, Charl. There aren't any scars on her. June Hayes should have some."

He watched the woman's eyes widen. "I should have thought of that myself."

He nodded. "You should."

She said, "But what are you doing here?"

He explained. "I wanted to find out who put her up to this. She wasn't very afraid of me. I guess she figured that she could handle a man. A lot of women put too much dependence on the lure of their body, but I thought she'd be afraid of you, afraid of what you might do. I thought she'd talk." His voice was bitter. "I guess the murderer thought the same thing. Where's Fields?"

Her eyes widened. "You think—"

He said. "Fields was attorney of the estate. He could have messed up the funds."

Her lips pursed and she looked at the butler. "Where's Fields?"

"Locked in the study." The man sounded sullen.

"Could he have gotten out?"

The butler shook his head. "Don't think so."

Lennox asked, "And the old man and woman, the uncle and aunt?"

"They're above the garage."

"Come on, let's have a look." He didn't wait for her, but led the way toward the rear door.

As he reached the steps which led upward beside the garage he stopped suddenly, sniffed, then started to run up the stairs. The smell of gas was strong, very strong.

HERE was a door at the top of the stairs, locked. He heaved against it, striking the panel with his shoulder. He succeeded only in hurting his shoulder as he bounced back.

He tried again, and this time the lock snapped, almost throwing him into the room beyond. Gas came around him in an eddying wave. He ducked his head and backed away, fumbling for a handkerchief. The motion probably saved his life for flame suddenly seemed to race up the far side of the building. There was a terrific explosion and the whole place was suddenly a mass of flame.

The explosion knocked Lennox backward from the platform. And in that flashing, falling moment he had time to realize that it would probably be his last.

But he failed to count on the row of California evergreens which grew like a hedge alongside the garage. His body was thrown directly against them. The narrow trunks bent under the sudden weight, and he found himself lying among the thick branches. held there as securely as if he had been in a cradle.

He lay for an instant, collecting himself. then he grabbed one branch and swung down, dropping to the ground a dozen feet below. The foliage tore at his clothes, ripping them in a dozen places, but he gained the ground unhurt, and went racing up the flaming stairs.

The wood had not thoroughly caught as yet and it looked much worse than it was. The heat however was bad and getting rapidly worse as more and more of the building browned and then burst into flame.

Both the old man and woman were dead. Lennox picked up their bodies and dragged them to the flaming platform and tumbled them down the stairs. It was the best he could do.

By the time he reached the ground his coat was smouldering in a dozen places, and he stood beating at it with his hands until a sudden stream of water struck him directly in the face.

He turned to see Charl Hayes spraying him with the garden hose. The building at his back was a mass of flame but the wind was coming from the other direction and Lennox thought that there was little danger that the house would catch.

He thanked Charl and started toward

the house. She followed. "Help me with the fire!"

He shook his head. "No. I want to see Fields. And where's your brother?"

She said, "He went down to the club. He should be back at almost any minute." As if in answer to her words, lights swung into the drive and a car slid up to their side.

Rubell was under the wheel. He stared at the burning building, then at his sister. "What the hell happened?"

She told him. "Lennox thinks it's Fields. Come on."

"But the fire?"

Bill shrugged. "You can't save the garage, and I don't think it will catch anything else. The fire department should be here in ten or twelve minutes."

Rubell followed Lennox and Charl. Lennox unbolted the study door to find Fields standing beside the window, watching the fire. He swung around and his eyes widened when he saw Lennox. "Bill!"

Lennox's voice was cold. "Yeah, Fields. Why didn't you come out and join us?"

The lawyer swore. "How could I? What's been going on? All the tramping and shooting and—"

Bill said, "The little Hayes girl is dead. The game's blown up. She wasn't June Hayes after all. She didn't have any scars."

The lawyer stared, then he swore. "I should have thought of that."

Lennox nodded. "Someone should. Why didn't you come out to join the fun?"

Fields snarled, "I was locked in, you fool."

Rubell brushed passed Lennox. He crossed the room and tried the French doors. The center one was unlocked. Rubell turned around, his dark face working, and there was a big gun in his hand.

"So you were locked in, shyster."

Fields was staring. "Hey, wait!"

Rubell was advancing toward him. "No soap, Fields. So you thought you

could ring in a false girl and then, when the game went sour, kill her and her supposed uncle and aunt off." He reached out to grab Field's collar, but Lennox stopped him.

"Drop the gun, Rubell."

The night-club man turned. Lennox cracked, "Any more and I'll blast you." He had his gun in his hand.

Rubell looked at him, then let the heavy automatic slide from his fingers. "What the hell?"

Lennox said, "Search him, Fields. I think we have the killer."

Charl Hayes was staring. Rubell laughed. "You're crazy. You can't make this stick."

Lennox said, "Save it. The woman over the garage talked before she died in my arms. You didn't count on that, did you?"

The man's face went livid. Fields was searching him. Suddenly the lawyer stopped as a heavy voice behind Lennox said, "Drop it."

Bill started to spin, but he had no chance. The big butler reached out, grabbed his arm and twisted it. The gun slid from his numbed fingers. Rubell laughed.

"O. K., smart guy. The last trick's mine." He said to the butler, "Hurry up. Knock 'em on the head and toss them into that fire. The engines will be here in a few minutes and then it will be too late."

Charl was white-faced. "Me too?"

He snarled at her. "Sure, you! If you hadn't been so tight I'd have never gotten in this jam. I owed a hell of a lot of dough. I got part of it from Frank. He wanted the dough back. When I couldn't pay, he threatened to expose some past deals that I can't afford to have come to light. I had to have him knocked off, so I did and made it look like an accident.

"Then I needed more dough, so I got in touch with Frank Hayes' uncle. Remember him and me used to be pals in the old days? I knew he had a daughter and I figured to pawn her off as June, have her come out here, scare you and get a cut. I thought you'd come to me for advice and that I'd advise you to pay.

"Come on," he snarled at the butler, "crack Lennox and let's get it over with."

"Wait." The little man with the funny eyes was standing in the open French window, a gun in his hand. Rubell swung around and the little man shot him directly in the chest.

The big butler jumped forward, but he wasn't fast enough. The little man's second bullet knocked him over before Lennox could move.

Then the little man stepped through the door, shoving his gun into his pocket. "Mind if I see her?"

Lennox stared at him. "See who?"

The little man said. "Mary Hayes. You know, the girl who has been calling herself June Hayes."

Lennox caught his breath. "Who are you?"

The little man said, "My name isn't important. I was in love with her back home, before she got the crazy idea of pretending to be her dead cousin. I followed her out here and have been trying to find her for two days. I hung around her hotel, but she knew I was here and has been hiding from me."

Lennox said, "Then that's where she was all day, hiding from you. You know that she's dead?"

The little man nodded. "I know. I've been watching the house. I saw this man," he indicated Rubell, "get into his car and drive out the driveway. He parked about a block down the road and walked back. I saw him stand at the French door and fire into the room, but I wasn't close enough to stop him. Before I could get here he hurried along the terrace, unlocked one of the doors to this room, but he didn't come in. Instead he ran to the garage."

Lennox nodded. "I figured it was something like that. Well, go on and see her."

The little man backed out onto the terrace. Lennox bent over Rubell. The man wasn't dead, but he was in bad shape. His eyes fluttered open as Lennox lifted him.

Bill said, "There's just one question I'd like to ask. Why'd you kill Carmen?"

The wounded man circled dry lips with the tip of his tongue. "Had to," he gasped. "She kept the girl over night, questioned her, and the kid admitted knowing me. We were afraid Carmen would tell you, afraid that maybe she'd written a note. We searched but couldn't find it, so we tried to make her tell us whether she had or not."

Lennox's voice was savage. "So you beat her to death."

The man's eyes were closed. "That damn little boy friend." He was mumbling. "I knew he'd cause trouble. I wanted to kill him, but the girl wouldn't let me. She said that she'd keep away from him until we put it over, and then she could handle him. That's a laugh! He handled me." The voice trailed off and his head rolled back.

Lennox laid him on the couch, then led Charl Hayes out onto the terrace. She was quiet, subdued, but she said, finally, "It was lucky for you that the woman in the garage lived long enough to talk."

Lennox was watching the fire. "She didn't."

"Didn't?" Fields had come out behind them.

Lennox nodded. "That was just a bluff to try and trap Rubell. It had to be either you or him, and I couldn't figure how you could have gotten out of that room, found a gun, had time to do all the things that were done, and get back without being seen.

"Then, too, he tripped himself when he mentioned that the man and woman were dead. I hadn't mentioned it and he couldn't have seen the bodies.

"Finally when he tried the French door to prove that you could have escaped from that room he didn't try them all. He acted as if he knew which one would be unlocked. It all added up so

I took a chance and . . . ." He broke off as the sirens sounded.

"Here come the fire engines." He started toward the steps.

Charl Hayes followed him. "Wait, Bill. I haven't thanked you for clearing this up. He was my brother but—well, those things I told you this afternoon go double now. I—I need someone, someone to help me. With Frank's money we could do things out here, be someone. Who knows how far we could go?"

He turned to look up at her. In the glow from the burning building she looked utterly desirable, yet, perhaps it was a trick of light, but there was a halo of danger about her, a warning to stay clear.

"Please!" she said.

His tone was gruff when he said, "Thanks, Charl. Let's skip it. You picked the wrong guy." Then he turned and walked away . . . .

When the fire was extinguished he bummed a ride on the hook and ladder back to Hollywood. It was dangerous, swinging around the steep horseshoe curves, but not as dangerous as it would have been to remain at the house. As he stepped down from the truck he grinned a little to himself, knowing that as long as he lived he would wonder a little just what he had missed.

LIGHTS, ACTION— KILLER!

A Bill Lennox Novelette

By

W. T. BALLARD

"All we need," said cameraman Jimmy North, on location in the Panta-lope Lumber Mill, "is little Nell, strapped to the saw carriage." But the old movie gag didn't seem so funny when trouble-shooter Bill Lennox found Director Roy Martin in the sawmill—neatly sliced in two. . . .

CHAPTER ONE

Ghost Camp

BILL LENNOX waited on the foggy Glendale station platform, glancing at his watch every two minutes. He was a big man, trim-looking and almost slender in his carefully tailored ulster.

His eyes were gray, level and thoughtful.

Had his life developed in different channels, he might have been an editor or a very human college professor. He had wanted an education well enough to work for it, sending himself through Northwestern.

At the time, he had hoped to teach, but a chance meeting with the editor of one of the Chicago dailies had led to a job, covering police and criminal courts.

From there he had graduated to the sports desk where he might have remained, had not the paper put on a beauty contest as a circulation builder.

The contest had been a success, due mainly to Lennox' ideas, and he had been offered a job with a Hollywood publicity firm. For three years he used his ability in publicizing the picture stars and did such an outstanding job that Sol Spurck, production chief of General Consolidated Studios, offered him a job.

The job had no title. He was Spurck's assistant, used to iron out whatever bottle necks developed in the production schedule.

At the moment, he was heading north to where a location company had run into script trouble. And Spurck was going with him. He hadn't wanted the production chief along. He knew that the fishing trip which Spurck was talking about too loudly was only a blind.

The little producer could not be content unless he had his fat finger in everything that went on around the sprawling lot.

But the train was coming. If Spurck did not hurry, Lennox would make the trip alone after all. And then, just as the multi-colored streamliner slid into the station, Spurck arrived.

The big limousine pulled in until its chrome snout was touching the platform. The uniformed chauffeur swung from under the wheel, but Lennox reached the rear door first.

"Come on. Get the bags, George," he said. He caught Spurck's arm and almost yanked him from the air-foam cushion.

Spurck ran. At least his heavy body went into motion and his arms moved like pumping pistons. He reached the train, seized the car handles and hoisted himself aboard.

"Some day," said Lennox, coming up the steps behind him, "you're going to miss a train."

Spurck sounded aggrieved. "Honest, Bill. It is not my fault, you understand. But apple strudel Mama made with her own hands, and for eight trains, I would not insult her by not eating." He reached the vestibule and Lennox had his first clear look at his chief's costume.

His exclamation was involuntary. "What the devil are you made up for?"

Spurck looked downward at his rotund form. "What's the matter? Ain't I going fishing?"

They both knew that the fishing was a stall. They also both knew that Spurck would play the part out to the end, and he had dressed carefully for the performance. His short legs were incased in Duxbak breeches which were stuffed into lace boots. His shirt was gray flannel and a heavy gold watch chain linked the two breast pockets. Over the shirt he wore a waterproof hunting coat with a corduroy collar, and on his round head was a cap of brown. Had it been green, and had there been a feather, it could have done service for Robin Hood.

Lennox made no effort to hide his laughter. He and the little producer understood each other. No one else on the big lot would have dared laugh at Spurck.

He said, "Come on, let's get into the compartment before someone shoots you for a Jap soldier," and pushed his chief ahead of him down the passage.

O NCE in the compartment, Spurck removed the hunting coat and settled down beside the blacked-out window in comfort. The sleeves of his shirt were too long and were held up by pink arm bands. Lennox had not seen anything like them for years.

Spurck saw the look. "For years I had them," he said. "And when the *schlemiel* made these sleeves too long, there was no time to have them changed. Now this script—" He leaned forward, opened an expensive bag, found a cigar and lighted it.

"The script," said Lennox, "stinks." When he had first come west, he had been surprised at the language which served the film colony, but after six years he spoke no other. He was too busy to think about himself, his likes or dislikes.

At first he had dreamed of writing a book, a lot of books, but as the weeks drifted into years, he still spoke of quitting pictures, of going east and really settling down to write.

That time never seemed to come. Through experience, he had learned to mask his interest, his enthusiasms, and his softer feelings under a shell of hardness which was the only phoney thing about him. He had become flippant, since the town understood nothing else. He had ceased to admit that he could read, or that he liked good books. He gambled when he could, needing the false excitement of the game as a safety valve for his nerves.

But although he refused to admit it, even to himself, he was still moved by enthusiasm for each new picture, still hoped that some day someone would cut loose and make, not the old formula story, but something really new, something different. All the bitterness and boredom of his job was in his voice when he said: "They dipped the barrel dry for hokum on this, Sol. If we had Pearl White, we could make the greatest serial out of it that was ever made."

"Funny," said Spurck. "Mama and I was just talking at dinner. Them old days was different. Pictures was fun then, and not always the headache which we have not got."

Lennox always liked to get his chief talking about the early days of the industry, when the combine controlled the patents, when the independents were fighting for their chance, when actresses were not stars but were billed under their studios!

Spurck was saying: "It was before I loaned money to my brother-in-law, and went into the business to protect it. In them days, a friend owned a nickelodeon in Newark, and was buying his pictures from Blackton and Smith at Vitrograph.

"Once he asked, did I want to see pictures made, so I said yes, and we go out and watch while they shoot *Carmen*.

"No extras much could they afford, so they shoot the picture through the arch which the bull uses to enter the ring. That way, they have a curtain with heads painted on it which looks like the crowd in the distance." He broke off to chuckle. "Well, they didn't have no bull either, you understand, but they have a cow, which they rent from a farmer, for Westerns.

"This cow, they put a brassiere onto so she can look like a bull, and everything is set, only the cow does not like her brassiere. She sulks, and no how can they get her to charge after the toreador.

"So a prop man lights a newspaper which he holds under the cow. She charges then, you understand, clear across the ring. She scatters the few extras that they had, catches the nice painted curtain on her horns and runs off home. It was that day which I first met Roy Martin."

Lennox said: "Let's forget Martin. I know that you made a deal to use his mill for this picture and in return he hopes to direct that Southern epic that you've got on the fire. But I still don't like him."

Spurck took the cigar carefully from his mouth. "If I treated him like the *schnorrer* which he is, we would be whistling for a mill in which to shoot this picture. Less people you catch with vinegar than sugar, just remember that. Now, I will prove further that I am smarter than you by beating you at gin-rummy. The cards, they are in the yellow bag."

HE diner was almost empty when Lennox came into it the next morning. Spurck was still sleeping heavily and he did not have the heart to wake the production executive. He was surprised when a woman at the far end of the car half rose and motioned to him. Not until he had traveled half the distance toward her did he recognize Hope Sutherland.

In his book, Hope was one of the best actresses in the business. She wasn't young. She dated well back into the Pickford-Gish era, but she might well have passed for thirty-five, sitting there with the morning sun coming through the window at her side.

"Come and sit down, William."

He sat down, ordered and then told her: "This is the last place I expected to find you. Where are you headed?"

"The same place you are," she told him. "Astoria."

His surprise grew, but she stopped it almost at once. "Listen, Bill." Her tone was deadly serious. "I knew that you were on the train. I saw you get on at Glendale last night. I got on downtown."

"But why?"

She said: "I've got to talk to Roy Martin. It's important, Bill, really a matter of life and death, and I don't want anyone to know that I'm in Astoria. I'm going to get off at a town twenty miles this side and drive over. I've already telegraphed for a room at the Lodge under another name."

He said, in surprise: "Is Roy in Astoria? I didn't know that he was up here."

She said: "I don't know exactly where he is, Bill. But he's in the mountains somewhere, and his brother Herb will know. All I want you to do is to tell Herbert that I'll meet Roy tonight at nine o'clock at the Waterfield Road corner. That's all, and please don't ask me any questions." She rose, gathering up her purse. "I waited here to see you. I hoped that Spurck would sleep late. Good-bye, and thanks."

He turned to stare after her, then went on with his breakfast. When he finished, he went back to wake Spurck. They had to change trains in an hour.

ASTORIA had been a mining town once, and there were still some quartz properties in the district, but the placer ground had played out in the late fifties and the town would have become another ghost camp, save for the railroad shops and the thick stand of heavy timber which threw a blanket of green across the rugged hills. It was also the center of a good fishing district and in season the Lodge and auto camps were filled with eager anglers.

Lennox had been there two months before, looking over the place and arranging for the location company. The town was built around a square in the center of which stood a weathered courthouse. The street traffic was heavy. Trucks and trailers, loaded dangerously with green lumber, went past as the town's single taxi took them first to the Lodge and then out to the lumber mill.

The Pantolope Mill was not large. None of these mountain mills were. It occupied a couple of acres of flat ground in a loop of the hurrying river.

Once, it had been run by water power, later by steam, but now electricity had replaced them both. The taxi turned into the rutted drive which wound through the maze of lumber piles toward the building and went into second for the pull through the deep sand.

Spurck, still dressed in what he thought a fisherman should wear, filled his big chest with the sharp air and exhaled slowly. "Wonderful. A new man this climate would make of a corpse," he said.

Lennox said: "It's the fresh wood that you smell." It was hard to speak against the screech of whirling saws that filled the quiet air.

Spurck was staring about as if he had stepped into another world and his round, slightly prominent eyes sparkled as the busy scene stirred his imagination.

Trucks, carrying logs, thick as the height of an average man, made a steady stream as they brought their cargoes down from the steep, timbered slopes to feed the hungry mill.

They left the cab, entered the building and crossed the sawdusted floor to where Jimmy North and his camera crew were taking stock shots of the running mill.

The main unit was working high up on the side of Mount Dunkin where the big trees were being felled, sawed into lengths, and canted onto the trucks.

Lennox left Spurck with Jimmy North and went on across to the mill office. The closing door cut off some of the sound and Lennox breathed deeply with relief. The ripping saws set his nerves on end.

Herbert Martin was at his littered desk, a big man whose hand was rough and firm as he offered it to Lennox. "Glad to see you again. Sorry the picture isn't going well."

Lennox shrugged. "We're used to that," he admitted. "The script's wrong. We'll have to change it. I wanted to see you about something else. I've got a message that you're supposed to deliver to Roy."

"Deliver to Roy?" Herbert Martin showed surprise. "But Roy isn't here."

Lennox' quick ear caught a false note in the man's tone. He sensed that Herbert Martin was lying, but at the moment, his mind was on his own troubles. He said: "I don't know anything about that. Hope Sutherland was on the same train with us coming up. She got off at a station twenty miles down the line. She said that you were to tell Roy to meet her at the Waterfield Road corner at nine tonight." He didn't wait for an answer. He turned and went back into the main body of the mill.

Spurck was watching Jimmy North ride a crane directly above the machinery. When he had his "take," North left the crane and joined them as the foreman cut off the power and the saws stopped.

In the surprising quiet which followed, North said: "All we need is little Nell, strapped to that saw carriage. I never saw such a murderous looking thing as that blade in my life."

"Remember what I said about Pearl White," Lennox reminded Spurck, "but this script is worse. It reads as if it had been plagiarized from Grimm's Fairy Tales. Come on, let's get uptown."

CHAPTER TWO

Man of Mystery

 THE lobby of the Lodge was a big room with a heavily beamed ceiling. The floor was not covered, save for a few scattered bear rugs. The clock on the stone mantel showed that it was a quarter to twelve.

Lennox had been gambling. Spurck had gone to bed early. "I gotta get up before dawn," he explained. "I gotta catch those trouts when they are still so asleep that they won't know the difference between these artificial flies and the real thing. You would think that even a fish would know better than that."

Lennox had been glad enough to be relieved of another session of gin-rummy. Outside, the poorly lit streets were still filled with noise and laughter and the half-dozen clubs which faced the courthouse square were still full. This town did not seem to know the meaning of rest.

Lennox turned toward the stairs but he never reached them for a man came out of the shadows of the rear hall to press against his side. "There's a gun in my hand, Lennox. I've orders to bring you over to talk to the boss. I'd as soon take you feet-first."

Surprise stopped Lennox for an instant, then anger flared up to grip him. But his back was toward the man. He had no chance to turn. "You seem to be holding the cards," he said, steadily. "Call the game."

"That," his captor assured him, "is one of the smartest things you ever said." He patted Lennox' pockets, found no gun and stepped back. "Come on."

Lennox did not answer. He turned and they went out through the double doors together.

The North Star Hotel was a four-story brick building at the corner of Pine and Gold Run Alley. Its ground floor was occupied on one side by a restaurant, on the other by a saloon, which in the parlance of the country was called a "club."

Joe Carren owned them both, as he owned the building, and the other clubs in Astoria.

Upstairs the rooms were arranged along a hall, pullman fashion, occupied by miners and lumber workers. As they mounted the steps, the gunman muttered to himself: "What a town, no one ever goes to bed."

Lennox was surprised. He'd assumed that the man was local, one of Carren's men, that he was being taken to see the gambling czar. Apparently he wasn't, and he puzzled about it all the way back along the old hall.

Figures on the front of the building said that the hotel had been erected in '58 and Lennox decided that it had not been thoroughly aired since.

All along the hall he tried to find the answer to the gunman's actions. Not until he pushed open the end door did he know who had sent for him. Then he stopped.

Manny Yarcovitch sat in an old rocking chair beside the window. He was a small man, this Yarcovitch, with an egg-shaped head that lacked hair of any kind. Nor had he eyebrows or eyelashes to break the smooth whiteness of his face.

Lennox did not know him very well, but he did know one thing—Yarcovitch was Hollywood's star money lender. Some said that he was a Serb, some claimed that he was Greek or Armenian. No one knew exactly and Manny never had bothered to tell them. He was a man of mystery, seldom appearing in public, never getting his name into the papers, but it was rumored about the movie capital that whenever anyone was very short of cash, he would receive an offer from Manny of a loan. Rumor also said that the interest was high and the repayment exacting, that several of Manny's debtors had been beaten up seriously for not living up to their agreements.

Lennox had never had anything to do with the man personally, and he resented him as he resented the horde of leeches who preyed upon the movie city.

"This is a pleasure, Lennox." The hairless man made no effort to rise. "A pleasure I have been looking forward to for years."

Lennox didn't answer and the money lender went on. "Roscoe is a rough boy." He looked fondly toward the gunman, his little brown eyes seeming to snap in his white hairless face. "I'm loving Roscoe like a son, but he ain't exactly a whirlwind when it comes to brains."

LENNOX still did not answer. He sat down on the edge of the sagging bed and looked at his host. The man's suit, although carefully tailored, seemed too large for his shrunken body. He wore no jewelry save for a gold tie pin, fashioned in the form of a skull. In the skull's mouth was a diamond. Lennox judged that it must be at least a four-carat stone.

"You wanted to see me." His voice was level, unhurried when he spoke. "If you ever want to see me again, don't send Roscoe. I don't like him."

Yarcovitch rubbed the side of his nose with a skinny forefinger. The nose was big, too big for his small face and it jutted out like the prow of a battleship.

"I send for men any way that I like," he said evenly. "When Manny sends, they come running."

Lennox did not dignify this by a reply. Instead he waited, still puzzled as to why the man had sent for him, what had brought this human leech to Astoria.

Yarcovitch rocked back and forth, making the old chair creak. "Where's Roy Martin, Lennox?"

William Lennox started, and stared hard at the money lender. His first impulse was to lie. Not because he liked Martin or owed him anything, but because he definitely disliked this money lender.

However, he realized that he would

gain nothing by lying now. Yarcovitch was too smart.

Instead Bill Lennox said: "I didn't know until this morning that Martin was within five hundred miles of this place. I still don't know where he is, but I understand that he's somewhere in the hills."

The money lender's mouth looked like a tight trap.

"Come, come," he said. "We aren't children, Mr. Lennox."

Behind Bill there was a protesting squeak as Roscoe moved forward. "Shall I bop him, boss?"

Yarcovitch said, "Not yet, Roscoe," and smiled gravely. "I have to use force in my business, Mr. Lennox. Mine body is frail. Roscoe, he is my strength." He appeared to study Lennox carefully, then sighed. "I'm beginning to believe that you do not know," he admitted. "Tell me, then, where is it that Hope Sutherland has gotten to? To fool people, she got off the train down the line, but she

drove into town by auto. That much we know."

Lennox stared. "Isn't she at the Lodge?"

"No," said Yarcovitch, watching him. "If she were, we would not be troubling you."

Lennox got slowly off the bed. At times his movements looked awkward, but this was not one of the times. "As far as Martin is concerned," he said evenly, "what you do is your business. But Hope Sutherland is a friend of mine. Remember that and keep your paws off of her."

Roscoe drew his breath hissingly. He brought his hand out of his overcoat pocket and there was a gun in it. "Careful," he growled.

"No," said Yarcovitch. "Not now, Roscoe. Sometime maybe, but not now. Please be leaving the thinking to me. Good-night, Mr. Lennox. A sound sleep I am wishing for you. You might need it."

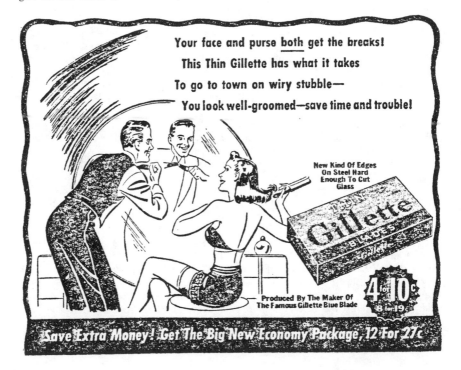

Your face and purse both get the breaks!
This Thin Gillette has what it takes
To go to town on wiry stubble—
You look well-groomed—save time and trouble!

New Kind Of Edges On Steel Hard Enough To Cut Glass

Gillette

Produced By The Maker Of The Famous Gillette Blue Blade

4 for 10c

Save Extra Money! Get The Big New Economy Package, 12 For 27c

ENNOX said, "Quit it," and tried to sit up. He had been sleeping so soundly that the shaking motion seemed a part of his dream. It wasn't. He managed to get his eyes open and found that his room was filled with men.

Herb Martin had a grip on his shoulder and the sawmill man gave no sign that he intended to let go. "Damn you," said Martin. "Damn you for a murderer."

His big hands tightened convulsively and he shook Lennox until his spine threatened to snap. Joe Carren grabbed his arm and pulled him back. Carren was a small man, with well-shaped features and careful clothes. He looked like a well-dressed bank clerk, not a gambler.

He said, "Stop it," and there was something in the cool levelness of his tone that made the big mill owner release his grip and step back grudgingly.

Lennox pushed the blankets aside and got out of bed. His legs were encased in bright blue silk. Pajamas, loud ones, were one of his weaknesses.

A sheriff's deputy said: "Boy, oh boy. Can I sleep with you?"

Lennox ignored him. He ignored Martin and the sheriff, sensing that Joe Carren could control them all. He said to the gambler: "What the devil goes on?"

"Be quiet," the sheriff cut in. "Get some clothes on. Quick."

Carren did not answer, and after a long look at the gambler, Lennox obeyed.

Outside, it was cold and the faint light which was beginning to show in the east seemed only to increase the chill. Lennox shivered as he got into the rear seat between Carren and the deputy. The sheriff and Martin were in front. The car cut through the empty streets and swept out the river road toward the lumber mill. Lennox guessed where they were going long before they turned into the private road.

The piles of raw cut planks blocked their view and they had almost reached the building before he could see it. When he did, he realized that every light in the place was burning.

The wet ground had frozen enough so that it broke like cardboard under his feet as he left the car and moved toward the entrance. No one said anything. Someone swung open the door and stood aside for Lennox to enter. He did so, and stopped. For a full minute, he was certain that he was going to be sick. He turned, choked and ran full into the broad chest of the big sheriff. The jar restored him a little and he turned back for a second look at the mill.

The big, ugly looking teeth of the circular saw were stained deeply with already darkening blood. There was blood on the saw carriage, on the log, and spattered thickly across the sawdust of the floor.

But it was the man's body which drew his horror-fascinated eyes. There could be no doubt that Roy Martin was dead. He had been sawed in two.

Never again would the director make a picture. Never again would his name figure in a divorce action. He had run his course, this orchid man who was no longer young.

But Lennox' thoughts were not for Martin. The man's death, save for the shock of method, brought no feeling. Lennox was remembering Jimmy North, remembering what the cameraman had said that afternoon: "All we need is little Nell, strapped to the saw carriage, being threatened by the whirling blades."

The thought had been in North's mind, and if any living man had reason to wish Roy Martin dead, Jimmy North had that reason.

THE cameraman had had a wife once, a wife who was cast in one of Martin's pictures. That picture had led to a Nevada divorce and the girl had expected Martin to marry her. But there had been no marriage and her body had been picked up in a Detroit street. The police never decided whether she had fallen or jumped from the hotel window.

114

The details were vague in Lennox'
mind, so much had happened since. But
at the time, Jimmy North had been a
crazy man, searching Hollywood for
Martin, carrying a gun until his friends
had disarmed him and sent him to Mexico to cool off.

He'd come back, but he'd never been
the same. He drank too heavily to hold
his first camera. He was an assistant
now, without ambition, without caring,
and he was big enough to have handled
Roy Martin, big enough to have bound
the director to the saw carriage single-
handed—

The sheriff said slowly: "Well, Lennox?"

Bill turned to face them. His reaction
was that of a wolf, brought to bay by
a pack of snarling dogs. There was no
softening in any of the faces of the men
before him.

They knew each other well, he was
a stranger, and by their attitudes they
showed clearly that they suspected him
of murder.

Again he centered his attention on
Joe Carren. The little gambler was the
natural leader, the levelest head present.
He alone was unswayed by his emotion,
but governed rather by a cold and careful brain.

Lennox said, never taking his eyes
from the careful features of Carren's
handsome face: "Where's the mill watchman? How did Roy Martin happen to
be here?"

They didn't know. They looked at
each other, and their uncertainty was
apparent.

"Why, hell," said the sheriff. "The
watchman should be here. He was here
when we left."

"I think," said Lennox, "that one
thing which this mill needs rather badly is a new watchman. Don't you,
Carren?"

The gambler did not answer with
words, but his smile, although thin,
seemed to indicate his agreement with
Lennox.

CHAPTER THREE

A Frightened Angel

THE big lobby of the
Lodge was cold and
bleak. A deputy stirred
the fire and threw on
fresh w o o d. Spurck
came down the wide
stairway, carrying an
already jointed rod in one hand and a
creel in the other. He paused at the
bottom of the stairs and his round face
grew more pink as surprise hit him.

"Bill—you up? And these men, what
is it that goes on?"

The sheriff turned around and
scowled at the rotund figure in the brown
Duxbak. "Who the hell is that, and
what's he made up for?"

Lennox explained, and the sheriff's
weathered face lightened a little. "Oh,
another movie gun." He rubbed his
hands as he went forward. "Say, you,
did you know Roy Martin?"

Lennox caught Joe Carren's eye and
stepped sideways toward the small gambler. "You're a businessman, Carren."

"So?" The gambler's expression had
not altered.

"So the man that your sheriff is questioning is the production chief of General
Consolidated. You people up here like
to have location companies. They bring
money to your town. Let the sheriff
make Spurck sore, and you won't get
another."

Carren considered Lennox carefully
as if he had never seen him before, then
without a word he turned and crossed
the room. Herb Martin had joined the
sheriff. Martin had lost control of himself again. "I know you Hollywood
people," he shouted. "For years, Roy
couldn't get a decent job in your pictures. So when you wanted to make a
lumber story, you got him to write to
me. But you threatened him. You
scared him so badly that he went up
into the hills to hide. Then you had him
tracked down and killed him."

Spurck's face showed plainly that he had no idea what was going on. Carren touched Martin's shoulder. "Lay off," he said.

Martin was sputtering. "But—"

"I said, lay off."

For a moment they faced each other, the big mill owner and the little gambler. It was the mill owner's eyes that dropped first. The sheriff hesitated, then turned away. Spurck came over to Lennox. His round, usually light eyes were almost black with anger.

didn't say anything. He placed the rod across the broad stone mantel, added his creel and turned around. "Tell me."

Lennox shrugged. "There isn't much to tell. A week after Roy Martin arranged with his brother for us to use the mill for pictures, he come rushing up here and told his brother that someone was going to kill him. That he had to hide.

"Herb put him up in the mountains

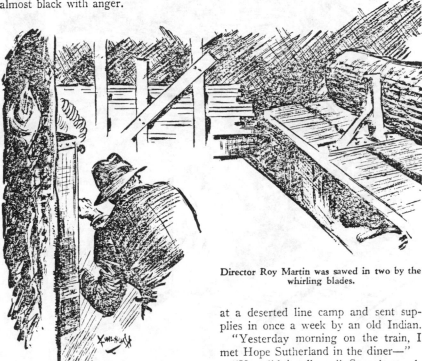

Director Roy Martin was sawed in two by the whirling blades.

"Bill, tell me one thing, is it that everyone has gone suddenly nuts, or are my ears playing screwy tricks on me?"

"Neither," Lennox told him in an undertone. "This is serious, Sol. Someone killed Roy Martin down at the mill, and the local law thinks that the murder goes back to Hollywood."

Spurck took a full breath, and then

at a deserted line camp and sent supplies in once a week by an old Indian.

"Yesterday morning on the train, I met Hope Sutherland in the diner—"

"You didn't tell me." Spurck sounded accusing.

Lennox was blunt. "It wasn't any of your business. She was coming up here to warn Roy Martin about something. She wanted me to get word to his brother that she'd meet Roy out on some road last night. I delivered the message and forgot the whole thing.

"It seems that Herb sent the message up the mountain by the Indian and the next thing they know, the watchman telephoned Herb at two thirty. He'd just found Roy, sawed in two."

Spurck caught his breath and his face paled. "Say that once more."

L ENNOX repeated himself. "The watchman," he added, "came up-town for a drink about twelve. The drink

you know it. The fishing was just an excuse. The trouble is that you have to have a fat finger in everything and you wouldn't trust me to straighten out this script."

knocked him out and he was out for a couple of hours. When he came to, he went back and found the corpse."

Spurck moaned a little. "And now, they are asking me questions, like may-be I was the sawman or something."

Lennox said: "I told you not to come."

"The fishing," said Spurck weakly.

"The fishing, hell." Lennox was sore. "You didn't come up here to fish and

Ordinarily Spurck would have flashed back, and they would have quarreled as they had for years, but at the moment his mind was too shocked by the method of Roy Martin's passing.

"Who killed him, Bill?" he said urgently.

Lennox' shrug was expressive. "For their money," he indicated the sheriff's men. "I did, or at least, I had something to do with it. Because I carried Hope

Sutherland's message to Herb, I'm in it somewhere. They've been questioning me for an hour. They're hunting the hills for Hope. As far as I'm concerned personally, Roy's death doesn't mean that." He snapped his long fingers. "The guy was a first class heel. He hasn't made a decent picture since the old days at Fort Lee. All he's done is snipe at other men's wives, and he was old enough so that he should have known better. He must have been better than sixty but he sure as the devil didn't look it."

Spurck said: "Hey, wait. I've got an idea. Jimmy North!"

Lennox seized his arm so tightly that Spurck cried out in protest. "Cut it," Bill said in an undertone, looking around quickly to see if the men at the other end of the big room had heard. "Jimmy's been through enough. Don't give those human bloodhounds any ideas."

Spurck was at once contrite. "I didn't mean nothing, Bill. Honest, I didn't think."

"I know." Lennox breathed easier, but an instant later he looked up and his mouth tightened—for Jimmy North, as if he were answering to his name, was coming down the broad stairs.

He saw Spurck and grinned. "I thought you were going fishing early. If you don't hurry, those trout will be taking their siesta."

Spurck opened his mouth, but he couldn't speak. It was as if his vocal cords were paralyzed. Lennox covered the pause by saying in a low voice: "There's been a little trouble, Jimmy. Roy Martin was murdered out at his brother's mill."

"Roy Martin." Jimmy North said the name slowly. "You mean the Hollywood Roy Martin?"

"Yes." Lennox was watching him closely without really meaning to. He saw North's face alter and said, urgently: "Get a grip on yourself. You look as if you'd seen a ghost."

"I've heard of one," North said slowly. "One that I've killed in my mind a hundred times. So that mill belonged to Roy's brother. I didn't know that."

Lennox couldn't be certain whether North was lying or not. It was entirely possible that the assistant cameraman might not have known. He cursed himself for assigning North to the picture. But as to that, it would have been difficult to get a crew together without having at least one member in it who had some grudge against the dead director. Roy Martin probably had been one of the most hated men in the film colony.

SPURCK caught Lennox' arm with his short fingers. "Bill, look—that girl!"

Lennox said: "What girl?" He said it absently. The morning had been hectic. Despite the murder, they had gone over the script with the director, the writer and the principals. Men died, but pictures still had to be made. Nor had Lennox confined himself to his own business. He was worried about Hope Sutherland. The search for her was almost state-wide.

All the neighboring counties had been warned by phone, every village and camp contacted and yet there was no trace of her or her rented car. Lennox feared that the same man who had struck down Martin, had finished off the girl, and that her car might be a twisted heap of metal at the bottom of one of the deep canyons which laced their way through this foothill country.

But he'd carried on his investigation separately from the sheriff. He had little faith in the law officer or his ability. He knew that he and Spurck were being watched, and that they might well be under arrest save for Carren's interference.

He was under no illusions in regard to the gambler. Carren was first a businessman, interested in the money which the movie players spent at his games. For that reason, he did not want them angered, but if it came to a real showdown, Lennox knew that they could not count on the man.

For that reason he had hunted up the mill watchman without consulting anyone. The watchman confirmed everything that the sheriff said save one detail. He claimed, and Lennox was not certain that he wasn't lying in an attempt to cover himself, that someone had called him at the mill, someone who claimed to be Herb Martin.

He said that the voice sounded strange, but he put it down to a bad connection. Martin had told him to come up to the North Star Club at once. The watchman had obeyed, but failing to find Martin at the club and being unable to reach his employer by telephone, he had taken a couple of drinks to ward off the spring cold. The next he remembered was awakening at two with a bad headache, going back to the mill and finding the body.

Lennox then questioned the bartender. His story was that the watchman was already tight when he came in. He phoned someone, the bartender did not know whom, then had not two, but four drinks and went to sleep at one of the empty poker tables.

After lunch Lennox managed to locate the old Indian who had carried the message to Roy Martin at the line camp. He learned exactly nothing, save that the message had been delivered and that Martin had appeared worried upon its receipt.

Spurck said again: "Look once, and tell me positively, did you ever see such a beautiful face?"

Lennox' thoughts, which had been a million miles away from the town's square, snapped back to the present and he turned. The girl was beautiful. There could be no argument on that score.

There was a soft, haunting quality about the face as if she had known great suffering, suffering which she was too timid to reveal.

She came toward them along the almost deserted walk, her head bent a little, her eyes never lifting from the sidewalk. Before Lennox realized what he was going to do, Spurck had stepped sideways so that his short bulk completely blocked the woman's path.

One pudgy hand went up to the brim of his Robin Hood cap, and as he raised the hand, the diamond on his finger caught the afternoon sun and threw its rays in blue refracted glory across the square.

The girl stopped. She could have done nothing else unless she had moved around where Lennox stood and stepped into the street. Spurck's body completely blocked the sidewalk between Lennox and the building.

The girl looked up, and she looked scared. Her eyes were almost purple. Lennox had never seen anything so startling in his life. Hardened as he was to beauty, after years of picture making, there was something about her face which made him think of an angel, a frightened angel.

She opened her mouth and her teeth were as white as pearls and just as regular. But she didn't say anything. Her

NO FINER DRINK... *At home or on the go*

lips moved, but no sound came out.

Even Spurck, who as a general thing was not sensitive to other people's feelings, felt that something was wrong and he got concerned.

"Look, miss. You got it wrong, see. I am no low-life which is trying to get smart with nice girls. A wife I have got for thirty-five years without one fight, hardly." He was getting more excited and as his excitement grew, his scrambling of words increased.

Lennox took a hand. He said: "There's nothing to worry about. Mr. Spurck makes pictures, movies, you know. He was struck by your beauty."

"That's it," said Spurck. "And I'm telling you that there is no malarkey when I say that in twenty-five years I have not seen such a face like yours. We got a company shooting here, now. All I'm asking is that you get in a car and ride out to where they are working. I would like to see your picture, y'understand."

SOMETHING about Spurck seemed to have reassured the girl and she found her voice. "Please, I can't stand talking to you. It isn't allowed. Let me pass."

But Spurck was not used to having anyone refuse his requests. He meant nothing. He was merely carried away by the enthusiasm which had made him one of the world's leading producers.

"It's that you don't understand," he explained with the patience of a teacher, talking to a backward child. "Fame and fortune is what I am offering you, like Joan Bennett and Hedy LaMarr—only, honest, for my money, you are better looking."

A spark of interest glowed in her oddly colored eyes and a little tension went out of her lithe body. "You really mean it?" There was wonder in her voice. "You really would make me an actress?"

"If the test comes out," Spurck's habitual caution reasserted itself, "but being an actress is hard work and not all peaches with cream, you understand.

I—" He stopped, and the unlighted cigar which he had just drawn from his pocket, fell from his suddenly lax fingers.

Joe Carren had appeared from one of the stores behind them and stepped forward. Later, Lennox realized that the man's arrival was no accident. He had seen them talking to the girl, made his way down the alley and through the store.

"Karma" he said in his soft, unhurried voice. "Go home."

Spurck had recovered himself. "Now wait, a business proposition was all that I was offering—"

"Go home," said Carren, and the girl turned and fled. The gambler put his eyes upon Spurck's face, and there was something in the expression that dried up the words forming in the producer's throat.

"You'd be wise," said Carren, "to concentrate on your picture and finish it as soon as possible." He turned on his heel and vanished into the store from which he had come.

Spurck let out his pent-up breath slowly. "Honest, did you see how he looked at me, Bill, like a snake looking at a bird which it is about to eat." He shuddered, found a red and blue handkerchief somewhere in the pockets of his fishing coat and wiped the beaded perspiration from his forehead.

Lennox had not spoken, but he caught movement from the corner of his eye and turning, saw Herb Martin coming across the street from the direction of the courthouse. "More trouble," Lennox muttered under his breath. "Get set, Sol." But he was wrong, for when Martin saw them, his long, weathered face broke a little into a strained smile and he altered his course slightly so that he would come up to the curb where they were standing.

"Hello, Mr. Lennox. I just wanted to tell you that I'm sorry that I acted like a damn fool this morning, but after finding Roy, I went a little screwy."

Surprise held Lennox silent for an instant, then he recovered.

"That's O.K. I understand."

But he didn't understand the change in the man's attitude until Martin said: "Since the sheriff made the arrest, I see how very foolish I acted."

"Arrest?" Spurck and Lennox made a chorus. "Who'd they arrest?"

"A man named North," Martin explained. "A cameraman with your company. It seems that Roy was mixed up with his wife or something."

Before Lennox could stop him, Spurck burst out: "Who told on Jimmy?"

Martin turned to look at Spurck, and some of the friendliness went out of his eyes leaving them bleak and chill. "A newspaperman," he said. "Several of them flew up from Hollywood. They got in an hour ago. This Greer told the sheriff the whole story." He hesitated for a moment, then turned on his heel and went on down the street.

Spurck sputtered under his breath. "That Greer, he always was a low-lifer. Come on, Bill, we can't leave Jimmy stuck in that jail."

Lennox said: "Wait. We don't want to go over there while all the reporters are at the courthouse. We'll find the sheriff later. Let's go down to the Lodge and clean up. We can't do anything now. In fact, we can't do much until we find out what happened to Hope Sutherland."

Spurck didn't want to go. When aroused, he believed in action, and he wanted action now. But Lennox did not give him a chance for argument. He turned and started down the street toward the sprawling log building.

THE restaurant was full when they entered and found seats at a rear booth. The counter was crowded with lumbermen and truckmen, but here and there in the crowd were groups of newspapermen from Los Angeles. Several called their greetings as Lennox followed Spurck's short figure toward the booth, but he ignored them. He didn't want to discuss the murder with anyone at the moment and he was glad to reach the semi-privacy of the booth.

Spurck was looking curiously at the pressed metal panels which formed the walls. "An antique, I would call this," he suggested as he unfolded his napkin.

Lennox said: "Built in '58. See the holes beside the kitchen door? Some punk put them there with a gun in the old days."

Spurck's eyes got round. "A tough place it must have been."

"Still is." Lennox gave his order. When the waitress had gone he continued. "You're O.K. in these mountain towns as long as you mind your own business. Try to get tough and—" He stopped for above the edge of the booth he had seen Yarcovitch come in the restaurant, followed by Roscoe.

Spurck had his back to the door. He did not know that Yarcovitch was within five hundred miles of Astoria until the hairless man paused beside the table. "Good evening. Seats, there are too few. Roscoe and I, we will join you." Without further word, he squeezed his small form in at Lennox' side.

Spurck looked as if he had seen an unwelcome ghost. He opened his mouth to protest, but Roscoe, who was always a man of action rather than words, crammed himself into the booth at Spurck's side.

Sol sputtered. "Such a world it is coming to, that a decent man cannot longer eat his dinner in peace without lice."

Roscoe growled. "Button the lip, fat boy, or I'll lace it shut for you."

The hairless man said: "Now Roscoe. Mr. Spurck does not mean anything. Mr. Spurck and I are the oldest of friends."

Spurck was bitter. "Friends we never were. Can a man help it if in a busy life, mice and rats run across his path? Please, Bill, my appetite, it is all gone. Shall we leave before we catch germs or even an epidemic?"

Yarcovitch said: "Sit still." His tone and manner had both changed. "No time

I have to waste with you." He turned to Lennox, reaching under his coat as he did so, and producing a gold-bond billfold. From this he extracted ten hundred-dollar bills.

"For Jimmy North's defense. A lawyer he needs, a local one. With a mountain jury, an outsider would lose before he began."

Lennox looked at the money in his hand, then lifted his eyes to meet the money lender's stare.

He said slowly: "Does this mean that you killed Roy Martin and don't want an innocent man . . . ?"

"It means," said Yarcovitch, "I want Jimmy North saved. A dead man pays no interest. Jimmy North owes me money. Thank you, pal. Manny Yarcovitch does not forget favors."

He rose and motioned to his bodyguard to follow.

Spurck's breath made gusty sound between his lips.

"*Koosh!*" he said. "Honest, I never saw such nerve. That *schnorrer* would cut a turnip for blood which wasn't there."

Lennox' eyes were still following the departing money lender. "I didn't know that you knew him."

"Knew him? Does one brag about knowing a snake? Honest, Bill, a hundred thousand he could sue me for what I am thinking at the moment. Certain, I know him. Everyone who has been in this business for twenty years, knows him. In every pie, he has a finger, and his money is everywhere. But even more he wants. Throw that away. Don't touch it."

Lennox said: "No harm in trying to help Jimmy with it. Besides, no sane man hunts trouble with Manny—if he can help it."

Spurck shivered a little. "You are right," he admitted. "And that gunman which sat beside me—I don't like him either. Gooseflesh I have from him being so close. I couldn't eat now for anything. Come on. Let us leave while I can still walk."

CHAPTER FOUR

No-Limit Game

THE courthouse h a d been a fine building in 1860. It wasn't now. They mounted the steps and went along wooden halls which were scuffed and worn from the passage of countless feet. Dust filled the air. Dust which had been gathering for a long time.

The sheriff was at his desk in the center of the cluttered office. He wasn't glad to see them and he said so, bluntly. "You can't talk to North, and that's final."

Lennox tried to argue. The sheriff was unerring in his shot toward the battered brass cuspidor. There was something insulting in the way he spat. "Look," he said. "You guys are big shots, down below, but here you're just another city guy getting out of line. Now, if you don't mind. I'm busy."

Outside on the worn steps Spurck said: "You didn't tell him about Yarcovitch."

Lennox asked: "What was I supposed to tell—that I don't like Manny?"

"So, he's up here for no good. If you ask me, it was him that Roy Martin was running away from when he hid out in the mountains."

Lennox had been thinking the same thing and he nodded. Spurck was pleased. "So then, Manny and that hoodlum catch Roy in the mill and saw him up, right?"

Lennox said: "We can't prove it. Remember, Sol, this is a real murder case, not a movie script. In life, you have to prove that a man's guilty of a crime—you can't get him to confess at the right moment."

"Confessions are for cops," said Spurck. "Honest, the way I feel, we should scrap the picture and go home. Under a montage of murder it is buried, you understand."

Lennox did not answer. Instead he led the way across the street to the Timber Club. "Sheldon usually comes in here for an evening drink," he explained, holding open the swinging door. "They tell me that Sheldon is the best lawyer in the county. He used to be a state senator. I met him once in Hollywood."

Spurck did not appear to hear. He was looking around at the gambling tables against the wall. "Open, they run it."

Lennox shrugged. "They're realists up here. They know that the only law is the kind they can enforce. If they closed these games, the boys would go over the hill to Reno and take most of the town money with them. Joe Carren has a good thing of it."

Spurck was interested. "The little guy who wouldn't let me talk to that girl?"

Lennox nodded. "There he is now."

Spurck turned around as Carren came through the door. He gave them the barest of nods and moved on toward the rear room where he disappeared. "Probably a big game in there," Lennox muttered under his breath. "Don't get in, Sol. These boys are good, even better than you."

Spurck showed no intention of joining the game. "They play a lot," he suggested idly.

"Half the night."

"I think I go out for some air," he decided, and moved toward the door.

Lennox was about to protest, but at that moment the lawyer entered the room and Lennox motioned him toward the bar. They shook hands, gave their orders and Lennox said in an undertone: "I suppose that you heard that the sheriff arrested one of my men for the Martin murder. I want you to represent him."

Sheldon was tall and lean. He had dark hair which was painfully straight, high cheek bones and a sallow face which spoke plainly of Indian blood. His voice was slightly hoarse and he did not waste words. "Sorry."

Lennox' mouth tightened. "There's a thousand dollars, more if needed."

"It's not money," said Sheldon. "I represent the Martin interests. It wouldn't look right. Try Judge Cline."

Lennox said: "You mean Herb Martin's interests?"

Sheldon took his brandy neat. He touched his thin lips with a handkerchief and returned it to his breast pocket. "They're Herb's now I suppose. Roy owned everything until he died."

Lennox was not easily surprised, but he was surprised now. "Why, hell, Roy Martin hasn't made enough money out of pictures in the last dozen years to have bought one tree. If it hadn't been for his women, he'd have starved."

The lawyer shrugged. "Not as long as he controlled a couple of hundred thousand acres of timber and three mills." He hesitated as if intending to say something else, changed his mind and with a nod, moved toward the door of the rear room. He vanished through it, leaving Lennox to stare after him.

For a full minute, Lennox remained on the bar stool. Then he rose and crossing to the entrance stepped out onto the street, expecting to find Spurck waiting for him.

The sidewalk was fairly filled with people, but the producer's squat form was not in sight. Lennox frowned his annoyance. Had Spurck circled down the alley which ran beside the building and slipped into the rear of the saloon by the side door? The little man prided himself on his ability to play cards and the thought of a no-limit game might pull him.

Lennox took a step backward, then seeing the town cabman loitering beside the wall he turned on impulse and asked: "You remember the man with me, the one in the hunting clothes—did you see where he went?"

THE cabman spat into the gutter. "Yeah. He asked me where the girl Karma lives. I offered to take him there, but he said that he'd walk." The man spat again. "Joe Carren better not catch your friend fooling around her. He'll get rough."

Lennox was thinking the same thing. "You can take me there," he said, and moved toward the taxi.

It was a Buick, and it wasn't new. The driver had some difficulty getting the engine started. He made the circuit of the courthouse square and pulled up before a small white house only a block from their starting point.

Lennox got out, told him to wait and went up the short walk. There was a light burning inside, but the blinds were drawn. He swore softly to himself as he punched the bell, his anger at Spurck mounting. If it were Joe Carren on the porch instead of him, the producer would be in a bad way.

He did not doubt Spurck's motives. He knew that the producer had come here for one purpose and one only, because he saw in the girl the possibility of a new screen personality. But others would not be so charitable in their judgment.

Inside there was the scrape of a chair followed by strained silence. Lennox could not help a grin. He could picture Spurck and the girl, frozen with fear by the sound of the bell.

He raised his voice, calling against the door: "Sol. Sol. It's me."

Sound came to life within the house. Someone was unlocking the door and he had a view of the girl's face. It was very white and her eyes were deep purple. Spurck had come to the living-room door and he was puffing a little as he always did when he was excited.

"Bill, don't ever do that again. A year I have lost from my life, or maybe two."

Lennox said, sharply: "This was a damn fool trick. You know how Carren acted this afternoon."

Spurck pouted like a misunderstood child. "But Bill, yourself, you said that almost all night they will play poker."

Lennox said, shortly: "I didn't guarantee anything. Come on, let's get out of here."

Spurck said: "Now, Bill, you gotta wait, see. This is very important, don't you understand?"

"Frankly," said Lennox, "I don't. We're in trouble enough without getting the town's leading hot-shot down on our necks."

"Is it," said Spurck in an unbelieving tone, "that you are afraid?"

"It is," Lennox told him. "If you want to know, I'm scared as hell."

Spurck's mouth opened to object, but his natural honesty stopped him. "Me too," he said somewhat shame-facedly. "But, Bill, there are times, when one cannot let fear grab the upper hand. This girl, she is beautiful. She wants to be an actress, and maybe she might be great."

"And maybe we might be dead." Lennox seized his arm, and almost dragged him to the door.

The girl had not spoken. Lennox turned to look at her, and suddenly he knew that he was acting like a heel. Her eyes were dark, purple pools of hopelessness. The hands which she held rigidly at her sides were little fists, the knuckles showing white through the warm skin.

"I'm sorry," he said. He wasn't exactly certain what he meant, but she seemed to understand.

"It's all right." Her voice was low and steady, but there was hopelessness in it. "Don't worry. You couldn't do anything else. The cards fell out of the deck wrong."

He would have stopped then. He was no hero, but he wasn't hardboiled either. Down deep, underneath, he was a sucker for anyone in trouble. It hurt him to see her standing there, and there was a lump in his throat. "I—we—" but she gave him no chance to say what was in his mind for already she was closing the door.

"Never," Spurck told him, "did I think to see the day when two men walk out and leave a girl like that with trouble."

Lennox was angry. He felt that he

was being put in the wrong through no fault of his. "Now look. What would Rose say if I let you get shot up for trying to help a gambler's wife?"

"Mama would understand." Spurck was confident. "Besides, that girl ain't Carren's wife. No man's wife is she."

"His sister then."

"Nor sister," said Spurck. "Honest, Bill, like a good screen play, her life reads. Never has she known who she is. Carren's mother raised her up like a daughter, but Carren, he does not look at her like a sister, you understand."

Lennox said: "I'm afraid that you've been kidded, pal. The girl probably has been reading too many stories."

Spurck was insulted. "Is it that you think I am too dumb to know when the truth is not being told? Honest, Bill, sometimes you would think I was a child in which you have no faith." He lapsed into hurt silence as they reached the cab and made no objection when Lennox told the driver to take them to the Lodge.

HERE was a piece of white paper lying in the exact center of the bureau top. Lennox saw it as soon as he switched on the room light. He'd made Spurck promise that he would not try and recontact the girl and had had to spend an hour in the producer's room, learning that he still could not play gin-rummy.

He shut the door, crossed to the bureau and stared down at the paper, realizing that it was a note, addressed to him, written on the Lodge stationery. He read it without picking it up.

Lennox:
Be smart. Shoot your picture, then get out of here. You'll only cause trouble by butting into something which is none of your business.

The note was printed crudely with a soft pencil, and it was not signed. He reread it slowly, then undressed and got into bed, but he did not sleep. He lay there in the darkness, listening to the street noise gradually die, and tried to think of some means of getting Spurck out of town. He was not particularly worried about himself. Self-worry had never been one of his characteristics.

He had no idea of how long he had been in bed. Nor had he heard any noise, but he was suddenly conscious that the hall door was moving inward.

For an instant he thought that someone must have a key, then he remembered in the surprise of finding the note, he had forgotten to lock the door.

He threw back the covers and an instant later was standing shivering beside the bed. There was a gun in his grip, but the grip was in the closet, and there was no time to reach it. He moved silently toward the opening door and as the shadow of the intruder moved into the room, he shot out one arm and locked it around the newcomer's neck. Not until he had his hold, did he realize that his uninvited visitor was a woman.

She did not scream, but she uttered a little stifled gasp which was all terror. Lennox swung her around so that the moonlight, coming in through the window, fell directly on her face. Then his grip was relaxed as relief surged through him. It was Hope Sutherland.

"Hope, where have you been?"

She was shaking, and she kept hold of his arm as if to assure herself that she was not alone. "It's Yarcovitch. The devil must have suspected that I'd try and come into town to see you." She drew a deep lungful of air to steady herself. "I heard Roy Martin was killed last night. It was terrible."

"Heard . . . what are you talking about? Didn't you meet him as you planned?"

She nodded. "We met. We talked for a couple of hours, driving around in my car. Then he said that he had an appointment to meet someone at the mill at one. I drove him to the footbridge which crosses the river just above the mill. I waited there. He was supposed to come back. I heard the mill machinery start suddenly, heard screams." She broke off, shuddering. "I knew that he was dead. I didn't know what to do. I drove up into the mountains over an old logging road. I've been there all day."

Lennox said: "Get a grip on yourself. Everything is all right now."

"No," she said. "It's too late. Everything will never be all right again. You do something wrong, Bill, and you think that you can live it down. You can't. It comes back to haunt you in your old age."

"You're not old," he said.

"I feel a million years." She shivered again. "If you feel that old, you shouldn't be afraid to die. But I am afraid. I'm terribly afraid."

She was so near hysteria that one wrong word would have acted as a switch. But he did not say that word. Instead he told her: "You're O.K. now. Yarcovitch isn't going to close in on you while I'm here. Do you want to tell me what this is all about?"

She nodded. "That's what I want to do, Bill, to tell someone. I've got to talk. I've got to."

He waited patiently for her to begin and after a full minute she said: "It goes back almost thirty years. It started there, I mean. I was in pictures even then. You didn't realize that, did you, Bill?

"We had a lot of fun. It wasn't a business then. It was a kind of game. Everyone knew everyone else and two reels made a long picture.

"There was another girl about my age. Her name was Vincent. You probably never heard of her, but she might have been a great actress had she lived. She was one of the most beautiful people that I've ever seen, and her eyes were her most striking feature. They were actually purple."

Lennox stiffened. "Say that again."

"Say what?"

"Nothing," he told her. "Go on."

"Well," she said. "There was a funny little man who used to hang around the lot. It was different in those days. Anyone who wanted to could go where they pleased, anywhere in the studio. As likely as not, a visitor would be crowded in as an extra. The scenarios weren't much either. I've got a couple of copies of the old ones we used. The whole company used to take a hand at helping to rewrite them as we went along."

"This funny little man?"

"Yes," she said. "His name was Yarcovitch. He was crazy about Helen, and she and I used to let him take us to dinner. He always had money, even then, and he would always loan it to anyone. We laughed about him, when he wasn't around and I never dreamed that Helen would marry him."

"She married Manny?" Lennox' surprise crept into his voice.

HOPE SUTHERLAND nodded. "She married him, and he loaded her with jewels. I suppose that that was the only way he knew to prove his love. I didn't learn until afterward that the reason Helen married him was because she and Roy Martin had had a fight. She was in love with Roy, and her marriage didn't make any difference. Roy and she continued to see each other. I don't mean that there was anything improper. I don't know anything about that.

"At any rate, after her baby was born, she didn't seem to gain back her strength. In fact she seemed to be growing worse and after consulting a doctor, she began to suspect that she was being slowly poisoned. Roy Martin finally persuaded her to leave her husband, taking her baby and her jewels with her. I helped her get away. I took charge and we all came out to the coast. Both Roy and I went to work at the old Edendale studios, after that we worked on the old Inch lot, and then for Triangle.

"But Helen died. As she was dying, she asked us to look after her daughter. We promised. She told us to sell her jewels to provide for the little girl.

"But there was no place that either Roy or I could care for the child so he sent her up to live with some friends of his in the mountains. She died in less than two years."

Lennox caught his breath. "You say that she died?"

Hope Sutherland nodded. "She died, and then I did something that I've regretted ever since. I have no excuse, save that I hated Manny Yarcovitch. He poisoned his wife, I know it. He suspected that she was seeing Roy Martin, and he was terribly jealous. I couldn't bear for him to have the money which had come from the sale of Helen's jewels. Things were bad in the picture business. It was during the last war and no one was working much. I took the three thousand dollars that was half of the money, Roy took the other half. Roy was murdered last night for taking it. I'll be killed if Manny Yarcovitch catches up with me."

"Three thousand," said Lennox, slowly. "That doesn't seem to be very much. Are you sure that that is all the jewels brought?"

She looked up in surprise. "Why yes, at least that's what Roy said."

Lennox told her: "It's strange that Yarcovitch waited all these years to strike."

"He didn't," she said. "He's been blackmailing Roy for years, taking a few dollars each time. Roy's luck hasn't been good for a long time, so Manny couldn't get very much. But a month ago Roy arranged for Spurck to shoot this picture up at Astoria. There was a writeup in all the columns. Roy did it in the hopes of getting to direct your new Southern picture, but it was a mistake, for Yarcovitch is like a bloodhound. He began making inquiries, and he found out that Roy really owned a lot of property up here.

"A friend of mine knows a girl in Yarcovitch's office. She dropped a remark about what Manny was doing. I warned Roy and he got out of town. I

stayed to learn all that I could and then came up on the same train with you. I warned Roy to get out of the country, but it's too late. Manny had his revenge, last night, at the mill."

"Then you think that Yarcovitch killed him?"

She looked her amazement. "Who else?" She shivered. "You don't know that Shylock. He's hated Roy for years. Last night, he got his pound of flesh."

"More than a pound," said Lennox, thinking of the mill. It was all that he could do to keep from shivering. Her fear was infectious. "Listen, I'm going to take you down to Spurck's rooms. If you're right, and Manny followed you here, the first place he'll look is this room." He moved quickly across the room, cut the light and opening the door, peered out into the dark hall.

Spurck's suite was at the end. Spurck thought he was roughing it in sitting-room, bedroom and bath—the best the Lodge afforded.

Nothing moved in the dark hall, and after an instant of listening, Lennox took the actress down to the producer's suite.

In short, sharp sentences, he told Spurck that the actress was in danger.

The production chief got excited. "Under the bed I will hide her, and if that low-life tries to get in, I will fix him, right on the noodle." He peered around near-sightedly for a weapon, saw a stick of wood on the hearth and caught it up.

Even with it in his hand, he did not look awe-inspiring. His short figure was draped in an expensive woolen robe which he wore over widely striped silk pajamas, but his eye glittered with resolve, and Lennox knew that at least the producer would try.

"Lock the door," he said, "and don't open it for anyone." He went hurriedly back down the hall and into his own room. He didn't know exactly what to do. Waiting was hard, but he forced himself to wait, slipping back into bed. But his every sense was alert as he lay there, listening. Finally he could stand it no longer. He rose and began to dress.

CHAPTER FIVE

Your Move, Mr. Lennox

E HAD almost finished knotting his tie when he heard a faint sound and glancing into the mirror, saw that the hall door had been p u s h e d wide. Roscoe stood in the entrance, looking like the angel of death, with his hands hidden in his bulging coat pockets and the snap-brim of his hat pulled well down to shade his eyes.

Lennox had been waiting for something like this. He had laid his gun on the bureau top, but he had expected more warning. His hand moved out now, sheltered by his body, but Roscoe must have seen the movement in the mirror.

"Don't," he said. "Turn around and walk over to the wall—careful."

Lennox obeyed. There was nothing else that he could do. He saw Roscoe step into the room, saw Yarcovitch follow. The overcoat was as much too big as the money lender's suit had been. It gave the effect of a walking circus tent as he advanced until only a few yards separated him from Lennox.

"Where's Hope Sutherland?"

Lennox said: "You asked me that once before. I still don't know."

"That time was different," said Manny Yarcovitch. "That time I believed you. Now, her car's in the street. Outside we wait for her to come back. She doesn't, and it is cold, waiting."

Lennox said: "That still doesn't mean that I know where she is."

Yarcovitch said: "A man wants to lie, first learns how. She comes in, and at once, almost, your light goes on. Not another light is there in the whole building. Does that make sense?"

Lennox did not answer. Roscoe said: "Let me." He stepped forward, bringing both hands out of his pockets. His right was empty. His left held a gun. He moved with incredible swiftness. His right shot out, grabbed Lennox' wrist, swung the trouble-shooter around and twisted the arm up between his shoulders.

The man's strength was enormous. Lennox realized what was coming, and tried to free himself. He failed. Sharp pain shot up through his arm to paralyze the shoulder muscles, and an involuntary cry escaped his lips.

"Enough," said Yarcovitch, and the gun guard released his hold and Lennox straightened, his arm useless for the moment. "Now," Yarcovitch told him. "You realize we mean business. Where's Hope?"

"So you can kill her as you killed Roy?"

The money lender seemed surprised. His pinched features tightened. "Had I wanted Roy Martin should be dead, I could have killed him years ago. Money, he took from me. My wife and child, he stole. They are dead, and nothing can now change that. But when I found that all these years when he has played so poor, he was really very rich, it was too much to stand. I came up here to make him give back what was mine. He's dead, and collecting debts from dead men is not easy. I need Hope Sutherland, to tell the truth, to tell how they stole jewels belonging to my wife."

"Jewels worth six thousand," Lennox said.

"Six!" Manny Yarcovitch for a moment had lost the power of speech. "Six, did you say—hah! Those jewels were worth ten, no, fifteen times that, and I want every dollar of it, every dime."

Lennox did not bother to hide his contempt. "Listen, you won't believe me, but Hope Sutherland got only three thousand dollars of that money. Martin must have kept the rest."

The hairless man said: "Of that rat, I would believe anything. Didn't he give my wife poison in small doses until she died?"

"Why didn't you kill him then?"

Yarcovitch said, slowly: "For such a man, death is too quick. He loved money, so for years I took money from him. But he was smarter than I." The money lender's voice rose with feeling. "He fooled me, but his brother should not get the mills and the forests which with my money were bought. I want Hope Sutherland. I want to make her go with me to see this Herb Martin. I want she should tell how she and Roy were thieves. Then maybe this brother will give me justice. Otherwise, I take them all into court."

Lennox almost believed the little man, but he could not be certain. He did not dare let Hope Sutherland fall into Yarcovitch's hand. He said: "Who killed Roy?"

Yarcovitch said: "That man should have a medal. Maybe it was the brother. Maybe Roy Martin was scared. Maybe he came up here to give me back what is mine. Maybe this brother did not want to lose the mills and the forests by this time, so he killed Roy. Me, I do not know."

Lennox said: "You've got something there. Let me talk to Herb. Let me see if I can't get your property back for you. Then you can let Hope Sutherland alone."

The hairless man hesitated. Roscoe said: "Don't trust him, boss. I'll make him tell where the dame is." He grinned at Lennox hopefully.

Yarcovitch decided. "A chance I will take, but if any foolishness you try, Roscoe will tend to you."

IT WAS with certain misgivings that Lennox turned into the Timber Club. Aside from two men at the bar, the place was empty. The bartender looked him over carefully as he asked for Carren. Finally he went to the door of the rear room, opened it, and then motioned Lennox to follow.

Cards littered the cloth top of a round table which occupied the center of the room. The air was heavy with stale smoke, but aside from the small gambler, the place was empty, the other players were gone.

Carren said: "What brings you out so late?"

Lennox told him: "I want to see Herb Martin, here. I want to straighten out this murder. Jimmy North did not kill Roy, and everyone but the sheriff knows it."

Carren's dark eyes were unreadable with thought. "Who did?"

Lennox shrugged. "Roy Martin came up here, scared. Years ago he stole a lot of money from a man. That money was put into mills and timber tracts. To save his life, Roy was ready to give them back. I figure that Herb wasn't."

"You think that Herb killed Roy?"

Lennox said: "He had a lot to gain."

"And why should I help you?" The gambler was direct.

"Because," said Lennox. "It's good business. The movie company drops plenty at your games. You'd like to see another unit come back to Astoria. They won't if I tell them not to."

Carren considered this carefully, then without a word he turned to the wall phone. Lennox heard him talking to Martin. He saw him hang up. Neither of them said anything. Lennox sat down at the table, gathered up the loose cards, shuffled them and dealt two hands of stud.

Carren played his without sitting down. He lost five dollars and dealt in turn. It was twenty minutes before Herb Martin came through the rear door. He stopped, just inside, his eyes narrowing when he saw Lennox. "What's the idea? Why'd you send for me?"

"Lennox wants to talk to you." Carren threw down his cards and wandered away from the table as if this was none of his affair. The door behind Martin opened and Roscoe came in, trailed by Yarcovitch.

Lennox looked at the hairless man angrily. "You promised to keep out of the play, to let me handle things."

Yarcovitch gave him a thin-lipped

smile. "My mind, it changed. I think maybe that it is better that I am here."

Roscoe had his gun out. Roscoe put his back to the wall beside the door so that he could cover the room. "Search them, boss."

Yarcovitch got a gun from Martin, nothing from either Carren or Lennox. "Now," said the hairless man, stepping back, "It is your move, Mr. Lennox."

Bill said, "We might as well sit down," and took a chair at the table. Martin hesitated, then followed suit. Carren obeyed silently, so did Yarcovitch. The little money lender's eyes glittered under the hairless brows.

Lennox took a deep breath. "Herb," he said, addressing Martin, "your brother stole some jewels about twenty-five years ago. He stole them from Manny Yarcovitch, the little man sitting opposite you. Manny thinks that all the timber lands and mills which your brother owned were bought with the money that came from selling those jewels."

Martin stirred. "You're crazy. The property was in Roy's name, but we both worked to get it, worked hard."

Lennox said: "Maybe. I'm afraid that you're going to have to prove it. But that isn't what concerns us most at the moment. It's murder that concerns us most. Roy was scared when he left Hollywood, so scared that he would have been willing to sell out everything and turn the money over to Yarcovitch to save his life. He was murdered before he could sell the property. You're the man who gained directly by his death.

"I talked to the mill watchman today. He was lured away from his post by a phone call, and fed a mickey when he came up here, supposedly to meet you. Now, you sent the Indian up to get your brother so that Roy could meet Hope Sutherland. You might have added that you'd meet him at the mill at one and—"

"You're crazy." Herb Martin had shoved back his chair. "I see it all now. You're framing me for Roy's death. I

didn't kill him. But I'll tell you who did, and why." He jerked suddenly erect, his hand still hidden by the table's edge.

There was a sharp, whip-like report. For an instant Herb Martin stood motionless, then he fell forward, across the table, carrying it with him to the floor.

Lennox had dived forward and grabbed Carren's wrist. He wrenched it sideways and a little gun jumped from the gambler's fingers, made an arch in the air, and lit on the worn flooring a dozen feet away.

Roscoe was coming forward on stiff legs. "What the hell? What the hell?"

Lennox said: "Carren had a sleeve gun."

The little gambler was unmoved. "You should thank me. I saved all our lives."

"What do yuh mean?" Roscoe was bristling. "That guy wasn't armed."

"That's what you think," Carren told him. "Look under the poker table. Martin was sitting in the dealer's chair. Sometimes the dealer needs a gun in a hurry."

Lennox turned over the broken table and they stared at the holster which was fastened beneath it.

Roscoe looked at the big gun which slid from its place and dropped to the floor. "What a country!"

ENNOX had stooped and r e c o v e r e d the sleeve gun. It was no longer than his index finger. It had two barrels and a tiny pearl handle. He'd seen ones like it in museums.

"Now," said Carren, "do you realize what I did?"

Lennox nodded. "Yes. Herb Martin didn't kill his brother. You did. And you shot Herb just now to close his mouth."

The gambler's eyes burned like two live coals. "You are crazy."

"No," said Lennox, and then raised

his voice. "Karma, you can come in now."

The rear door was pushed open slowly. The girl stood there in the entrance, looking around uncertainly. Fear was deep in the oddly colored eyes, fear was in every line of her slender body. Looking at her, Lennox had a momentary doubt. From her appearance, she seemed not more than a young girl, but she must be almost thirty if he was right.

Carren's breath made a whistling sound through his tight lips, but the effect on Yarcovitch was the more startling. He was staring at the girl as if he had suddenly met a ghost.

"Helen," he said, as if he were being strangled. "Helen."

"No," said Lennox. "Your daughter Karma." He had never taken his eyes from Carren, and the little sleeve gun was in his hand.

Carren turned slowly and he tried to smile. "You're wrong, Lennox, all wrong."

"No," Lennox told him. "I'm right, Carren. Those eyes mark her as Manny's daughter. Roy Martin didn't come up here to sell his mills and timber land. He knew that the thing which Manny Yarcovitch wanted more than anything else was to have his daughter, the daughter that Roy Martin had claimed was dead. He thought that by taking the girl back to Hollywood, he would be allowed to keep the property.

"But he figured without you, Joe. The girl had been raised by your mother, and although she wouldn't marry you, you'd supported her. You got scared when Spurck spoke to her."

Carren's smile was faint. "You can prove nothing, Lennox." He had recovered his complete control.

"You're wrong, Joe. You forget that Hope Sutherland drove Roy to the mill. What you don't know is that she followed him across the foot-bridge, and saw his murderer."

Joe Carren's face drained of all expression. "I—" He stopped, for the rear door had burst open and Spurck, trailed by Hope Sutherland, dashed into the room.

"Hands up." Spurck had a gun, and he was excited. Then he realized that the situation seemed well in hand and he stopped. "Bill, you O.K.?"

"Sure," said Lennox. "I told you to stay in your room."

Spurck looked hurt. "I should stay safe when you are going to death or worse. In the Lodge office, I find this gun and—"

But Lennox was not listening. "Well, Joe?" He was looking at the small gambler.

Carren shrugged. "You win. I'll call the sheriff for you." He turned and moved toward the wall phone.

He had taken less than a dozen steps when a voice said: "Drop the guns."

Carren was out of the line of fire. He laughed. "That's Baldy," he said, referring to the bartender. "He's at the lookout post."

Roscoe ignored the order. He had raised his heavy revolver, looking for someone to shoot.

Above their heads a shotgun roared, smoke curled out of an aperture in the partition. The slugs caught Roscoe directly in the chest with terrible force. He fell, and the unseen bartender said: "There's another barrel, gents. Who's next?"

Both Lennox and Spurck had dropped their guns. Yarcovitch had not moved since his daughter had entered the room. He moved now, placing his frail body between her and the unseen bartender.

Carren laughed. He stooped, caught up Spurck's fallen gun. "They don't want any more. You can come down from your perch, Baldy."

They heard sounds from the other room as the bartender climbed down from the peek hole through which he had fired. Lennox said, huskily: "You haven't a chance, Carren."

"Haven't I?" The gambler was cool. "This is my country, Lennox. I'll say that Herb Martin learned that Yarcovitch killed his brother. They had a gun fight in here—you, Spurck, and the actress happened to get in the middle."

"And the girl, Karma."

He looked toward her, and his expression was soft. "I can handle her."

Spurck was stepping sideways, an expression of intense concentration on his moonlike face. Lennox wanted to shout at him to stand, but the producer kept moving, and Carren saw the movement from the corner of his eye. He swung, and Lennox heard the click as Carren squeezed the trigger. He expected a shot which did not come.

Spurck let go a haymaker which caught the smaller man along the side of the head. Carren did not go down. He backed away, still squeezing the trigger, but he backed toward Lennox.

Bill jumped forward. His fist crashed into the man's neck, just below the ear, with such force that Carren was knocked over like a falling tenpin. Lennox did not even look toward the fallen gambler. He pivoted and jumped toward the door which led inward from the saloon. Even as he reached it, the bartender was opening the door. Lennox reached around the jamb, grasped the shotgun barrel and wrenched it from the astonished Baldy's grasp. He used it as a club, saw the stock splinter against the bartender's head, and turned back, still wondering why Spurck's chest was not filled with holes from Carren's gun. Or—had Spurck come to his rescue with an unloaded gun . . .

COMING out of the courthouse an hour later, he found Spurck waiting for him at the bottom of the steps.

Spurck sighed. "That Manny Yarcovitch, after all we've done, getting his daughter back. All I say is that I would give her a screen test, and you would think it would make him happy. But no. He tells me that no actresses does he wish in his family. Away, he is going to take her, as if any girl wouldn't rather be an actress than a lady."

"QUICK! WHERE'S THE D.A.?"

HE'S OUT FOR A PACK OF NEW **STAR** DOUBLE EDGE BLADES!

INTRODUCTORY OFFER
5 for 10¢
15 for 25¢

STAR

Made by the Amazing **6NX** Process!

MAKES YOUR DOUBLE EDGE RAZOR PERFORM MIRACLES!

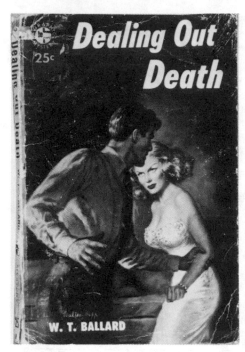

The two different covers for *Dealing Out Death*. Left, the more sedate 2nd edition.
Below, the more hard-boiled one of the first edition.

W.T. Ballard

Novels

Bill Lennox Series
Say Yes to Murder. New York: Putnam, 1942; Penguin, 1945; Reprinted as *The Demise of a Louse* (as by John Shepherd), Belmont, 1962.

Murder Can't Stop. Philadelphia: McKay, 1946; Graphic, 1950.

Dealing Out Death. Philadelphia: McKay, 1948; Graphic, 1950.

Lights, Camera, Murder. (as John Shepherd). Belmont, 1960.

Max Hunter Series
Pretty Miss Murder. Permabooks, 1961.

The Seven Sisters. Permabooks, 1962.

Three For the Money. Permabooks 1962; originally published in *Argosy*, August 1963.

Mark Foran (series character)
Murder, Las Vegas Style. Tower, 1967.

Non-series books
Walk in Fear. Gold Medal, 1952; originally published in *Shadow Magazine*, February/March, 1948, under the pen name Willard Kilgore as "I Could Kill You."

The Package Deal. New York: Appleton Century Crofts, 1956; Bantam, 1957.

Fury in the Heart. Monarch, 1959.

Chance Elson. Pocket Books, Cardinal Edition, 1959.

As P.D. Ballard
Age of the Junkman. Gold Medal, 1963.

End of a Millionaire. Gold Medal, 1964.

Brothers in Blood. Gold Medal, 1972.

The Death Brokers. Gold Medal, 1973.

As Todhunter and Phoebe Ballard
The Man Who Stole a University. New York: Doubleday, 1967; Curtis, 1967.

134

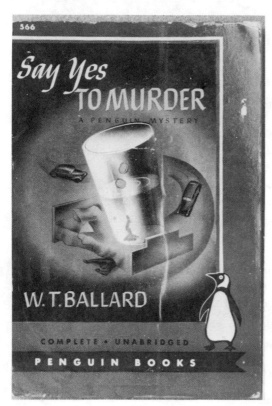

Left, the first Bill Lennox novel published under its re
title in 1945 as a Penguin paperback.

Below, the same novel retitled for Belmont's 1962 reprin
Neither front cover mentioned Lennox.

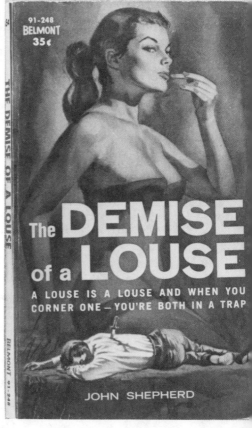

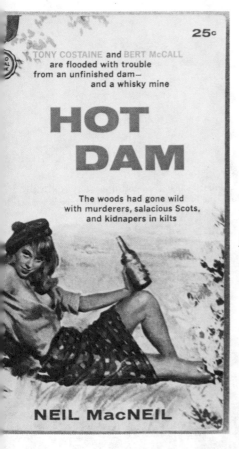

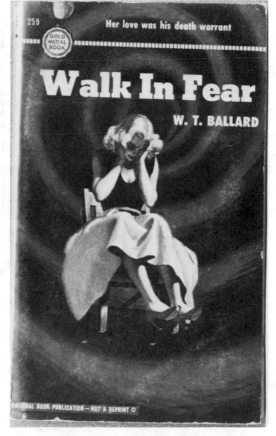

Even while concentrating on westerns, Ballard wrote several action/adventure novels for Gold Medal. Left, *Hot Dam,* one of seven Neil MacNeil novels. Below, Ballard's first mystery novel for Gold Medal (1952).

MARK FORAN, NEWEST
OF THE PRIVATE OPS—
OUT-HARPERS HARPER

50c

TOWER
42-778

MURDER
LAS VEGAS
STYLE

W. T. BALLARD

Left, Ballard's last hard-boiled mystery (1967).
Below, one of the Max Hunter crime novels written for
Perma books.

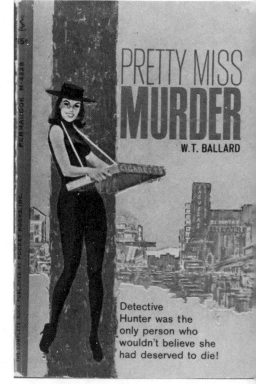

PRETTY MISS
MURDER

W. T. BALLARD

Detective
Hunter was the
only person who
wouldn't believe she
had deserved to die!

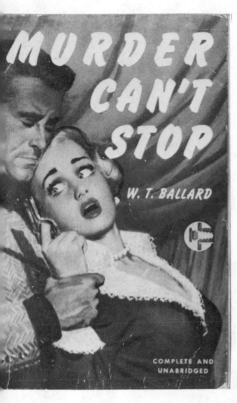

Left, the second Bill Lennox novel.
Below, the fourth and last Bill Lennox novel, published under the penname John Shepherd.

MURDER PICKS
THE JURY
By Harrison Hunt

Hate, like a point of flame, burned in Lee's brain, hate for Vale City and all it represented. Vale City, corrupt, cruel and uncaring, had murdered his only friend—the one man who had stood by him through his degradation. As surely as if it had plunged a knife into his back, Vale City had murdered him. And Randolph Lee determined that he would make the city pay for its crime, if it was the last thing he did.

Not that there seemed much likelihood that he would have the opportunity. For Randolph Lee, once the state's most brilliant young prosecutor, was now a down-and-outer, a vagrant in the Vale City jail. Then unexpectedly Fate dealt a lucky card. Through an error in a planned escape, Lee suddenly found himself a free man. And through the same error he met pretty, blue-eyed Susan Drake—who needed him.

His chance had come. Susan's father, white-haired Gregory Drake, philanthropist and reformer, was about to go on trial for murder. Whether Drake was guilty or innocent made no difference to Randolph Lee. Here was the way to tear Vale City wide open, and he did not hesitate.

Mystery House

Ballard's collaboration with Norbert Davis. The dedication is to Robert Leslie Bellem and his wife Bebe. Ballard and Bellem shared offices for many years in Pasadena while writing for *Super Detective* and *Popular Detective*.

As Nick Carter
The Kremlin File. Award, 1973.

As Neil MacNeil
(All books with characters Tony Costaine and Bert McCall)
Death Takes an Option. Gold Medal, 1958.
Third on a Seesaw. Gold Medal, 1959.
Two Guns for Hire. Gold Medal, 1959.
Hot Dam. Gold Medal, 1960.
The Death Ride. Gold Medal, 1960.
Mexican Slay Ride. Gold Medal, 1962.
The Spy Catchers. Gold Medal, 1966; originally published in
Argosy.

As Harrison Hunt (with Norbert Davis)
Murder Picks the Jury. Samuel Curl, 1947; Bestseller Mystery,
No. B108.

Todhunter Ballard
Two-edged Vengeance. New York: Macmillan, 1951; Popular,
1952; originally published in *Esquire*, June/July 1950; also
published as *The Circle C Feud.* London: Sampson Low, 1952.
Incident at Sun Mountain. Boston: Houghton Mifflin, 1952;
London: Rich and Cowan, 1954; Popular, 1953.
West of Quarantine. Boston: Houghton Mifflin, 1953; London:
Richard Cowan, 1954; Popular, 1953.
Showdown (with James C. Lynch). Popular, 1953.
High Iron. Boston: Houghton Mifflin, 1953; London: Rich and
Cowan, 1955; Popular, 1954; originally appeared in *Blue Book*, 1952.
Rawhide Gunman. Popular, 1954.
Blizzard Range. Popular, 1955; originally appeared in *Ranch
Romances*, 1954.
Trigger Trail. Popular, 1955; originally appeared in   *Ranch
Romances, as "Empire West," 1954.*
Gunman from Texas. Popular, 1956; originally appeared in
Toronto Star Weekly, 1955.
Guns of the Lawless. Popular, 1956; originally appeared in
Ranch Romances, 1955.
Roundup. Popular-Eagle, 1957, originally appeared in *Toronto
Star Weekly*, 1956.
Trailtown Marshall. Popular-Eagle, 1957; originally appeared
in *Ranch Romances*, 1956.

Saddle Tramp. Popular, 1958; originally appeared in *Toronto Star Weekly*, 1957.

Trouble on the Massacre. Popular, 1959.

The Long Trail Back. New York: Doubleday, 1960; London: Herbert Jenkins, 1961; Avon, 1962 .

The Night Riders. New York: Doubleday, 1961; London: Herbert Jenkins, 1962; Pocket, 1963.

Gopher Gold. New York: Doubleday, 1962; as *Gold Fever in Gopher*, London: Herbert Jenkins, 1962.

Westward the Monitors Roar. New York: Doubleday, 1963; London: Herbert Jenkins, 1963; originally appeared in the *Toronto Star Weekly*, March 23, 1963; also published as *Flight or Die*, Tower, 1967.

Gold in California! New York: Doubleday, 1965.

The Californian. New York: Doubleday, 1971; Popular, 1972.

Nowhere Left to Run. New York: Doubleday, 1972; Leisure Books.

Loco and the Wolf. New York: Doubleday, 1973; Manor, 1974.

Home to Texas. New York: Doubleday, 1974; Dell, 1979.

Trails of Rage. New York: Doubleday, 1975; Ace, 1977.

Sheriff of Tombstone. New York: Doubleday, 1977.

As John Hunter

West of Justice. Boston: Houghton Mifflin, 1954.

Ride the Wind South. Permabooks, 1957.

The Marshall from Deadwood. Permabooks, 1958.

Badlands Buccaneer. Pocket, 1959.

Desperation Valley: A Novel of the Cherokee Strip. New York: Macmillan, 1964; originally appeared in *Argosy*.

Duke. Paperback Library, 1965.

Man From Yuma. Berkley, 1967.

A Canyon Called Death. Berkley, 1968.

Death in the Mountain. Ballantine, 1969.

Lost Valley. Ballantine, 1971.

Hell Hole. Ballantine, 1972.

The Burning Land. Ballantine, 1973.

Gambler's Gun. Ballantine, 1973.

The Higraders. Ballantine, 1974.

This Range is Mine. Ballantine, 1975.

Manhunt. Ballantine, 1975.

As Parker Bonner

Superstition Range. Popular, 1953.

Outlaw Brand. Popular, 1954; originally appeared in *Ranch Romances* as "Railroad Doctor," 1953.

Tough in the Saddle. Monarch, 1964, No. 452.

Applegate's Gold. Avon, 1967.

Plunder Canyon. Paperback Library, 1968.

The Town Tamer. Paperback Library, 1968.

Look to Your Guns. Paperback Library, 1969.

Borders To Cross. Paperback Library, 1969.

As Jack Slade

Lassiter. Tower, 1967.

Bandido: Lassiter No. 2. Tower, 1968.

The Man from Yuma: Lassiter No. 3. Tower,1968.

The Man from Cheyenne: Lassiter No. 4. Tower, 1968.

As Clint Reno

Sun Mountain Slaughter: Vigilante No. 1. Gold Medal, 1974.

Sierra Massacre: Vigilante No. 2. Gold Medal, 1974.

As Sam Bowie

Thunderhead Range. Monarch, 1959.

Gunlock. Award, 1968.

Canyon War. Ace, 1969.

Chisum. Ace, 1970. (Novelization of John Wayne film).

The Train Robbers. Ace, 1973. (Novelization of John Wayne film).

As Hunter D'Allard

The Long Sword. Avon, 1962.

As Clay Turner

Give a Man a Gun. Paperback Library, 1971.

Gold Goes to the Mountain. Paperback Library, 1974.

Go West, Ben Gold! Paperback Library, 1974.

As Brian Fox

A Dollar to Die For. Award, 1968. (Also published as by Joe Millard).

The Wild Bunch. Award, 1969.

Outlaw Trail. Award, 1969. (Novelization using "Alias Smith and Jones" TV characters).

Unholy Angel. Award. 1969. (Novelization using "Alias Smith and Jones" TV characters).

Sabata. Award, 1970. (Novelization from screenplay).

Dead Ringer. Award, 1971. (Novelization using "Alias Smith and Jones" TV characters).

Apache Gold. Award, 1971. (Novelization using "Alias Smith and Jones" TV characters).

Dragooned. Award, 1971. (Novelization using "Alias Smith and Jones" TV characters).

Return of Sabata. Award, 1972.

Bearcats! Ballantine, 1973.

As Brian Agar

Have Love, Will Share. Monarch, 1961.

The Sex Web. Soft Cover Library, 1967.

W.T. Ballard
Detective/Crime Stories

Black Mask
Bill Lennox Stories

"A Little Different." September 1933.

"A Million Dollar Tramp." October 1933.

"Positively the Best Liar." November 1933.

"Trouble-Hunted." January 1934.

"Tears Don't Help." April 1934.

"That's Hollywood." May 1934.

"Whatta Guy." July 1934.

"Crime's Web." September 1934.

"Snatching is Dynamite." October 1934.

"In Dead Man's Alley." November 1934.

"Murder Isn't Legal." December 1934.

"Gamblers Don't Win." April 1935.

"Numbers With Lead." January 1936.

"Blackmailers Die Hard." May 1936.

"There's No Excuse for Murder." September 1936.

"Whipsawed." December 1936.

"This is Murder." March 1937.

"Fortune Deals Death." July 1937.

"Mobster Guns." November 1938.

"No Parole from Death." February 1939.
"Scars of Murder." November 1939.
"Pictures for Murder." September 1940.
"The Lady With the Light Blue Hair." January 1941.
"Not in the Script." July 1941.
"Murder is a Swell Idea." November 1941.
"The Colt and the Killer." February 1942.
"Lights, Action—Killer!" May 1942.

Red Drake Stories
"You Never Know About Women." October 1935.
"After Breakfast." December 1935.
"Blood on the Moon." April 1936.
"Fugitive for Justice." August 1936.
"A Ride in the Rain." October 1936.
"Call a Dead Man." May 1937.
"Only Proof Counts." December 1937.

Jimmy DeHaven Stories
"Confession Means Death." February 1935.
"Murder Makes a Difference." June 1935.

Don Tomaso Sherman Stories
"Stones of Death." April 1937.
"Friends Sometimes Kill." November 1937.

Non-series Stories
"Death in the Zoo." July 1939.
"Thirty Miles to Albuquerque." March 1941.
"The Con Man and the Cop." December 1942.
"Sing for Your Slaughter." July 1944.
"Dressed to Kill." May 1945.

Other Detective/Crime Stories

Ace G-Man
"Masquerading Corpse." January/February 1938.
"G-Man on the Dodge." March/April 1938.
"Live Bait for Suckers." June/July 1938.
"Special Agent from Hell." September/October 1938.
"Murder on Approval." September/October 1938.
"G-Man Corpse Catcher." March/April 1939.

All-Star Detective
   "Murder Merry Go Round." May 1942.

Argosy
   "Dancer Kills a Horse." February 3, 1941.
   "Contention at Red Gulch." June 1945.
   "The Fiddler & the Gunman." May 1946.

Big Book Detective
   "Murder's Not My Line." February 1942.

Black Bat Detective
   "Masked Detective Bets on Death." May 1941.

Black Book Detective
   "Don't Bury Me Yet." April 1948.
   (Reprinted in *Triple Detective*. Winter 1955)

Captain Satan
   "Never Trust a Cop." May 1938.

Clues
   "Death in the Patio." May 1936.

Crack Detective
   "Deferred to Death." July 1942.

Crime Busters
   "Drake Deals Death." October 1938. Red Drake.
   "Tickets for Murder." February 1939. Red Drake.
   "Suicide for Killers." April 1939. Red Drake.
   "Wise' Girl." May 1939. Red Drake.
   "Women's Work." November 1939. Red Drake.
   "Blind Date with Death." August 1939. Red Drake.

Detective Novel
   "No Body Knows." Spring 1948.

Detective Short Stories
   "Letter of the Law. March 1939.
   "The Alibi That Was Too Air Tight." February 1941.
   "Four Killers and a Kid." April 1941.

"Look for a Luscioius Redhead." January 1943.

Detective Story
"Murder Takes the Stage." November 1942 (with Norbert Davis).

"The Accidental Case." 1945 (with Norbert Davis).

Detective Tales
"Death is on Board." October 1938.

"I've Seen that Corpse Before." October 1943.

"Front Page Obituary." November 1943.

"Murder Has Green Eyes." April 1945.

"It Could Happen To You." May 1945.

"The Very Silent Partner." June 1945.

"Head South to Murder." July 1945.

"Case of the Climbing Corpse." September 1945.

"Murder on the Meter." August 1945. Hymie Beerman.

"Hide-Out in Hell." December 1945.

"Murder the Girl Said." May 1946.

"Murder Stakes the Claim." June 1946.

"The Clock Reads Death." July 1946. Hymie Beerman.

"Redheads is Poison." August 1946. Hymie Beerman.

"Don't Look Now—It's Murder." October 1946.

"Toehold on a Torpedo." December 1946. Hymie Beerman.

"The Model in the Morgue." December 1946.

"Hymie's Christmas Carol." January 1947. Hymie Beerman.

"Red Hot Ice." April 1947. Hymie Beerman.

"Hell on Wheels." May 1947. Hymie Beerman.

"A Dame Called Flame." September 1947.

"Can't Keep a Dead Man Down." October 1947. Hymie Beerman

"Having a Wonderful Crime." December 1947.

"Hymie on the Spot." January 1948. Hymie Beerman.

"Hymie & the Homemade Lettuce." February 1948. Hymie Beerman.

"Hymie & the Double-Dome." May 1948. Hymie Beerman.
(All Hymie Beerman stories were published as by Parker Bonner.)

Detective Yarns
"The Devil's Warehouse." December 1938.

Dime Detective
"Eight Hours to Doom." December 1941.

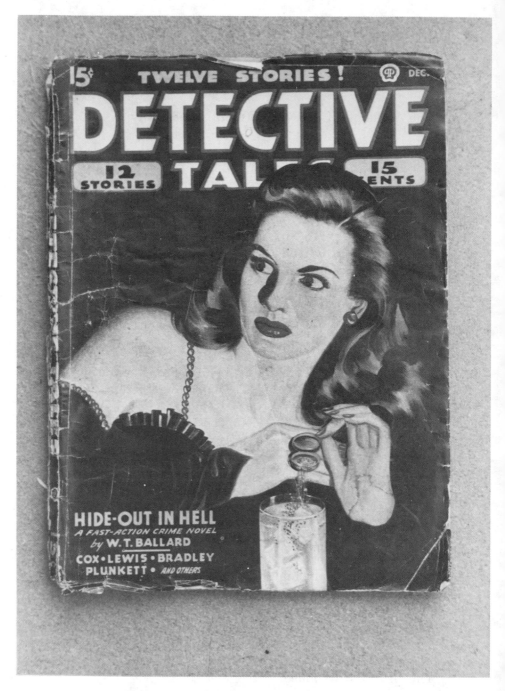

The December 1945 issue with a typical pulp title

"A Heel of the First Water." May 1943.
"Murder Warden." March 1943.
"Mister Six Feet Deep." June 1943.
"All's Fair in Murder." September 1945.
"Blood on the Stars." July 1947.
"The Dead Don't Care." January 1948.

Dime Mystery
"Murder Tavern" September 1940.
"Hearse Ride to Murder." March 1944.
"Dig Your Own Murder" September 1946.

Double Action Detective
"Nosey Guy." October 1938.

Exciting Mystery
"The Corpse That Died Twice." Winter 1942.

Feds
"Contact Man." October 1936.

Flynn's Detective Fiction
"Homicide House." May 1942. Charley Trask.
"Combination for Murder." October 1942.

Lone Wolf Detective
"The Body in Drawer 13." Februry 1941.

Mammoth Detective
"Just One More Case Uncle Sam." March 1943.
"I'm a Dead Man!" January 1946.

Mystery Magazine
"Murders Aren't Nice." February 1940. Red Drake.
"Odds on Death." April 1940. Red Drake.
"I Stole a Horse." June 1940.
"Wired for Death." February 1941. Red Drake.
"You Can't Forget Murder." March 1941. Red Drake.
"Flames of Death." July 1941. Red Drake.
"Men With Guns." January 1942. Red Drake.
"Death Writes the Bond." March 1942. Red Drake.
"A Toast to Crime." May 1942. Red Drake.

"A Horse on Death." July 1942. Red Drake.
"Death Wears a Horseshoe." September 1942. Red Drake.
"Death Rides Iron Horses." January 1943. Red Drake.

New Detective
"Night is for Dying." 1935.
"Bodyguard." June 1935.
"Deep in the Heart of Murder." September 1942.
"Ninety-six Hours to Kill." November 1942.
"Don't Turn on Me." January 1945.
"Death is Like That." September 1945.
"Make-Up for Murder." January 1946.
"Accent on Trouble." March 1947.
"Bury Me Not." July 1947.
"Death Before Breakfast." November 1947.

Phantom Detective
"The Phantom Clue." May 1935.
"The Phantom Strikes Back." October 1939.

NOTE: In the 1940s almost all stories published in *Phantom Detective* were ghostwritten by Ballard in collaboration with Robert Leslie Bellem.)

Popular Detective
"More Than Blood." June 1939.
"The Whole Scenario." June 1939.
"Women Are Funny." August 1939.
"Not Too Blind." November 1939.
"Murder's No Accident." January 1940.
"Engraving for Death." February 1940.
"Sauce for a Rat." February 1940.
"Murder Resort." 1940.
"Heads It's Murder. February 1941.
"The Diamond Bride." September 1941.
"Kidnapped for What." September 1941.
"Heads It's Murder." February 1941.
"Shark Bait." December 1941.
"He's in the Death House." August 1941.
"And Here Comes Murder." January 1942.
"Sinister House." October 1942. Dr. Zeng Tse-Lin.
"Lion's Loot." June 1943. Zeng.

"Camelback Kill." February 1943. Zeng.
"Blackmail Clinic." December 1944. Zeng.
"Corpse Cargo." August 1944. Zeng.
(The Dr. Zeng stories were published as by Walt Bruce.)

Private Detective
"Models for Murder." April 1945.
"Slay Ride." November 1947.

Shadow
"New Orleans Limited." October 1943. Red Drake.
"I Could Kill You." February/March 1948. (As Willard Kilgore).

Strange Detective Mysteries
"Bride of Death." July 1940.

Super Detective
"Murdered in Reno." November 1934.
"Hell's Ice Box." July 1942. Jim Anthony.
"Days of Death." August 1942. Anthony.
"Caribbean Cask." November 1942. Anthony.
"Murder Between Shifts." December 1942. Anthony.
"Cauldron of Death." January 1943. Anthony.
"Murder's Migrants." February 1943. Anthony.
"Death is a Flying Dutchman." March 1943. Anthony.
"Homicide Heiress." April 1943. Anthony.
"Curse of the Masters." May 1943. Anthony.
"Pipeline to Murder." August 1943. Anthony.
"The Noose Hangs High." June 1945.
"Mary Took a Little Lam." January 1946.

NOTE: In the 1940s almost all issues of *Super Detective* were ghostwritten by Ballard in collaboration with Robert Leslie Bellem. All Jim Anthony stories were published as by John Grange.

Ten Detective Aces
"Case of the Cluttered Corpses." June 1938.
"Lady Won't Die." September 1938.
"Homicide Blues." October 1938.
"Stooge for Murder." December 1938.
"Decoy Dame." February 1939.
"Hell's Hangover." April 1939.
"Five-Star Fraud." September 1939.

"Black Gold Doom." August 1940.
"Preview to Crime." June 1942.
"Contract with Death." August 1942.
"Hell is My Hangout." September 1942.
"Death Knows No Dimout." December 1942.
"There's That Corpse Again." February 1943.
"Countess and the Killer." April 1943. Bill French.
"The Man Who Killed Twice." July 1943.
"Death on the Way." December 1943.
"My Kingdom for a Corpse." April 1943.
"Stand-In for a Corpse." March 1938.
"Lady Fingers." April 1938.
"Ruckus in Reno." September 1948.

Ten Story Detective
"Death Doubles on Red." March/April 1939.
"Murder in the Mirror." March 1940.
"Water for the San Pasquel." September 1941.
"Death Comes with the Fog." December 1941.
"All Set for a Death Rehearsal." May 1943.
"The Knave of Diamonds." December 1944.

This Week
"Cop's Choice." June 20, 1937.

Thrilling Detective
"Death Holds the Stakes." January 1939.
"The Name is Kelly." September 1939.
"Death Deals in Diamonds." December 1941.
"Key to Murder." January 1942.
"Death Takes a Vacancy." September 1942.
"Murder Takes Priority." December 1942.
"You Gotta Have Homicide." January 1943.
"Murder Calls the Tune." February 1945.
"Murder's Mandate." September 1945.
"The Second Act is Murder." January 1946.
"Let's Have Some Murder." February 1949.

Thrilling Mystery
"No Escape from the Dead." May 1939.

Top-Notch Detective
"Rogue's Gallery Galahad." March 1939.

The February 1949 issue. By some coincidence Ballard often appeared on the same cover with Carroll John Daly.

A typical pulp action scene from February 1949 *Thrilling Detective.*

Triple Detective
"Don't Bury Me Yet." Winter 1955.
(Reprint of *Black Book*, April 1948).

Underworld Novelettes
"Three Reasons." Winter 1933/34.
"A Busy Day." March 1934.
"Dead Men Don't Walk." May 1935.
"Night Club Murder." June 1935.
"Killer's Bait." July 1935.
"How About Murder." July 1936.

Variety Detective
"Murder Merchant." February 1939.
"Routine with Death." August 1939.

W.T. Ballard

Western & General Short Fiction

All Sports
"A Bird in the Bush League." November 1948.

Brief Stories
"Gambler's Luck." October 1927.

Century
Thespian of Wood's Creek." 1947.

Collier's
"Money Rider." March 9, 1946.

Cowboy Stories
"The Bandit Chief." May 1936.

Esquire
"Two-Edged Vengeance." June/July 1950. (Filmed as "The Outcast" 1954).

Frontier Stories
"Miner Wear Your Guns." December 1943.

Giant Western
   "Dry Camp." December 1949.

Lariat
   "Drifter's Choice." July 1948.

McCalls
   "First Class All The Way." September 1948.

*McClure's (*newspaper)
   "Ladd's Gate." November 19, 1941.

New Western
   "Bait for Bushwackers." July/August 1936.
   "Satan Rides for Dead Man's Gold." February/March 1937.

Popular Western
   "Bar X Ranny." November 1938.

Ranch Romances
   "Come Ride With Me." January 1947.
   "Squabble by Gaslight." September 1948.
   "Pat Hand for Kepps." September 1949.
   "The Dragon was a Lady." July 1949.
   "Sell It to Sweeny." July 1949.
   "Let the Flag Fly Free." May 1956.

Romance
   "King for an Hour." April 1940.

Saturday Evening Post
   "The Builder of Murderer's Bar." June 23, 1945.
   "The Mayor of Strawberry Hill." November 3, 1945.
   "She Has to Have Music." February 9, 1946.
   "Three Rooms Wanted" (with James C. Lynch). July 21, 1946.
   "Kelly Makes a Deal" (with Norbert Davis). May 17, 1947.
   "The Magnificent Hoax" (with James C. Lynch). December 4, 1948.
   "Run Out of Town." September 30, 1950.

Short Stories
   "Mooch's Gleam." May 1938.

Sports Action
    "Tiger Kid." December 1938.

Thrilling Western
    "Careless Guns." November 1937.

Toronto Star
    "Not An Angry Man." February 27, 1946.

Turf & Sport Digest
    "Bug Rider." August 1938.
    "No Bet's Good if you Lose." January 1939.

Western Short Stories
    "Jughead for Catfish Business." December 1938.

Writer
    "Put Yourself in the Background." November 1946 (non-fiction).

W.T. Ballard
Teleplays

Wild Bill Hickok **(TV series) 1951**
    Six episodes.

Dick Tracy **(TV series) 1951-52**
    "Dick Tracy and the Sapphire Mystery."
    "Dick Tracy and the Smugglers."
    "Dick Tracy is Missing."
    "Last Man Murderers."

Cowboy G-Men **(TV series) 1952**
    "Hangfire."
    "Silver Fraud."
    "Hush Money."
    "Salted Mines."

Shotgun Slade **(TV series) 1959**
    "Too Smart to Live" (with Bill S. Ballinger).
    "Bob Ford" (with Dwight Newton).

Manhunt (TV series) 1961
   "Guest of Honor" (with John Hawkins).

Shannon (TV series) 1961
   "Pacific State Report (with John Hawkins).
   "The Idlers."
   "The Patriarch."
   "The Sports Car Story."
   "Delayed Delivery."

Death Valley Days (TV series) 1964-65
   "Fighting Sky Pilot."
   "A City is Born."
   "Dry Water Sailors."
   "Temporary Warden."
(All with Robert Leslie Bellem.)

W.T. Ballard
Anthology Appearances

"The Builder of Murderer's Bar," in *Branded West*, ed. Don Ward. Houghton Mifflin, 1956. (A Western Writers of America Anthology).Also appeared in WWA Silver Anniversary Anthology, ed. August Lenninger, Ace. 1977.

"The Bridegroom Came Late," in *Frontiers West*, ed. William R. Cox. (A WWA Anthology).

"Johnny Who Rode the Ghost Train" (with Phoebe Ballard) in *Great Ghost Stories of the Old West*, ed. B. Baker.

"The Saga of Toby Riddle," in *With Guidons Flying,* ed. by Charles N. Heckelmann, Doubleday, 1970 (A WWA Anthology).